Others Available by DK Holmberg

The Cloud Warrior Saga

Chased by Fire
Bound by Fire
Changed by Fire
Fortress of Fire
Forged in Fire

The Painter Mage

Shifted Agony
Arcane Mark
Painter for Hire

The Lost Garden

Keeper of the Forest
The Desolate Bond
Keeper of Light

Assassin's Sight:

The Painted Girl
The Forgotten

CHANGED BY FIRE

THE CLOUD WARRIOR SAGA
BOOK 3

ASH Publishing
dkholmberg.com

Changed by Fire

Published by ASH Publishing

ISBN-13: 978-1512145854
ISBN-10: 1512145858

ASH Publishing
dkholmberg.com

CHANGED BY FIRE

THE CLOUD WARRIOR SAGA
BOOK 3

CHAPTER 1

A Warrior's Plan

SMOKE HUNG LOW OVER THE VALLEY like nothing more than an early morning fog. Had it not been for the stink of charred bodies—lives Tan had watched burned alive—it might have been peaceful. Perched on an outcropping of rock, he looked down on the lake. Clear water tinged with the hint of green spilled down from the wide river flowing from the mountains, emptying into the lake below. Tall pines and oak trees lined the lake, though fewer now than before the attack.

If he focused and stretched his sensing out and around him, he could still feel fires burning on the edge of the lake in places the water elemental nymid could not reach and extinguish. The great earth elemental golud could not be moved to extinguish the fire. The wind elemental, ara, flittered through the air, barely enough to make its presence known, careful not to stir up any embers, knowing the danger were the twisted fire from Incendin shapers to rekindle. Only the draasin, the great winged fire elementals, did not fear those flames.

Here, in this place of convergence, all the elementals mingled.

Even spirit, though calling spirit required more effort than the others. And spirit had been the reason this place had experienced what it had.

"How long will you sit here?"

Amia stood over him, early morning sunlight catching her golden hair so that it nearly glowed. The narrow band of silver around her neck—the mark of her people—seemed wider than he remembered. Had bathing in a pool of liquid spirit changed it? She pulled a long, grey cloak over her shoulders, leaving the hood to fall around the back. It took him a moment to realize where she had found it; the dead archivist wouldn't miss it.

"I'm just thinking," he answered.

He felt her concern through the shaped connection between them. The shaping had come on accidentally, made by a spirit shaping placed on him by Amia in a time of great need as they ran from the lisincend. It was stronger now, especially after what he had done to save her.

Amia crouched on a rock next to him. "I wonder if we will be able to find this place again when we leave."

Tan nodded. He hadn't been certain he could find this place again either, but the draasin had known. "Asboel can find it, but I'm not certain he wants to return after what he's been through here."

"It's amazing, isn't it, the sacrifice they made."

Tan turned to her, tearing his eyes off the lake. "Did you know? When you went into the pool of spirit the first time, did you know what this place could do?"

Amia inhaled deeply. "I sensed the importance of the other elementals, but it was not the same as this time. Maybe because the draasin had already departed?" She pushed strands of golden hair behind her ears. She leaned against him, resting her head on his shoulder. "This time was different. Until you healed me, I couldn't sense anything."

Her contentment came through the connection. Amia would stay here with him as long as he wanted, but she understood he could not stay. Not knowing what he did.

"There's so much to do," he whispered. "I'm… I'm not certain I can do it."

Amia pressed her palm up to his chest. "You might not be certain, but I am. You've stopped Incendin twice already."

"Did I? The first time, the draasin stopped Incendin, hunting the lisincend to keep us safe. And the last time… had it not been for Lacertin appearing—"

A shout rang up from the valley, interrupting them, and they both turned. One of the shapers had found something.

Amia grabbed his hand and started down the slope. She moved quickly and easily, hurrying down the side of the rocks. Tan followed her, using earth sensing to find the safest way down.

At the bottom of the valley, Master Ferran stood over a fallen body. Ash covered the body's face and fire streaked through his chest, but Tan recognized him all the same: the archivist who had attacked during his rescue of Amia. The archivist he'd killed—or thought he'd killed.

A low groan worked from his throat.

Ferran stood over him. Earth swirled up and around in a controlled shaping, trapping the fallen archivist and preventing him from moving.

Next to him, Amia performed a shaping. Tan felt it as pressure building behind his ears, a soft and steady buildup that she slowly released, easing out in her shaping.

The archivist convulsed softly, his back arching into the dirt. His eyes flickered wide before turning and looking up at Amia. A dark laugh escaped his lips. “You,” he spat. “You should have been the one sacrificed.”

Tan started toward him, boot already moving to kick the man. After what happened with Amia—how the archivists had nearly killed her—he felt a certain crazed anger. Amia held him back, sending a soothing shaping of spirit through him to calm him.

He took a deep breath and relaxed, lowering his foot.

Master Ferran watched. “I found this one when searching through the wreckage. I did not expect to find any living.” His eyes darted over all the damaged wagons, destroyed by water and fire during the attack. More Aeta, fallen because of Incendin desires.

“He shouldn’t be,” Tan said. “I thought I’d killed him.”

The archivist grunted and thrashed. Tan turned to him and crouched down before him. Any empathy he might have felt for the man faded as he remembered the painful scars down Amia’s back. The time in the pool of spirit had healed them but didn’t take away the memory Tan had of what the archivists had done to her.

“Why would you do this to your kingdoms?” Tan asked.

The archivist laughed and turned his head toward Tan. A pointed nose stabbed at the air. Spittle and blood coated his lips. A deep gash split his forehead. Without healing, he would not survive long. “*My* kingdoms? You think I can claim these lands?”

Tan glanced at Amia. The archivists were descended from the Aeta, but could they be more than that? Could they *be* Aeta, not merely their descendants? But why would they have attacked Amia? What would have motivated them to hurt one of their own? What could Incendin offer that would entice them?

He leaned close to the archivist. “You won’t harm her again. You will never harm her.”

The archivist looked up at him with eyes that alternated between glassy and clear. In one of the moments of clarity, a dark smile twisted his mouth. "You might control much power, Warrior, but you are untrained. And there is much you don't know."

"Then tell me."

His laughed continued. "It is too late for that. Now that we have the artifact…"

"But you don't. Incendin has the artifact. The archivists have fallen, dead and gone. You have failed."

The archivist blinked. "Failed? The plan is only now in place."

Tan frowned. "What plan?"

The archivist coughed. Blood burbled to his lips.

"What plan?" Tan repeated.

The archivist gasped one time and then breathed no more.

Tan crouched next to him, eyes closed. A hand gripped his shoulder and squeezed. He opened his eyes and turned to Amia. "Could you tell what he meant?"

"He's a spirit shaper. I can't tell anything from him."

Tan stood slowly and wiped his hands on his cloak. What could the archivist have meant? What plan did they mean?

Too much remained uncertain. The archivists could have shaped the king. Incendin had the artifact—and a new, twisted lisincend. And the draasin were in danger. Where did he even begin?

Ferran shifted his attention from Tan to Amia. "When I first met you, I thought you exaggerated what you went through. If anything, you underestimated."

The master shaper had taught one of the earliest classes Tan tried attending, but he hadn't believed what Tan said about the lisincend, and he certainly hadn't been willing to teach. "Doesn't change anything, does it?"

"It does not." With that, Ferran turned and left Tan and Amia standing with the lifeless body of the archivist.

They stood for a moment until Tan could no longer tolerate the proximity to the fallen archivist. Amia took his hand and led him away, back to where the ground sloped back toward the cavern. As much beauty as there was in having all the elementals converge, part of him hated this place. Each time he'd been here, he'd nearly died.

"Some good has come from here," Amia said, reading his thoughts.

"The draasin. You." Tan stared at the valley and the rocks where he'd once died. If not for the nymid, he would have been gone. Amia would have been gone. "Other than that? I've nearly died here twice. If not for the draasin, I *would* have died here twice."

"You really think so little of what you did?"

Lacertin stood behind them. He wore a short sword with runes carved along the surface, nearly a twin of the one Roine carried. A warrior's sword, one only those capable of shaping all the elements could carry and use. He was dressed strangely for the kingdoms in pants of deep red leather and a black jacket buttoned tight across his chest. Hard lines worked around the corners of his eyes.

How had he appeared without Tan sensing him? Earth sensing was his strength. He'd spent years climbing mountains like these with his father—a man he only recently learned was an earth shaper—learning to stretch his sensing so that it became easy. Somehow, Lacertin still avoided detection.

Tan stood, putting himself between Lacertin and Amia.

"Lacertin. I thought you'd left."

Lacertin considered Tan with an amused smile. "Theondar would like it if I left," he agreed. "As would the others, I think. But this place is not theirs to defend. As shapers, they recognize that."

"What do you want from me?"

Tan asked it with more agitation than intended. He *should* be thankful. Had Lacertin not arrived, the Incendin shaper likely would have succeeded and they would have been destroyed. But it was hard thinking of him as anything different than the warrior who had led the lisincend into the cavern after the artifact. Could they really forgive him for what he'd done?

Lacertin looked at him askance. "When you stop thinking others have power you do not, you will be formidable, Tannen." He smiled. It appeared forced, stretching the corners of his eyes even more. "Besides, you alone in the kingdoms recognized that it was not simply the draasin attacking, but that Incendin was behind the attack as well. Had the kingdoms succeeded—had they destroyed the last of the draasin—Incendin would be one step closer to their end goal."

"You knew what they were after?"

"Not at first, but Incendin has records dating back nearly as far as the archives at the university. As I had seen both…"

Amia looked from Tan to Lacertin. "What is Incendin after?"

"You've already seen it," Lacertin said.

"The twisting of fire?"

"They wish to connect to fire more directly. That has always been their goal. From the first of the Incendin to this…new creature. They claim the shaping allows them to serve fire more directly. And that is what Fur tells the king. But even Fur must serve—not control, not like the draasin."

Amia's eyes grew dark the way they did when she was troubled. "I still don't understand."

"Incendin wanted the draasin destroyed, but not because they attacked the lisincend," Lacertin explained. "There was another reason, a reason they were willing to risk a bargain with spirit shapers."

"If the draasin were destroyed, another elemental would replace them," Tan explained. "I found records of it in the book I took from the archives."

"But the other fire elementals are saa and inferin. They're almost too weak to be considered lesser elementals," Amia said.

"Which was Incendin's plan all along," Lacertin said.

The archivist said the plan was in place. Could that really be it? Had they worked with Incendin to displace the draasin? But for what reason?

"There has to be a greater elemental," Tan answered. "When I stood in the pool of spirit, that became clear to me. They have not always been static. Even the udilm have weakened over time, with the nymid growing stronger as the kingdoms were claimed from the ocean."

Lacertin studied Tan. "How is it you know? It took me years of studying to learn."

"I found it in the archives," he answered.

He considered telling Lacertin more, explaining the book on the draasin he'd come across in the race to escape the Incendin fire shaper and the archives, but how much should he trust Lacertin? After everything he'd heard of him, *could* he trust him?

"Much of what is written in the archives is done in *Ishthin*." Lacertin waited. When Tan didn't say anything more, he chuckled. "Even knowing what I do, you still surprise me, Tannen."

Amia looked at Lacertin. "Are you implying the lisincend sought to become one of the elementals?"

Lacertin took a deep breath. "It is the artifact," he began. "A creation made by the oldest scholars and likely with the best intentions, but it is apparent there were other uses for its power."

"What is it? What does it do?" Tan asked. "And how is it you know so much about the artifact?" Roine suspected it allowed the user to communicate with the elementals, but Tan thought that unlikely to be the only reason. If that were the case, the ancient warriors would not have placed such heavy protections around it.

Lacertin motioned toward the rock and raised his eyebrows as if waiting for Tan's approval. Tan stepped to the side, letting the warrior pass. He stood atop the rock, staring out over the valley, looking from the lake to the trees and finally to the sky.

"I have spent the last twenty-five years trying to understand the artifact. It was the last assignment given to me by King Ilton before he passed."

Tan blinked. "You were serving the king all this time?"

Lacertin's face hardened and his body stiffened. "I have never stopped serving the king. Everything I have done has been at his command."

"But when he died… what they claim you did…"

"In a way, all of it was true. I entered the king's chambers after his passing. I went to Ilianna's quarters. I tried to convince..." Lacertin trailed off and shook his head. "It no longer matters. Not after all this time. Only reclaiming the artifact matters. The ancient warriors knew they needed to protect it. That's why they placed it here. But there must have been another reason for placing the artifact here, in this place of convergence."

"What does the artifact do to the elementals?" Tan asked.

"Why do you think it does something to the elementals?" Lacertin asked.

"It's the only reason I could think why the ancients would need to protect it so well."

"Protect," Lacertin agreed, nodding. "It was protected here, kept from us until one with the ability to shape spirit recovered it." He watched Amia. "But once, such an ability was not uncommon. Once, the ancient warriors could shape all the elements, including spirit."

Tan frowned as he began to understand what Lacertin implied. "Then it wouldn't have been protected at all. At least, not from the warriors of that time."

"It would have been protected. Think of how difficult it was for you to reach it. Had you not been enabled somehow…" He waited, as if expecting Tan to reveal how he'd managed to slip past the barrier the first time, but Tan would not share the secret of the nymid, not with Lacertin, who smiled anyway. "As I said, had you not been enabled, it is unlikely you would have managed to reach the artifact. You have potential, Tannen Minden, but you are no warrior yet. And none of us is anything like the warriors of that time. But even to them, passing through the protections around the artifact would have been challenging."

Tan thought about how the Incendin shaper tried to reach the pool of spirit. That must have been why they wanted Amia, though as a spirit shaper, the archivist would have been equally able to reach it. What could they have wanted with the pool of spirit?

What use could they have for spirit at a place where the elementals gathered?

"What do you think it does?" Amia asked.

Lacertin turned toward the mountain peak, the place where the protections once hid the artifact, a place he had once battled Roine and then the Incendin shaper. "A place of convergence," he repeated. "A place where pure spirit can be found. I have found no other place like it in all my years. For all I know, there is no other place like it, where spirit burbles from the ground, summoned by the great elementals."

Tan noted how he emphasized the word *summoned.*

And he thought about what the world might have been like one thousand years ago. It was a time when shapers were more powerful, when many spoke to the elementals—learned from them. It was a time when the draasin still roamed and, at times, hunted. Most of the ancient warriors feared the draasin, and for good reason. But Amia had shown a way to control the draasin, to shape them.

Had she only been able to do so in this place? Was that why the archivists could only twist her shaping, not recreate it?

"Does the artifact control the elementals?" he whispered.

Lacertin met his eyes. "That is my fear."

"But Incendin has it now. The lisincend… or whatever she is… took it."

"And we should fear what they will use it for."

"Without access to spirit, is there anything they *can* do with it?" Amia asked.

"I don't know. As I said, the artifact is not well documented. I found what I could in the archives of Ethea. Incendin kept their own records from a time before they separated from the rest of the kingdoms. Between the two, I still couldn't find what I needed. There might be more, but I could not discover it."

Tan thought of the lowest level of the archives, the place where he and Roine had found the dead archivist, rooms where no shaper could reach. Could the archivists hide additional records there? If so, it made sense that Incendin would want to work with the archivists, or at least make a show of working with them. Now the oldest of the archivists were dead. How many remained who knew the answers?

"Do they need spirit to shape more of…" Tan trailed off, uncertain what word to use to describe the creature. She wasn't a lisincend, at least not like Fur or the others. She was something different, twisted in an altogether new way. A threat to the draasin.

Lacertin nodded slightly. "A form of spirit has always been needed to create the lisincend. It is why the Aeta refuse to travel too deeply into Incendin."

Tan shot Amia a look. When he first met her, the Aeta had returned from Incendin after risking a deeper run. Had the Mother known the risk?

"How do they use spirit?" Amia asked. Her voice lowered to a whisper.

"That is a secret Fur kept closely guarded. Only those willing to make the change—Embrace Fire, as they called it—were given the secret of the shaping."

"I thought not many succeeded."

Lacertin nodded. "Failure is high. Those who don't succeed are considered unworthy to fully embrace fire. It is why the lisincend are so revered within Incendin."

"Did that shaper know the secret?"

"No. Alisz sought to embrace fire for nearly a decade, but Fur always refused. I think he sensed in her too much like him, one who might eventually challenge him for supremacy over the lisincend. Even after he was injured, he still didn't share that secret with her, though he did with several others, none of who succeeded in embracing fire." Lacertin frowned. "How did she transform?"

Tan wished he could forget what she'd done, but the image burned into his mind. "She used the artifact. She… cut… the archivist, and he bled into that bowl of hers. Then she used his blood in some shaping. I thought it was the same as Fur used."

Lacertin's eyes closed as he considered. "Perhaps she learned more of the shaping than I realized. Alisz has always been dangerous, even for a fire shaper. And now—"

"Now she's more than even one of the lisincend, isn't she?"

"It seems she drew her inspiration from the draasin. Perhaps that was where Fur went wrong, thinking to shape himself into something more akin to saa."

Lacertin made a point of meeting Tan's eyes. He wore a hard expression, but mixed with it was pain. Tan couldn't help but wonder what he had seen while in Incendin. What must it have been like, being so close to the lisincend?

"You understand why I must return?" Lacertin asked.

"But you don't. You've shown that you don't work for Incendin. You can return to the kingdoms, help fortify the barrier—"

Lacertin shook his head. "The barrier will fall if it hasn't already. That has always been the plan, the reason so many are taken from places like Doma and Chenir. Even after all the time I spent in Incendin, they kept them from me. I know little of what they do—or their strength—but with enough numbers, they can overwhelm the barrier."

"It's held for so long!" Amia said. "Even my people recognize the value of the barrier."

Lacertin turned and stared again over the valley. "Like so much else before it, the barrier will fall."

"How can you be so certain?" Amia asked.

"Because I helped build it in the first place."

"What will you do?" Tan asked. "If you won't return to the kingdoms, what then?"

Lacertin sighed. "The kingdoms were my home for many years. Ilton was my king. Althem?" He shook his head. "He is nothing like his father. He thinks to use those around him and refuses to listen. No—I can't return to Ethea even were I to want to. Besides, there is much I have yet to do. Which is why I need your help, Tan."

Tan frowned. "What do you think I can do? I'm no warrior."

"No, you are more than a warrior. And you are not pledged to Althem, freeing you to do what is needed. The kingdoms *have* a warrior who serves willingly, though he might call himself by another name. Theondar would have failed. Yet you, a boy with minimal shaping, managed to handle Incendin not once, but twice. I think you are exactly what I need."

Tan started to shake his head, but he couldn't deny the truth. He might have shaping skill, but that was not where his gifts truly lay. He could speak to the elementals. And they answered his call. Without the elementals, everything would have been lost.

"What is it that you plan?" Tan asked.

Lacertin fixed Tan with his stare, his back turned on the kingdoms. "The barrier will fall. When it does, Incendin will attack. Their shapers may be weak, but they have more of them than the kingdoms. As long as there is the threat of the lisincend, those stolen shapers will answer."

Tan blinked. "You plan to go into Incendin and attack the lisincend?"

"If I don't—if no one does—there is a real possibility that the lisincend will succeed in their plan. And if they become one of the greater elementals, there is no stopping Incendin."

CHAPTER 2

An Argument Renewed

AMIA HELD TAN'S HAND. After the connection they shared in the pool of liquid spirit, the physical touch seemed both inadequate and comforting. A soft breeze caught at her hair, pulling it from behind her ears so that strands flicked into her face, almost as if ara played games with her.

"You didn't ask about her," Amia said, looking down the trail where Lacertin had disappeared. She kept her eyes fixed straight ahead, but tension simmered through the shaped connection.

Her. His mother. He should have asked Lacertin more about her, maybe learn why she hadn't come to him when she survived the attack in Nor, but did it matter? "What would he say?"

"You don't want to know where she is or why she didn't come to you?"

Tan swallowed back the lump rising in his throat. He had thought of little else at first, but what would Lacertin say if he even answered? Would he explain where Tan's mother had gone? Would he know why she didn't come searching for him? Or would he not care, so focused as he was on what he needed to do?

Perhaps Ephra truly had died in Nor. Only Zephra remained.

"Had she found me in Ethea, what would have happened?" Tan asked. Would he have gone to help Elle? Would he have sought the draasin, or spoken to udilm, or even found Amia, had his mother found him in Ethea? Or would he have stayed, letting her continue to protect him?

"You wonder whether you would still have learned what you did."

Tan nodded.

"When I think of losing my family, I have the same questions. Then I hate myself for the thoughts. Had our caravan not been attacked, had we never gone through Incendin? What would have become of me?" She squeezed his hand. "In time, I would have become Mother. Being blessed by the Great Mother would have given me much standing among the People. Possibly enough to direct another caravan. Maybe I would have been one of the few who settles." A faraway look crossed her face.

Through their connection, Tan felt none of the contentment he would have expected from the look on her face. Instead, there was anxiety. "The Aeta settle?"

She blinked, the lost expression clearing, and turned to him. "Some. There is a place where those who cannot travel will go. It was..." She swallowed. "It was where I thought I would find healing."

"I thought the Aeta were wanderers?"

She nodded. "Most are. Even in this place, the wagons can be moved... only they never are. We would visit once a year in a gathering of Mothers. It is where I saw the only other of my people blessed by the Great Mother."

"Did you ever find out why they betrayed you?"

One hand slipped up to the band of silver around her neck and fidgeted with it, running her fingers around it. "The archivist," she began. "He was Aeta. What he chose did not serve the Great Mother. He traveled with them, using the caravan as a way for him to chase his studies. With it, he could pass through any border. But he was no longer Aeta."

"Why would the Mother allow it?"

Amia swallowed. "When I learned, that was when they… restrained me," she began. "They are blood. More than simply of the same caravan. He was her brother, I think."

Tan let out a slow breath. It would explain why the Aeta would allow the archivist to travel with them, though not why the Mother would allow him to capture Amia. As one of the Aeta—and one blessed by the Great Mother—she should be revered among her people. Instead, she was treated with violence.

"Will you go there now?" he asked.

She pulled him toward her, standing on her toes and kissing him on the mouth.

The suddenness surprised him and it took a moment for him to kiss her back. When he did, his mouth covered hers with hunger.

"There was only one reason I would have gone," she said. "And I no longer have that need."

He smiled and kissed her again, gently this time. "But the others need to know of the archivists. There were others. How many of the archivists were born of the Aeta? How many would use the caravans in such a way?"

A troubled look crossed Amia's face. "I…I don't know. I hadn't thought it possible." She forced a smile at him. "You could come with me. Learn what it means to travel like the People."

Once, Tan would have welcomed an invitation like that. So much had changed for him. "I'm not certain what I should do."

He could search for his mother—as much as he tried to deny it, he wanted to see her, to know she was well, and for her to know Amia—but there were other things he *should* do.

They made their way down a narrow path leading toward the lake. All around him, the woods were quiet, none of the usual life active in the forest. Distantly, he sensed the kingdom's shapers lingering around the water, fewer now than there had been earlier. Many had already begun to return to Ethea.

One shaper stood out and was nearer than the others, as if waiting for Tan and Amia to make their way back down. When Roine stepped onto the narrow trail, Tan was not surprised.

His face had aged since they were last in Ethea, most since the Incendin shaper attacked. Lines wrinkled the corners of his eyes and his mouth twisted in a pursed line. He stepped toward them hesitantly. "Tan," he said in greeting.

"I thought you would have returned to Ethea by now."

"I need to return. After what happened here, the king needs to know."

"You think he'll listen?" Tan asked. One of the king's Athan—advisors he kept closest to him—had been an archivist. And Incendin had sacrificed the archivist Jishun to create a new lisincend.

"That's why I've come to you," Roine said.

"We found the other archivist," Tan said.

"Does he still live?"

Tan shook his head, moving along the trail. Roine followed. "He did."

"What did you do?"

Tan stopped and turned to face Roine. "Me? You think me capable of killing him?"

Roine gave Amia a pointed look. "There are many reasons men kill, Tannen."

Tan followed Roine's gaze to Amia. He raised his chin, refocusing his attention on the warrior. "No. I didn't kill him." He had tried. When it meant saving Amia, Tan had been willing to do anything, even kill. "Not that he didn't deserve it."

"Did he say anything?"

"He said a plan was already in place. Lacertin thinks it is the same as Incendin's plan."

Roine grunted. "About Lacertin…"

"I know you don't trust him."

Roine went still. "That's an understatement." He took a deep breath. A shaping built as pressure in Tan's ears before releasing softly. "You don't understand what happened, what I have seen of Lacertin. He comes and tells you that he's worked against Incendin all this time and makes claims about your mother, but he can't be trusted, Tan. I remember what he was like before he left Ethea. Even then, he wasn't to be trusted."

Tan met Roine's gaze. "He said he has always served King Ilton."

"Does he? And how much do you know about King Ilton?"

His father used to tell him stories around the hearth at night, tales he later learned must have come from his time in Ethea, but none of them were about King Ilton. "Not much."

Roine grunted again. "Probably kind of your father to leave those out. Ilton was a reasonable king. At first. He bargained with Ylin for control of the fishing lanes and made a point of welcoming trade from Doma. That hadn't always been the case. As he aged, something changed. He developed a hardness to him. There was an uprising in

Nara, and he sent warriors to contain it. Many died. And then his mind began to slip. He started making outrageous claims, drawing only a select few to him."

Tan wondered what kind of outrageous claims. Would it not once have been outrageous to claim the archivists attempted to shape him? "Lacertin was one?"

Roine nodded. "Lacertin had always been one of Ilton's closest advisors."

"But Lacertin fought alongside you. Without him, Incendin would have won."

"Are you so certain Incendin did not win? That everything that happened here was not part of their plan?"

Tan frowned.

"She escaped with the artifact. The archivists are gone. And Lacertin has practically convinced you that he has always worked on behalf of the kingdoms." Roine fixed him with a determined stare. "I would say that is success for Incendin."

"He spoke the truth," Amia said.

Roine looked over to her. "Can you be sure? After everything you've been through, you're so confident in your sensing to know he spoke the truth?"

"Yes."

A dark smile twisted Roine's mouth as he studied Amia. "I wish I felt the same. Too much has been lost fighting against him over the years."

"Is that why you came here, Roine? You wanted to warn me against trusting Lacertin?" Tan asked.

Roine took a deep breath. "No. You must decide that on your own. I only ask that you learn as much about him as you can before trusting him with something important. Like your life."

"Why do you hate him so much?" Tan asked.

"Hate is not a strong enough word." Roine's eyes blazed with the heat of his comment. He took a breath and looked back to the lake, staring over the water.

"Has it always been like this between you?" Tan asked.

Roine shook his head slightly. "We were friends once. Back when we first studied. There was always competition between us, always a rivalry. Both of us wanted to be the best, each reaching for the next shaping. When we both managed to become warriors, it continued."

"If you were both warriors, why didn't you help each other rather than competing?"

Roine snorted. "To answer your question, you need to understand what it was like back then. This was nearly forty years ago, Tan, and the kingdoms were a different place. The king—Ilton—*loved* his warriors, and each warrior strove for his attention."

"And Lacertin managed to get his attention?"

Roine turned. With his eyes closed, a slight smile crossed his mouth. "Lacertin managed to get everyone's attention. That was how he was. Not just the king, but within the palace as well and among the other warriors." Roine's smile deepened. "He was… powerful and confident. Not much different than he is now, to be honest, only then, he clearly served the kingdoms. It was captivating, even to me." He inhaled deeply. "I can honestly say that without Lacertin, I would never have been pushed to be the warrior I am today. We challenged each other. Most of the time, that was a helpful thing."

"Until it wasn't," Amia said.

Roine paused, his eyes narrowing as he studied her, as if expecting her to shape him. Any spirit shaping would likely set Roine off after how the archivist had used him.

"Until it wasn't," he agreed. "He took the competition too far and someone got hurt."

Amia stepped alongside Tan. "Who got hurt?"

"It doesn't really matter anymore, does it? All of that is in the past."

"Except it isn't," Amia said. "It separates you both, keeps you from seeing him as willing to help. If you really serve the kingdoms, you need to move past that history."

Roine grunted. "Like I said, it doesn't matter. What matters is what we must do now." He turned to Amia. "Jishun shaped me, twisting my mind until I was willing to act in ways I would not have. I don't know how long he worked on me, shaping me, but I fear he has done the same to Althem."

Tan had not forgotten about the possibility that the king had been shaped. What would the archivists have asked of him? What darkness now twisted the king's mind?

"That's why I came to you. I need you, Amia. I need you to return to Ethea and remove the shaping," Roine said.

Amia shifted her weight uncomfortably. "Will he allow it?"

Roine grimaced. "That's part of the problem. The palace is protected. Few can enter, and those who can are limited in using their shaping. It is a trick of the ancients, something few understand."

Tan touched the pocket where the dark ring of silver rested, the twin of the one on Roine's index finger. It was much like the silver necklace Amia wore. The ring granted access to the palace, but would it also let him shape while there?

"If I can't shape to remove the work of the archivist, how do you expect me to help him?" Amia asked.

"Jishun must have worked his shaping over many months. Years, possibly. It makes me fear what decisions were Althem's and what was Jishun's influence. I will need you to peel away the shaping slowly so as not to destroy him, giving him time to decide which decisions were his."

Amia bit her lip and glanced at Tan. Uncertainty drifted through the bond. "What you ask… I don't know if I can do it."

"Why can't she simply remove the shaping as she did with you?" Tan asked.

"Because I don't know what the shaping intended. The archivists had a purpose. Until we know what it was, we need caution. Short of convincing the archivists to share—" he looked at Amia, and she shook her head. The archivists could not be shaped with spirit, not like others. Tan and Amia had already seen how the archivists were immune to her shaping. "This is the only way I know of to learn their plan."

Tan closed his eyes, thinking about what Roine asked. "You don't think their plan included Incendin?"

"We have lived with the threat from Incendin for decades. We are only now learning of the threat from the archivists. If they are connected, I need to know."

"The archivists have moved in the shadows. It is what Incendin plans openly that we should fear."

Tan turned and saw Lacertin behind them.

Again, he had snuck up on Tan, bypassing his ability to sense Lacertin. There wasn't anything else that managed to surprise him so easily. Could Roine be right—should he still fear Lacertin?

Roine glared at the old warrior. His hand went to his sword.

Lacertin smiled widely and raised his hands in front of him. "Easy, Theondar. Or would you prefer I call you Roine?"

Roine made as if to move past Tan and Amia, but Tan stepped between them, keeping the two warriors apart.

"What have you been telling them, Lacertin? That you have been working in Incendin, helping the kingdoms all this time?"

Lacertin smiled. "Yes."

"I won't make the mistake of trusting you again. I pray Tan will not either."

"As you said, that is for him to decide."

Roine's eyes narrowed.

How long had Lacertin been there, listening?

From what Roine had told him, even the warriors were stronger in some areas than others. Roine had been a wind shaper first and still claimed the strongest connection to wind. Could Lacertin be an earth shaper? Was that how he managed to conceal himself from Tan?

"You saw what she became, Theondar. If she creates others like her—"

"And I felt what the archivists were able to accomplish with only two of them. What happens if a half dozen work a shaping? Perhaps they already have and we don't know."

Roine did not meet Amia's eyes. Tan felt a surge of irritation from her at the accusation. Somehow, she stayed silent.

"And perhaps you are weak enough to let them shape you."

"You believe you haven't been shaped?"

Lacertin sniffed again. "Live among the lisincend long enough and you will learn there are tricks needed to survive. If I couldn't protect my mind, I wouldn't have survived a year."

A wide smile split Roine's face. "Now you claim to be a spirit shaper?"

Lacertin shook his head. "You don't need to be a spirit shaper to protect yourself from one."

"Water and air," Tan said softly.

The comment caught the two warriors off guard. Lacertin grinned. Roine only frowned at him.

"It's a buffer. When the archivist tried shaping As—the draasin." He caught himself before revealing Asboel's name. That wasn't his to share. "I used a shaping of air and water to protect it. I'm not really sure what I did."

Lacertin studied Tan intently.

Roine continued to frown. "You shouldn't have been able to protect yourself from spirit with those two elements," he said.

Lacertin chuckled softly. "You *are* dangerous, Tan." He shifted his attention to Roine. "Wind to buffer the shaping, water to heal. It is quite simple, actually, and takes very little strength to maintain."

A soft shaping built. Roine's eyes widened slightly as he regarded Tan and Lacertin.

"I'm not who you think I am, Theondar," Lacertin said.

Roine's frown returned. "And I'm not Theondar anymore. I tried, but even in that, I failed, letting an archivist of all people shape me."

Lacertin laughed again, this time bitterly. "You think I should pity you for what you've been through? You think your life the last twenty years has been so terrible? Try living in Incendin for the same time, not leaving the Fire Fortress for nearly two years, all the time assailed by lisincend trying to determine what other motive you might have for coming to them. And the lisincend were not even the worst. They are blunt and powerful, but power is not the only thing to fear. There are shapers, subtle and skilled, working quiet shapings on you in a constant torture." He fixed Roine with an amused expression. "So pardon me if I do not accept whatever torment you've placed upon yourself."

Roine took a deep breath to compose himself. "You chose your fate. You entered Ilton's quarters after he passed. You went to Ilianna and stole from her. In whatever happened to you, you were complicit."

Lacertin sniffed softly. "I will not discuss the past with you, Theondar. Not when you are incapable of understanding my motive. But know this—what Incendin has planned for the last hundred years nears completion. And as a servant of the kingdoms, that should frighten you very much."

Roine met Lacertin's gaze. He took a few slow breaths and addressed Tan. "I don't deny that Incendin remains a threat, but there is a more immediate threat. And that is what I care about."

"The archivists and Althem? Even if Amia removes the shaping, the month or years the archivists have spent shaping him is nothing compared to the time Incendin has spent planning—"

"Enough!" Tan said.

Lacertin and Roine studied him, the expression on their faces similar.

Frustration bubbled up within Tan. Someone built a shaping nearby. "You both want the same thing. Can't you see that? Roine, you want the kingdoms safe and you'll do anything to ensure their safety. And Lacertin, you've spent the last two-dozen years living a lie to learn what Incendin planned, all because you served your king. It is time you work together again."

Lacertin's jaw clenched.

Roine frowned, narrowing his eyes as he looked at Amia. "Do *not* shape me." He spoke in a low growl, anger building behind his words.

Amia shook her head. "I did not…"

Lacertin considered Tan for a moment and laughed. "Spirit? Of course you can shape spirit, how else would you have managed to tolerate the pool of spirit?" He said the last mostly to himself.

Roine glanced from Lacertin to Tan. "Tan? That was you?"

"I didn't… I don't know—"

Roine squeezed his eyes shut and rubbed his fists against them. "I should have wondered. When you were able to speak to the nymid and draasin, it should have raised the question. And now that I know you've spoken to udilm…"

Tan held back sharing how he spoke to ara and possibly golud, though the earth elemental was trickier to know.

"Whatever either of us wants," Roine went on, watching Lacertin carefully, "you need to control your shapings. And spirit most of all. Accidents with any shaping are dangerous, but spirit can be devastating." Roine turned to Amia. "You will teach him?"

Amia bit her lip as she considered the question. "I have never taught another how to use this gift."

"But you know how you do it?" Roine asked.

Lacertin frowned. "We don't have time to spend on him learning to control spirit. The boy speaks to elementals. That will be enough."

Roine stepped past Tan, shaking the younger man off as Tan tried to grab his arm. "No. I promised his mother I would keep him safe."

"And a fine job of it you did."

"Don't press me on this, Lacertin."

Lacertin leaned forward, glaring at Roine. "And you will do what, Theondar?"

Tan watched the two warriors, not sure what to think. If he *could* shape spirit—and he must; otherwise he wouldn't have survived stepping into the pool of spirit—then he needed to understand it. And who better to teach than Amia?

"If you want me to help with the king, I may not have time to teach," Amia said, separating the two older men. She turned to Tan. "Roine is right. You need to understand what you're doing or a shaping like I placed on you could happen again. Or worse."

"Tan—" Lacertin started. "Every day we hesitate, we risk Incendin using the artifact."

He felt pulled in too many directions. In every way, he felt he was needed. How to argue with the fact that the king had been shaped by the archivists? Or the danger Incendin posed, not only to the kingdoms, but also to the draasin? But what if he was a danger to those around him, simply by virtue of abilities he possessed but had not yet learned to control?

Tan glanced at Amia. The decision tore at him. If he went with Lacertin, he could learn what had happened to his mother. He might eventually find her and understand why she hadn't revealed herself to him before now. Why leave him thinking she died?

But before he could be helpful against Incendin—before he could do anything more than rely on his connection to the elementals—he had to learn to control his shapings and understand what it meant that he could shape spirit. Amia might not think she could help, but she knew about spirit shaping. If anyone could help, it had to be her.

"Amia is right," he said. He made a point of not agreeing with Roine or Lacertin. "If I can't control even a part of my shaping, I put others at risk. I won't do that."

Lacertin closed his eyes and sucked in a quick breath. "It is your choice. I cannot help but think I will need the elementals to stop Incendin."

Roine shot Lacertin an angry look. "At least recognize what he needs to do for himself."

Lacertin glared at Roine a moment longer, and then turned to leave. As he started up the slope, he looked over his shoulder. "When you're ready, Tan. You know what's at stake. And if you don't, ask your draasin friend."

A shaping built with enormous pressure, culminating in a strike of lightning crashing to the ground. The air sizzled with it. When it cleared, Lacertin was gone.

Roine stared after him. "Do you really believe he still thinks to serve the kingdoms?"

Tan nodded. "With what Incendin plans, I do."

Roine sighed. "The Great Mother help us if we have to rely on him for salvation." He turned and headed down the slope, walking slowly. There was a slight stoop to his back and his shoulders slumped. He took another deep breath, straightening himself, and then disappeared around a bend in the trail.

CHAPTER 3

The Road Back

THE RETURN TO ETHEA TOOK the better part of a week.

Most of the other kingdom shapers traveled with them, keeping to themselves. That was fine by Tan and Amia, who rode mares rescued from the Aeta wagons. Roine, who could have shaped his return to Ethea, chose to walk along with them. Tan could feel his concern for the king roiling off him.

"The shapers worry about what they did," Amia said as they stopped near a stream.

Tan climbed down from the saddle and regarded the shapers. "They were shaped. What they did couldn't be helped."

"They haven't lived knowing spirit shapers. They struggle with what it means."

Tan took a drink from a narrow stream that reminded him of the streams he found in the forests around his home village of Nor. His horse gulped at the water as well before nibbling on the long grasses.

Tan considered the wide expanse of Ter. Master Ferran was leading them over a different path than the one Tan had last used when he went this way. It was a faster route, and Tan noted Roine let the Master shaper guide them. Tan stretched out with his sensing, reaching all around. There was a city nearby, but Master Ferran avoided it, choosing a straight path that led away from the city. Nothing else moved, nothing like within the forest, where wolves and squirrels and birds all competed for his attention.

"I think we all struggle to understand what it means now that the archivists are known," Tan said.

Amia started to say something but cut off as Master Ferran made his way toward them. He pushed the hood of his cloak back from his head and looked from Amia, his eyes lingering on the silver band around her neck, to Tan, blinking slowly as he did. "I never thanked you for what you did." He spoke slowly and with a deep voice. "Had you not come, Aeta, I fear what I would have done."

"You only did what he made you do," Tan said.

Master Ferran squeezed his hands into tight fists. "I'm not certain that is entirely accurate. I might not have attacked, but it felt like the shaping only encouraged action I would have taken on my own."

Tan glanced over at Amia, thinking of the shaping that had forged the bond between them, the one demanding that he protect her. He would have done it anyway, but the shaping certainly augmented the desire.

"Much has been lost," Master Ferran continued. "And much more remains to be understood. I cannot claim expertise in any of this. The Great Mother knows I didn't know Theondar still lived until he revealed himself during the attack. But I serve the king and will do what I can to oppose Incendin." He turned to Tan and hesitated before continuing. "You have much strength shaping earth. Your father would have been proud."

"I wish he would have lived long enough to teach me how to shape."

Master Ferran furrowed his brow. "And still you shielded the draasin from me? Perhaps he taught you more than you realize."

"I didn't…" Tan started, but stopped. He *had* shielded Asboel from the kingdom shapers, not willing to reveal the draasin before he was ready. Had he not, would they have harmed him? As one of the great fire elementals, Asboel was more powerful than any single shaper, but together, they might have overwhelmed him. Tan still didn't understand the draasin well, but they were different than the other elementals in some ways.

Master Ferran shook his head. "You did what was needed. You did what fully trained shapers could not when you recognized the risk Incendin posed. We came to hunt the draasin, thinking them the enemy. I am still not certain what it means to have draasin free once again, but after seeing how the creature helped, I no longer believe they are to blame."

"It was Incendin," Tan started. "Or at least the archivists working with Incendin. They wanted it to look like the draasin attacked Ethea so you would hunt them. Incendin thinks to challenge the elemental power of the draasin."

Master Ferran studied the ground and the grasses growing up around them. "All my life I wanted nothing more than to serve the kingdoms. I always knew I was an earth senser, but Master Digush found me and convinced me to visit the university, convinced I could learn to shape. And there, I met your father. Grethan was a skilled earth shaper. I can't help but think even he would have struggled against the challenges we face today."

"He won't have the chance. Incendin already took his life."

Ferran nodded, almost more to himself. "A great loss." He met Tan's eyes. "If you wish it, I am willing to teach what I know of earth shaping. As a warrior candidate, Theondar may wish you to learn from him, but there is much you can learn from me Theondar can't teach."

He nodded at Amia and took his leave.

Tan watched him leave, confused. "He had no interest in teaching when I was in Ethea before. He seemed to want nothing more than to find out where everyone came from. When he learned I came from the Galen region, he seemed disinterested."

Amia frowned at Master Ferran. "He regrets something he has done."

"They all regret letting the archivists shape them."

"It is more than that." She inhaled slowly. "Whatever he regrets is buried deeply. Without shaping him directly, I doubt I can learn."

"Probably best not to shape him."

Roine crouched near the stream, somehow having slipped past Tan's attention. He cupped his hands to his face, taking a long drink. Then he splashed water across his face. "After what we've been through, probably best not to shape any of us, Amia."

"You can't blame me for what happened."

He stood, wiping his hands on his pants. "Not you. You had nothing to do with what happened to us. But the others feel guilty about it. There is a certain awareness of the shaping but a helplessness to stop yourself. If they feel it happen again, I fear how they would react."

Tan remembered how the shaping had felt as it settled on him. He had run to the water, hoping the nymid would somehow help protect him from the shaping, but they had not answered. Not until he managed to free himself from the shaping had he been able to reach the nymid.

"What *was* it like?" Tan asked.

Roine's eyes took on a pained expression and he bit his top lip. "Like your mind was no longer your own. The things I did—the shapings I worked—they weren't mine."

Tan wondered how difficult it had been to convince Roine to attack Lacertin. They already practically hated each other for things that happened decades ago; would it really have taken much effort to convince Roine to attack him?

Roine took a deep breath and considered the other shapers.

Other than Master Ferran, Tan recognized Alan, the wind shaper who had known his mother. What would Alan say now that they knew his mother lived? Would he care?

A fire shaper, Seanan, crouched away from most of the others. He fidgeted with his hands and didn't look at anyone. Tan remembered him eagerly attacking the draasin, sending lances of flames at the fire elemental. The other kingdom fire shaper, a wisp of a woman with deep brown eyes and bright red hair named Cianna, sat close to Seanan. Neither said anything.

A tall water shaper, Nel, watched the fire shapers, studying them suspiciously. The others glanced over at them as well, eyes narrowing each time they did.

"Is it always like that?"

Roine followed the direction of Tan's gaze and saw him staring at the fire shapers. "Since the last Incendin war," Roine said. "Fire shapers have always been different. Most fire shapers come from Nara, which is different than the rest of the kingdoms. Hot and arid. More like Incendin in that way. Fire shapers haven't always been set apart, only screened differently than others. There has always been the fear that Incendin would send a shaper to join the university."

"And have they?"

Roine shook his head. "Not in all the time I've been there."

"Why do you think that is?" Amia asked.

Roine shrugged. "Probably because they learn more from their own shapers than they ever could learn from the university. After seeing some of the fire shapings Lacertin managed, I can't imagine what else he's learned during his time in Incendin."

"Was Lacertin a fire shaper first?" Tan asked. Roine admitted he was a wind shaper first. It was how he knew Tan's mother.

Roine tilted his head. "Is that what he told you?" When Tan shook his head, Roine nodded slowly. "Not something he used to be proud of. Even then, fire shapers had a certain stigma. Coming from Nara will do that."

"But shapers come from all over the kingdoms," Tan said.

Roine nodded. "For most shapers, that is true enough. You'll find water shapers from Ter or wind shapers from Vatten." He looked at Tan. "Or earth sensers from Galen."

"I'm more than only an earth senser," Tan said.

"We know that now. But your sensing ability is not *so* rare that I was surprised to find you in Galen. Had you been a fire senser, it would have been different."

Tan watched Seanan, who glanced up at times, long enough to catch others watching him, and glared at them. As he did, a shaping built and the air flashed slightly warmer, almost as if he struggled to keep control of his shaping. The other shaper near him did not look up. Instead, she ran the edge of her finger along a piece of bark. Smoke trailed where she touched.

"Why are fire shapers different?" Tan asked.

"They weren't always that way. Fire *is* different than shaping other elementals. It was the hardest for me to master, and I still can only manage shapings on a large scale, nothing requiring a delicate touch, and certainly nothing like Cianna does so easily." He nodded toward the woman. "You would have to ask them about why fire is different."

"Why do the others treat them differently?" Tan asked.

Amia answered. "Fear. The others fear another Incendin shaper. If they could be manipulated by archivists, they fear what would happen if Incendin were to send one of their shapers to them."

Roine sighed. "Worse than that is the fear they have about what happened to the king."

They rode mostly silently for the next few days, stopping only to eat and sleep. Between Tan and Master Ferran, they managed to catch enough to eat. Ferran found fruits and edible roots along the way to season the food. The fire shapers cooked what they caught, but did so in silence. Even Amia had fallen quiet.

As they neared Ethea, a growing awareness of the city pressed on Tan through his earth sensing. He had left the city to help Elle and instead was pulled into something greater. He returned intending to help the king, hoping to free him from the archivist shaping. Only then would Tan feel free to search for the Incendin shapers before they harmed the draasin.

The small fire shaper, Cianna, nudged her horse toward him. Her red hair hung in a braid down her back that bobbed with each of the horse's steps. She watched him for a few moments, almost as if waiting for him to say something.

Amia rode alongside Tan and kept close, keeping a watchful eye on Cianna.

"You speak to them, don't you?" she finally asked. She had a soft voice that lilted in a strange accent.

Tan looked over. "Who?"

She snorted. Scorn twisted her deep brown eyes. "You ask who. I thought Theondar would teach you better than to feign ignorance."

"Theondar doesn't teach," Tan said. Neither had Ferran, in spite of his offer.

"So you are ignorant?" she asked. Her arms crossed over her chest, guiding the horse with her knees.

Tan didn't know how to take the comment. Amia laughed. She covered her mouth with her hand. Amusement flowed through the shaped connection.

Tan studied Amia. At least she found humor in this. Since leaving the place of convergence, she had been so quiet. It worsened the closer they got to Ethea. He turned back to Cianna. "Consider me ignorant."

Cianna shifted her horse so she rode closer to Tan. She watched Amia as she did. "I haven't thanked you for what you did. Probably none of these others have, either. Most are too proud to admit they needed help. Or maybe stupid."

Tan blinked in surprise. "Stupid?"

"See?" Cianna said. "Stupid. Can't even realize what I'm saying. Does he need your help finding your mouth or can he at least manage that much on his own?"

Amia flushed slightly and shrugged.

Cianna laughed again, her voice a husky rasp. Her horse practically touched Tan's now.

Tan shifted in his saddle, uncomfortable with how close Cianna was. Heat radiated from her, but not unpleasantly like with the lisincend. "What do you want to know about the draasin?"

Cianna tilted her head, looking over at Amia. "Maybe not *quite* as stupid as I thought." Her accent made the words come out in a singsong. She turned to Tan. "How do you do it?"

If this was how all the fire shapers spoke, it was no wonder other shapers treated them differently. Not her accent—Tan found that more intriguing than anything else—but the direct and blunt way she spoke to him. "I don't really know how I do it. I was trying to speak to the nymid when it sort of happened."

Cianna leaned toward him, practically tipping out of her saddle. Her face was close enough now that he could feel the warmth of her breath. "Wait. You speak to nymid, too?"

"I can speak to all of the elementals," he admitted. With Cianna, being direct seemed best.

"Great Mother," she swore. She leaned back in her saddle and looked up toward Roine, who rode alongside Master Ferran. Since leaving the place of convergence, they had ridden together more often. "Theondar knows, then?"

Tan nodded.

Cianna grunted. "Figures he'd keep you for himself. Probably thinks he can learn to speak to the elementals."

"He didn't think freeing the draasin was a good idea."

Cianna shot Tan a look of amusement. "Of course not."

"You're a fire shaper. You don't think it was a good idea to free the draasin?"

"That's not what I said." She leaned even closer.

Amia watched Cianna, eyes fixed on how close she rode to Tan. Amusement changed into a flash of irritation surging through their connection.

"I said Theondar wouldn't want the draasin free. Too much unknown. Most fear fire when they should embrace it. Fire is as much a part of the world as water and wind and dirt." Smoke trailed from her hands where they gripped the reins. "Tell me. What's it like?"

Tan thought of the first time he spoke to the draasin, the way his mind had practically exploded. Only through a force of will had he managed to push Asboel back in his mind. "Like your mind is being consumed."

Tan regretted the answer as soon as he said it. Like the other shapers, the archivist had shaped Cianna.

Instead of anger, she nodded. "Or course. That's how it is with fire. You have to know your limits or it will consume you. Might be why so few fire sensers attempt a shaping, even when they have the potential." She practically touched him now. "So. Where did they go?"

The sense of Asboel was distant within his mind. Wherever he was, Asboel wanted to be left alone. Tan would honor that for now, but soon—when Tan had a better sense of shaping and after the king had been healed—he would need the draasin to hunt lisincend.

"Not going to say?" Cianna said. "That's fine. Probably best anyway. Safer that way."

"For who?" Tan asked. He couldn't decide if he liked Cianna or not.

She brought one leg up so now she leaned way out of the saddle. Her eyes drifted toward the front of the line of horses. "For them."

She glanced again at Amia with a grin and then dropped back into her saddle.

As she started forward, Tan said, "Wait."

Cianna turned and looked at him. Near her, Seanan glanced back. Tan realized he had been listening the entire time.

"Why did you go?" Tan asked. If Cianna was blunt with him, he would ask the question that troubled him. "Why were you willing to attack the draasin?"

Seanan blinked and turned away, trying again to look like he hadn't listened.

Cianna let her horse drift back to him. She bit her top lip before answering. "Nara is a hard place. Not like your Galen."

Tan frowned. "What kind of answer is that?"

Cianna spurred her horse forward. "The only one you need."

CHAPTER 4

Ride through Ethea

ROINE HAD ELECTED TO REST outside the city another night, wanting to reach Ethea during the daylight. The master shapers all seemed to understand, though Tan did not until they actually reached the outskirts of the capital. As they reached Ethea in the early morning, the stink hanging over it became nearly cloying from the lingering scent of burning bodies and buildings destroyed in the attack.

A shimmering fog draped over the city. Strange, considering the cool breeze blowing through. It took Tan a while to realize that it wasn't fog but the smoke from still-smoldering fires in spite of the weeks since the attack.

"How is it they still burn?" he asked as they crossed through the city's outer wall.

All around him were signs of the destruction worked by the

Incendin shapers. Places where fires had burned, leaving charred wooden buildings or crumbling stone. Ash and soot stained everything. A few people milled about in the street, but not nearly as many as Tan would have expected. Most moved hurriedly, carrying damaged clothes or other stacks of goods through the street, still attempting to recover from what had happened.

Cianna and Amia rode on either side of him, leaving Tan feeling uncomfortably flanked by the two smaller women, both such skilled shapers. It was almost as if they formed a sort of protection around him.

The other shapers left as soon as they reached the city. Only Cianna stayed with them. Tan hadn't figured out why, but the small fire shaper seemed to have taken an interest in him. Or maybe her interest was more in the draasin.

"Incendin shapings," Cianna said. She pulled on the black leather overcoat she wore, shifting it to drape over her legs. "Or maybe draasin. Difficult to extinguish either way."

"I thought the shapers took care of the fires before they left."

Tan hadn't stuck around the city to observe what happened. His focus had been on doing what he needed to help Elle. Hopefully the udilm had returned her to her people. Hopefully she was still safe.

"Controlled them. Kept them from spreading. That is all that *can* be done. You know fire," she admonished him. "Sense what they did."

Tan focused on the smoke drifting from just inside the wall. As he did, he became aware of the warmth. It pulled on him, drawing him, almost as if asking him to shape the fire larger again. He had to fight the urge as he pushed through the shaping, reaching for the embers he sensed still smoldered. Then he understood: The shaping was powerful. Too much energy would be needed to put the fire out completely, but in time it would disappear, burning itself out.

Earth and water shapings surrounded the fire. Even the air around the fire had been shaped still, keeping it from feeding the coals. Contained but not extinguished.

Tan focused on the fire. With an effort, he asked earth to soften, pull the remaining coals deep underground before closing atop them. At the same time, he pulled on his connection to the draasin to draw away the remaining energy from the fire, pulling it through him.

Weakness washed over him and he sagged in the saddle.

Cianna laughed. "See? Powerful shapings. You probably weren't even able to modify the shaping."

He didn't bother to correct her. He hadn't actually shaped anything. What he did involved the elementals, not any shaping of his own. Even when he thought he'd managed shaping when attacking Incendin, it had been the elementals helping. Learning to shape on his own was part of the reason he had returned to Ethea.

She continued to laugh as they worked through the streets. Patches of the city were unharmed, as if the shapings had missed them. Other parts of the city were entirely destroyed.

Tan hadn't realized the damage was so widespread. Could all of this have been from Enya—the youngest of the draasin—or had the Incendin fire shapers been a part? If this had been only one of the draasin—and the youngest and smallest of them—what would happen if all the draasin attacked?

For the first time, he had to wonder if maybe Roine was right. How dangerous had the world become now that the draasin had returned?

"Think of what it would be like without them," Amia said, leaning toward him.

She spoke softly, pitching her words for his ears only, but Cianna smiled tightly and turned to study him. She pursed her lips but didn't say anything.

"They needed to be free," Tan agreed. They were elementals trapped against their will at the bottom of the lake. Even had they gone willingly, one thousand years frozen within the lake had been long enough. "But what if they come again? What if this happens somewhere else, someplace where there aren't any shapers to protect them?"

"Do you think they would?" Amia asked.

Tan thought of Asboel, of the pride he took in hunting, but the creature Tan knew wouldn't do this, not without reason. And when the youngest had attacked, the archivists had used Amia's shaping, twisting it to coerce the youngest draasin into attacking the city.

"Some think the draasin were always deadly," Cianna said. She had released her reins and once again guided the horse with her knees. "But only the ancients know what it was like when draasin filled the skies. Even then, cities grew and flourished. The other elementals are different but not necessarily harmless. Udilm has claimed ships traveling the seas. Golud has sucked entire buildings underground. And ara..." She snorted. "Who is to know with ara? They say she is too fickle to care."

He hadn't thought the wind elemental fickle, but certainly difficult to connect to. There was a playfulness to ara that wasn't there with the other elementals.

"To them, we are nothing particularly special," Roine said. His gaze settled on Cianna.

"Theondar," she said, tipping her head. "You claim to know the mind of the elementals?"

He glanced at Tan. "Few enough speak to the elementals, let alone claim to know how they think. But how can we grasp the mind of the elemental? It would be like an ant trying to understand us."

Cianna barked out a laugh. Roine stared at her. "Is that really what you think, Theondar?" she asked. "That we're ants?"

Roine shrugged.

"Have you ever gone out of your way to help an ant?" Amia asked.

Roine turned to her. "You think the elementals help if it doesn't serve them?"

"Yes," she answered simply.

Roine sat taller in his saddle. "I wish I believed that to be true."

Cianna frowned at him. "I liked you better when you played as Roine."

He shook his head. "We'll reach the palace soon." Roine made a point of not looking at Cianna. "And I'll need you to begin freeing the king's mind."

"And if he hasn't been shaped?" she asked.

"Why would the archivists shape us but not the king?" Roine asked.

Amia met his eyes. "How can you be so certain he didn't know what they did?"

"Then you will learn that as well." Roine directed his attention to Tan. "You should stay away from the palace until this is done."

Sunlight sliced through the smoke and played across Amia's golden hair. One hand touched her neck, running around the silver band there.

"You will keep her safe?" Tan asked.

Amia fixed Roine with a hard expression. "He will not have to."

Roine stared at her. "Careful…"

"No, Roine. I will help, but if there is any sign of danger, I will not hesitate to do what I need."

Roine inhaled deeply. Then he glanced at Cianna. "See that he stays safe?"

Cianna looked at Tan. "You think someone able to ride the draasin is in danger within Ethea?"

"How many shapers remained in Ethea? How many may have

been influenced by the archivists? We know nothing about what they planned, nothing about how many shapers they had. You are one of the king's shapers. Be vigilant."

"Is that the Athan or the warrior?" Cianna asked.

"Yes."

Roine started away, turning off onto a different street leading toward the palace, which was visible in the distance. Amia touched Tan's arm, sending a reassuring shaping toward him, and then followed.

Tan stared up at the palace. Smoke swirled around, giving lingering images of the walls but obscuring much of the upper levels. Fires still simmered around the palace. How much longer before they burned themselves out?

"What was he like before?" Tan asked.

"Theondar? Don't know. I'm not old enough to know what he was like."

With her small face and long, wavy red hair, she could have been twenty or forty. Tan would have believed either. "How long have you been in Ethea?"

She laughed. "You want to know how long it took to master fire?"

He shrugged. "Yes."

"I've known I was a fire senser since I was nearly ten. Nara is different. The land is hot and dry. But I learned to find places that were cooler, almost as if drawn to them. That was my first sign." She looked over to the palace. "Fire sensers in Nara have a choice. Ignore it or attempt to chase it and learn to shape."

"Why would you want to ignore it?"

Cianna frowned at him. "You don't know your geography very well, do you?"

"Galen borders Incendin the same way Nara does."

"Not the same way," Cianna said. "Galen is separated from Incendin by the Gholund Mountains. Not so easy to pass through, even without the barrier. You're protected. Not the same with Nara."

"Because Nara was part of Incendin?"

"Not Incendin," she said quickly. "Rens. And what we call Nara was a part of it."

Tan remembered Roine mentioning Rens when telling him about King Weston. "And Rens took part of Nara from the kingdoms."

Cianna nodded. "Not as stupid as you pretend," she said with a smile. "Rens always had two different peoples. There were those who eventually came to Nara and joined the kingdoms, and those who eventually became Incendin. Irashers and Selanders. Back before Incendin existed, back when that land was still known as Rens, it was sometimes hard to tell people apart. There were similarities, but differences, too." She smiled and touched the braid in her hair. "I'm lucky. There's no confusing me for a Selander."

"And Seanan?" Tan asked. The other fire shaper didn't look anything like Cianna.

She nodded. "Seanan has some Selander blood. Many people in Nara do. There are still some people who believe all of Nara should rejoin with Incendin. That is why Nara is so different than Galen, even though we both share the border."

Tan couldn't imagine anyone in Galen thinking they should join Incendin. "You haven't told me when you came here."

Cianna snorted. "I came when I was fifteen. It was either come here and learn so I didn't destroy myself, or risk the crossing into Incendin."

"People do that?"

Her face turned serious. "Plenty of fire sensers from Nara make the journey across the border. They think that if they are to learn fire, they should learn it from those who truly serve it."

"Lacertin said he learned much from Incendin fire shapers," Tan said.

Cianna nodded. "And he's said to be one of the most accomplished fire shapers in generations."

Tan studied her. "You were never curious? Never thought to cross the border to learn?"

"I am committed to the king."

"That's no answer."

"No? You were raised in Galen, where there are trees and grass and plentiful water. Nara is different. Hot. Sandy. Harsh. Even that is nothing compared to Incendin."

Tan nodded. "I've seen Incendin."

Cianna laughed. "Seen Incendin? From your side of Galen? That is nothing like the Incendin I watched growing up. There, Incendin has stunted growth, but there are still trees and water."

"Now who's stupid?" Tan asked.

Cianna glared at him.

"I have ridden the draasin. What makes you think I haven't visited Incendin?"

She considered him a moment and then laughed. "Well, maybe I am being stupid now. Probably my turn anyway. Couldn't let you be the only one."

They rode onward, Cianna continuing to follow Tan. He wondered if she had somewhere to be. He did: Amia might be able to help the king, but there was something he could do that might bring him answers.

"So. You were in Incendin?" she asked after awhile.

Tan smiled. As blunt as Cianna seemed, he decided he was beginning to like her. "Not intentionally."

She laughed again. She undid the top clasp of her leather overcoat to reveal a burnt orange shirt beneath. Maroon embroidery worked around the neck. "How do you end up in Incendin accidentally?"

He shrugged. "It's a long story."

"See? Now you're stupid again. How else to explain you 'accidentally' end up in Incendin?"

"That's a different story," he said. "But Incendin was bleak. The sun burned down. Nothing but rocks and stunted plants, some which tried to kill me, all around. And then the sound of the hounds calling all around." Tan couldn't imagine being there for long periods of time.

How had Lacertin managed to survive *years* there?

Cianna nodded slowly. "That is Incendin. Nara is not quite so... barren. Still harsh. You wonder why I don't go to Incendin to learn? I would have to go there, survive the worst of Incendin to reach the Fire Fortress. And then?" She shook her head. "Lacertin might have been willing to risk it—the Great Mother only knows why—but I am unwilling."

"That's why you want to speak to the draasin?"

She turned her head toward him and smiled. "Sometimes you're almost smart."

"I don't know that the draasin teach," Tan said. "I'm not certain any of the elementals ever teach."

"No? Then how do you think the first shapers learned?"

"That's what I intend to find out."

She frowned as he pulled the horse to a stop and jumped from the saddle. A cluster of fallen rubble lay across the road in front of them. Behind the rocks, men wearing the king's colors—deep brown and a forest green like the one Roine wore when Tan first met him—worked, trying to clear the road. They nodded at Cianna and then at him but said nothing.

He tied the reins around a loose boulder to keep the horse from bolting. He'd have to find a stable to house it, but Cianna likely knew of one.

She waited, looking down from her saddle at him. "Why here? What do you hope to find?"

Tan turned and surveyed the city from this vantage point. It hadn't been long since he'd been here, but it felt ages ago. How much had changed in the weeks he had been gone? How much had *he* changed? It seemed each time he faced Incendin he changed even more. How much of that change had been for the good?

Tan turned to the low, squat stone building of the archives. Fires that had swept through the city had not harmed the archives, not like the surrounding buildings. Golud had helped build the archives, and the elemental power still protected them.

Tan sighed. What *did* he hope to find here?

"Answers," he finally said.

Cianna frowned, hesitating for a moment as if she considered what she would do.

Would she try to stop him? She was a Master shaper. She could stop him from accessing the archives, prevent him from accessing the hidden demesne of the archivists.

"What do you think to find in the archives?" Cianna asked.

Tan stared at the building. If not for his ability to sense, he wouldn't even know golud pressed beneath him, supporting—and protecting—the archives. What he wanted to know wasn't even in the archives, but below it. Answers had to be there, else why would the archivists work so hard to protect it?

Cianna waited for his answer, sitting in her saddle and staring down at him.

Tan sighed. "I don't want to go into the archives."

She frowned.

"What I want is below it."

A flash of understanding turned back her frown. She nodded and hopped from the saddle, barking an amused laugh. “Nothing there but more mysteries,” she said. “But I’ll go with you. Not much I can do—or you, I’d wager—but seeing as there aren’t many archivists to stop us, it doesn’t hurt to look.”

CHAPTER 5

Return to the Archives

CIANNA LIT THE SMALL LANTERNS hanging around the archives. Once the flickering orange light began glowing, Tan saw how the place appeared deserted but not abandoned. Books were stacked atop tables, picked up from where they must have fallen in the explosion. A few shelves were tipped to the side, but someone had been through and stacked the contents that had fallen.

"Who was here?" he wondered.

Cianna shrugged. "Archivists, likely."

"They were exposed. They would not have stayed. And you said they were gone."

"You think *all* the archivists were to blame? How many spirit shapers do you think there are hidden in the archives?"

Tan shrugged. "How many fire shapers have come from Nara?"

She cocked her head. "Why?"

"We don't have any idea how many spirit shapers the archivists hid. Besides, had this been archivists, they would have righted the shelves."

Tan made his way toward the door at the back of the archives. Behind the door were restricted works and then a staircase leading down. It was there that the valuable works were kept.

Cianna moved to block him. "Those are restricted."

"They are, but I've been there before. I've been *trapped* there before."

"That was you?"

Tan nodded.

"Roine—Theondar—never said who reported the attack in the archives."

"The archivist wanted Amia and brought the fire shaper to capture her."

Cianna frowned. "Are you sure they wanted her?"

He nodded. "She was the one captured by the archivists."

"But you're the one who speaks to the draasin."

Tan hadn't considered that. What if the archivist hadn't been after Amia? What if they had wanted him instead? Had they used her to get to him? Could he have done exactly what they wanted?

The idea gave him shivers. What would have happened had they succeeded? If they would have reached—and accessed—the pool of spirit in the cavern at the place of convergence?

Now that Cianna suggested it, the idea made a twisted sort of sense. Amia might have shaped the draasin, but he was the one who spoke to them. Would they have known?

Of course they would have known. Jishun would have heard from the king what Tan had done.

Maybe he *was* as stupid as Cianna teased.

She opened the door to the restricted section of the archives. With a quick shaping of fire, all of the lanterns here suddenly blazed brightly.

The air smelled musty but there was another scent to it, like that of rot and decay. Her nose wrinkled at the smell.

"Was it like this before?"

The shelves were intact here, not tipped like they were in the main section. A few small tables rested at the end of rows of shelves. Stacks of paper and a few rolls of parchment perched on the tables.

"It looked the same. Didn't smell like this."

"Well? What did you want to see here?"

Tan pointed toward the door along the back wall. The last time he'd been here, Roine had to shape it open.

Cianna hurried toward the door. She touched the lock and performed a quick shaping.

Tan felt the pull of the shaping differently this time, almost as if he could see what she did. With a jab of fire, she shaped through the lock on the door, destroying it. Cianna pulled it away and dragged the door open. Darkness greeted them.

"Any lanterns?" she asked, peering into the darkness.

This might be a shaping he could do. Shapers lanterns only required there be a shaper, not any particular shaping. With a focus of effort, Tan lit them. A steady white light lit the way down the stairs.

Cianna snorted. With a quick shaping, she flickered the lanterns on, then off. "More than I'm used to seeing." She turned and looked over at Tan. "There are a couple in the university, but not many. How do you know how to light them?"

"They lined the cavern in the place of the cavern…" He trailed off, not wanting to remind Cianna of that time.

Cianna's face tightened for a moment and then she nodded. "I think I remember. Too much of that time remains blank for me. Ever since your girl lifted the shaping, there are gaps."

Tan frowned. "Was it like that for the others?"

"Don't know," she said, shrugging. "Most of us didn't talk about it much. Too proud. Too stupid, maybe."

Tan wondered what would happen when Amia lifted the shaping from the king. Would he have gaps like the others? If he did, could they use those to determine how far back the archivists shaped him?

But what if he forgot too much? What would it mean for the kingdoms?

Cianna started down the stairs, moving into the shadows between the lanterns. After a few steps, she looked back at Tan. "You're the one who wanted to come down here. Aren't you coming?"

Tan forced a smile and started after her. The last time he had been down these steps, they had found the body of the only archivist who had been kind to him. They made their way quickly down the steps. Cianna paused at each door, looking into each. When she reached the room where Tan and Amia were captured, she paused and studied the ceiling.

"Incendin do that?"

Tan shook his head. "Me."

Cianna regarded him strangely and stepped into the room. She climbed onto the shelving and reached the top, where she ran her hand along the stone. Her eyes drifted shut and a soft shaping built. When she opened her eyes, she let out a soft whistle.

"Fire. And strong enough to melt stone." She jumped down. "With focus, too. You didn't bring the entire ceiling down on you." She laughed. "Probably knew that, though."

"I didn't really know what I was doing. All I could think about was escaping the shaper." And Amia's shaped command that still lingered in the back of his mind, the request for him to protect her. When they were chased, the command had practically overwhelmed him again, the same as it had when they ran from the lisincend through the mountains of Galen.

Cianna frowned. "Theondar does you a disservice. You need better teaching."

Tan snorted. "From who?"

She shrugged. "Me, for starters. To melt stone like that means you're a strong fire shaper. Makes sense you can speak to the draasin."

"I can speak to the other elementals as well. And I was an earth senser first."

Cianna grinned at him. "But look what you reached for when you needed to escape." She smacked him on the shoulder as she passed, moving back onto the stairs. "It'll be good to teach again. Not many come looking to learn fire."

Tan didn't know what to say. None of the other masters had seemed particularly interested in teaching. Only Ferran had offered, though hadn't made much of an effort during their return to the city. Even Roine hadn't really wanted to teach. Finally, he had a willing instructor, but why did he wonder if his time would be better spent elsewhere?

"Well?" Cianna asked.

He needed to learn. That was the reason he returned to Ethea. "I'm ready to learn."

Cianna started down the stairs again, not waiting to see if he would follow.

Tan frowned, a thought crossing his mind. He raced down the stairs to catch her. "How many fire shapers are there?" he asked.

Cianna looked back at him and shrugged. "Not many. Kingdoms probably only have ten or so. Most are deployed along the border to fortify the barrier. Not nearly as many as wind and water shapers. Earth shapers are less common, but not quite as rare as fire shapers."

"Why were you here?"

She laughed. "What—don't like me now that we're down in the

dark?" Her red hair seemed to glow with the lantern light.

"I like you fine," Tan said hurriedly.

Cianna laughed. "Some compliment. If I wasn't sure before, now I know why the Aeta girl is drawn to you."

Tan ignored the comment. "How is it decided who stays at the university?"

She nodded. "Not sure how it is with the others, but with fire, we rotate. Each serves along the barrier for three cycles before returning. Keeps suspicions at a minimum."

"Suspicions?"

They had nearly reached the lowest level where the strange doors ringed a circular area.

Cianna paused and looked back at him. "Fire shapers along the border raise questions, even with other shapers." She shrugged. "Most feel it best we return to Ethea regularly to prove our loyalty."

What would it have been like had his parents returned to Ethea during his childhood? Would he have learned about his abilities sooner, or wouldn't it have mattered? Would his father have still been called to service? Probably sooner. And his mother might have been drawn back into service as well. Instead, they served in a different way, working to preserve the barrier.

"How many fire sensers do you think there are?"

Cianna shrugged. Her braid bobbed as she did. "Not always easy to determine who can sense fire. How many earth sensers do you think there are?" She shook her head. "Get to your point. What are you trying to determine?"

"I'm only wondering why there are so few fire shapers."

"Only here. Incendin has more."

She turned, as if that answered everything, and reached the lowest level.

Tan wasn't as certain. If Incendin had more fire shapers, why hadn't they attacked before now? Maybe Incendin had as few fire shapers as the kingdoms. But why would that be the case?

"Great Mother!" Cianna said.

Tan hurried down the last few steps and reached her. The shapers lanterns gave the circular area a warm glow, but shadows remained in between them, drifting back toward the doors, almost as if drawn there.

"What?" he asked.

"You know what this is?"

"Roine said it was the first archive."

She whistled softly to herself. "First Archive," she said, emphasizing it like a title. "Ethea is old, but this place?" She shook her head again. "This place is *old*. Most of the buildings in Ethea are hundreds of years old. Much of the archive overhead is even older, somehow shaped into being."

Golud helped create the archive above. Did Cianna know that?

"But this? This place is even older than that. A thousand years? Maybe more? And look how well preserved it is!"

Tan touched the nearest door. A humming sense came from it, working through his fingers. He focused on it, wondering where it came from, and started building a shaping.

Then he released it. He didn't know what type of shaping would work. Doing anything blindly only risked wasting his energy.

"Roine said there should be a key."

Cianna looked over. "Probably. And I imagine the archivists would never admit if there was."

"What do you think is behind the doors?"

Roine had offered his ideas about what might be behind the doors but hadn't really known. None but the archivists truly knew.

Cianna crouched before one of the doors. The ends of her fingers glowed, giving gentle light.

Tan studied the shaping and thought he understood how she did it, pushing fire to the tips of her fingers and holding it there, but how did she keep from burning herself?

"Look at the markings on the door," she whispered. She traced her finger along them.

Tan leaned over her shoulder to see better. With the light coming from her fingertips, the shadows around the door dispersed. Some folded into the markings on the door, as if pulled there. His eyes traced over them but were drawn to a particular set of shapes.

"I've seen these before," he said, framing them with his fingers, not quite willing to touch them.

Cianna shot him an appraising expression. "These were made by the earliest scholars. When would you have seen them?"

Tan reached over Cianna and touched the runes. They felt cool, but not like the stone of the higher level shaped by golud. This was different, heavy and ancient, as if drawn from the depths of the earth.

"Incendin had something with these on them," he said. The dark obsidian bowl had runes like this. Amia had known that he shouldn't touch it but hadn't said anything more.

Cianna's eyes widened slightly. "I remember a shaping," she started, "but it's unclear, more like a dream than a memory."

"She used the bowl for her transformation. She pulled her shaping through the bowl." And through the artifact, but he didn't know how much Cianna knew about the artifact.

Cianna jerked her hand back and the light at the ends of her fingers died. "You've been here before. How did you intend to open the doors?"

Tan hadn't known. When he had come before, he had been with Roine. Any exploring they might have done was cut short when they found the body of the archivist. "I didn't really know, but there has to be a way to open them. If the ancient scholars could open these doors, then we should be able to."

Cianna stood and gave him an amused look. "You think we should be able to recreate what the ancient scholars did? You've been to the cavern. The place they *shaped* a forest into existence?"

Tan began to understand her point.

"Great Mother," she swore, looking up at him. "And I thought I was backward coming from Nara. Didn't realize Galen was worse. We might have their records, but they lived in a different time. They knew so much more about shaping than we've ever managed to learn. Those scholars were more skilled than us in nearly every way."

"Because they spoke to the elementals?" Tan asked.

Cianna shrugged. "Don't know. Maybe because they could shape spirit, too. No warrior has shaped spirit in hundreds of years."

She moved on to the other doors, leaving Tan staring at the door in front of him. The runes must have some meaning, if only he could determine what it might be. Incendin must know about the runes, at least enough to use in their shapings like the one on the obsidian bowl Alisz intended to use in her shaping.

But there was another place he had seen runes like this—Roine's sword.

Tan closed his eyes, trying to visualize what he remembered of the sword. Roine must have known they were the same, but why hadn't he said anything?

And then there was what Cianna suggested. The earliest scholars were nothing like the shapers of today. They were warriors able to shape all the elements, including spirit. Could spirit be the key?

Tan traced his finger around the door, focusing on the runes. The challenge would be intentionally shaping spirit. The only times he had done it had been accidental, just like when he first shaped wind.

But he'd learned to shape with some intent by thinking of how he spoke to the elementals. Would it work with spirit?

The silver pool in the cavern had been liquid spirit. Wading through it gave him insight, a sense of connection, that he had never experienced before. He had shared a connection to Amia, binding them together in a way he could never have imagined possible.

Tan used this sense and reached for what he thought to be a spirit shaping.

Pain surged in his head, pounding and powerful.

And then he collapsed.

Chapter 6

A Lesson in Fire

FAINT LIGHT FILTERED THROUGH DARKNESS. Tan blinked his eyes open slowly. His head throbbed, so much like it had when he thought the connection to the draasin to be the problem. Waves of nausea threatened to roll through his stomach. He moved, and the nausea no longer threatened. He turned his head to the side and vomited.

"Careful!"

He wiped his arm across his mouth, wishing to rinse the taste of bile from his burned throat. "Cianna?"

She laughed and stepped toward him, making certain not to step in his pool of vomit. Her nose crinkled. "You finally awake?"

Tan tried to nod, but it only set his head pounding more. "What happened? Where am I?"

She touched a finger to his chest and forehead. Her hand did not feel hot but a soft glow came from her fingers. Tan recognized the shaping as the same as she'd done in the lower level of the archives. "I don't know. I was looking at the doors. There was a sudden explosion of air. I looked back to see you on your back. Brought you to my place to rest." She pulled her finger away, apparently satisfied with what she'd discovered. "I hoped you would be able to tell me what happened."

The pounding in his head made it difficult to think clearly. He remembered the runes and attempting a shaping of spirit, but then… nothing.

"I tried to shape the door," he admitted.

Cianna moved around the cot he found himself on, making him need to twist to keep her in view. Nausea threatened to overwhelm him again and he closed his eyes until it passed.

"I tried the same thing. Didn't collapse, though. What did you do different?" She took a seat and leaned toward him. She smelled of heat and a strange spice. Neither seemed unpleasant. Red hair pulled free from the braid in places, and she pulled its thickness around her shoulder.

Tan took a deep breath. "Tried to shape spirit."

Cianna was silent for a moment. "You can sense spirit?" she asked softly.

He opened his eyes. His vision had cleared enough for him to see dark gray stone overhead. A small lantern hung from the stone, glowing with dim orange light. It took a moment to realize the light was shaped, but differently than the shapers lanterns. Warm, dry air pressed on him, also shaped.

"Probably can shape it, too."

She leaned toward him. The heat from her body pressed on him, making him acutely aware of how close she was. Tan turned his head enough to see her. She had changed from the dark traveling cloak she'd worn. She wore a tight-fitting jacket of a sleek material that shimmered in the light from the lantern overhead, cut low to reveal the cleft of her chest.

How long had it been since he passed out?

"You can shape spirit." She let out a slow breath. "Does Theondar know?"

"He knows."

She laughed softly and touched him on the arm. Her fingers danced across the inside of his wrist, making a surge of heat wash through him. As it did, the pain and nausea eased. She shaped him, but not a shaping he recognized.

"What did you do?"

"The only thing I can," she said. "I wasn't sure it would even work. How do you feel?"

Tan turned his head. The nausea was still there, but lessened considerably. "Better. But why wouldn't it work?"

Cianna shrugged. "That shaping only really works on fire shapers. Figured it couldn't hurt to try on you, seeing as what you are."

"And what is that?"

She leaned in so her face was close to his. Dark eyes blinked slowly. "Something not seen in the kingdoms in a long time." She tilted her head. "Maybe you could have opened the First Archive. Can't believe that's even possible. Not anymore."

Tan stared at her for a moment. "I'm not sure I can be that person."

Cianna grabbed his cheek, pulling him to look at her. "Can't be that person? Who do you think you've been?"

He pulled away from her grip. The way she held his face had felt too familiar. "I've only done what I needed to help my friends."

"And why do you think I serve?"

Tan shrugged. "The debt you owe." He knew all about the debt to the king. That was the price his parents had paid for learning to shape. It was the reason his father had died.

"That's only a part of it," she said. "And not enough to force me to do anything. There comes a time when you have to decide for yourself what's right and what's wrong. And when you do, you'll want to make sure you're on the side of right."

Tan pushed up. The nausea faded to little more than nothing. Pain still pressed on him, squeezing lightly on his temples, but not the way it had when he first woke. "I've been on that side and nearly died. My father was on that side, and I saw where it got him."

"Trust me when I say the other side is worse."

Tan started to tell her that he knew Incendin was worse, but something in the way she said it gave him reason to pause. She knew more about Incendin than she admitted.

"Tell me what you tried to do with the door," she suggested.

"I thought I could shape it," he began, thankful for the change in conversation. "The archivists shape spirit. I figured if I could do the same, I might be able to open it." Except he wasn't even sure he shaped spirit. When he shaped, there was no control, nothing like what he'd seen from Cianna.

She laughed. "Without knowing the right shaping? You're lucky it was only a small explosion. A shaping on something like that could just as easily kill." She nodded when he gaped at her. "From what I can tell, that place takes a particular shaping. It's sort of like finding the right key for a lock. Without the key, the door won't open. Only, in this case, without knowing the right key, the door might kill you. Or the key." She frowned. "I'm not sure which is which in this analogy."

Tan studied his hands. How could he have been so foolish to think he could perform a shaping where Roine couldn't?

He needed to know more about shaping before he *really* did

something dangerous.

"You said you'd teach?" he asked without looking up.

"You could be a strong fire shaper," Cianna said. "And you're stubborn."

He tensed.

Cianna smiled. "Those are a good combination. Don't worry, if you're *too* stupid—or stubborn—you won't survive the lessons."

Tan stood in a walled area with nothing but a dirt ground. Cianna had led him here, claiming she had the perfect place for him to practice. By the time they reached the yard, the sun had drifted toward the horizon. The hazy fog swirling around left him only able to see a few paces in front of him but once inside the practice yard, the smoke dissipated, almost as if anticipating what they would do.

One end of the yard was cluttered with refuse. A bale of hay. A small metal post, already twisted and rusting. An old saddle, the leather cracked and faded. A few other items, none of which looked as if they belonged here.

Cianna pointed at the saddle. A shaping built, steady and powerful. When it eased, the saddle began smoking. Cianna held the shaping for a moment before releasing it and turning to him.

"Your turn. Smoke, not fire."

"Don't you want me to learn fire?"

She nodded. "Shaping fire is both easy and hard. Starting a fire is the easy part. Fire *wants* to exist. Controlling a fire is not as easy. That's where real skill comes into play."

"I don't have any skill," he said.

Cianna snorted. "None," she agreed. "But you have strength or you wouldn't have been able to melt through stone like you did in the archives. Now we just need to teach you the control."

"And making smoke will teach that?"

Cianna held her hand out to Tan and waited for him to take it. He did so reluctantly, watching her carefully. Since his awakening in the small room, she had been acting differently toward him.

"You can sense?" she asked.

He nodded.

"Good. Not sure how to teach you otherwise." She pointed toward the end of the yard. "Pay attention. Sense what I do. There will be several examples."

Cianna breathed out. Steam hissed from her nose in a soft shaping. Pressure and heat built in her hand, slow but rising steadily.

Tan sensed for the shaping. It was there, a faint sensation tickling the back of his mind. He closed his eyes, trying to recreate the shaping Cianna made. Pressure built in his ears, but sharp—too quickly for smoke.

Cianna cursed.

Tan snapped his eyes open.

Flames worked up her arm and she quickly extinguished them with a shaping. Tan worried he hurt her but saw her skin was unharmed. The shimmery jacket she wore hadn't even taken on any damage.

"Control," she said. Again, she formed a shaping.

This time, Tan felt it beginning. The shaping formed slowly, as if drawn out of Cianna, pulled from inside her. It worked through her skin until reaching her fingers. There, heat and pressure built as she held his hand.

"Try again," she demanded. "But be more careful. I can control most fire, but you've almost got too much strength."

Tan's heart fluttered as he nodded. "I don't want to hurt you."

Cianna barked out a short laugh. "It will take more than your clumsy attempts to hurt me," she said. "Make it soft, like a caress."

His skin tingled where her shaping touched him but didn't burn.

Tan inhaled slowly and tried to create the shaping like Cianna's. Pulling from within him, he tried taking the shaping and drawing it through his skin and toward his fingers as he sensed her doing. This time, nothing happened.

He tried again, reaching within himself, but there was no fire there.

How had he shaped the fire the first time? How had he shaped it when he almost burned Cianna's arm?

Not from a shaping that started within him. His shaping had come from outside of him, drawn from the heat of the air all around him. Why should this be different?

Tan sighed and called out toward fire as if speaking to the draasin. Connected to his fire sensing, he recognized another presence around him, not as strong as Asboel, but still connected to fire. Saa? Would speaking to the lesser elemental even work?

Gently, he urged.

With the thought, smoke simmered from his hand and along his arm.

Cianna nodded. "Good. A good start with control. Now you will need to work on focusing it only where you want it. Fingers. Toes. Stomach." She smiled at him. "Lips."

"Why is my shaping different than yours?" he asked.

"The shaping was the same. Yours may have been less focused, but the concept is there. I think with more practice, you will learn the necessary control."

"It wasn't the same for me. When you drew out your shaping, it came from inside you, drawn down through you before reaching your hand."

Cianna studied him, a strange expression on her face. "You sensed *where* the shaping came from?"

"You told me to sense fire."

Cianna studied him. "Not many have the patience to sense so closely."

He shrugged. "My father taught me earth sensing. He made certain I focused on all details as I did. He said I never knew which would be important."

"Maybe. My shaping comes from within. All shapings do. That's how we draw on the elemental power. I've seen you do it before, just pull from within." She nodded toward the end of the practice yard, as if it was decided. "Now. You've shown control close, but you'll need it at a distance, too. That's harder."

Cianna began a shaping. She still held his hand and her skin pressed against his, dry and comfortable. This time, Tan made certain to focus closely on it. Again, it drew from deep within Cianna, drawn out slowly and pushed toward the saddle on the far end of the practice yard. Even before the shaping struck, Tan knew what it would do.

Smoke rose from the saddle, as if heated on a stove. No flames rose. The scent of burning leather drifted toward them. Cianna held the shaping a moment before releasing it and turning back to Tan.

"Try that."

Tan took a deep breath and focused on the saddle. He tried drawing the shaping through him as Cianna had done but again, nothing happened. Again, he called out as if speaking to the draasin. This time, he focused on the saddle as he sent the command. *Smoke.*

The shaping left him in a soft rush. Smoke rose from the saddle, billowing away. It was much like what Cianna had done. And nothing like it.

Could it be that he didn't shape the same way she did? For him to control fire, he had to use the elemental power. Cianna controlled it herself.

She looked over at him and smiled. "Good. Most can't maintain control at a distance so quickly. There's room for improving your control, but it's a start."

Tan thought about telling her he hadn't done it the same way, that his control was not what she believed, but how could he explain that he shaped differently than her? The results were similar, but he sensed how she created her shaping. What he did was different. Was it like that with each of the elements or only with fire? Maybe working with the draasin changed something for him, or maybe he simply had learned it a different way. But if he had, could he learn to have the delicate control Cianna managed?

"Try it again." She released his hand and pointed to the saddle. With a snap of her fingers, heat shimmered up from within her, radiating from her body as it raced toward the saddle. Smoke simmered around the saddle, slowly rising into the air. She snapped again and the smoke faded. "This time, hold it low and steady. Focus on trying to heat only the surface of the leather. If you do this, then you can build from there, increase your control."

Tan took a deep breath and fixed his eyes on the saddle. He focused on where she'd held her shaping and tried to recreate the same by drawing it through him. This time, there came a sense of a flutter, but nothing more. He let out his breath and called fire as if calling to the draasin. The shaping came easily then, pressing softly against the inside of his ears and releasing with something like a soft breath of air.

Heat shimmered above the saddle, barely creating any smoke, doing nothing more than creating translucent streamers of heat.

Cianna stared and then ran over to it. She touched the surface of the saddle and turned to him, a smile on her face. "Can you intensify it now?"

Tan focused on the heat and called for it to increase.

Smoke quickly drifted up in response.

Cianna nodded. "If you can do that, if you have control like that, then you can make other shapings more easily." She touched his shoulder, her hand lingering as she did. "Keep practicing. Next time, we can work on more complex shapings."

She started toward the door to the practice yard and paused, looking back. "Most take a long time to learn any sort of shaping. You learn quickly. I think you might be able to be a powerful fire shaper in time. Now. Time for me to see what Seanan has done since I left him. Probably pissed I haven't come help rebuild our wing of the university." She waved. "See you next time."

After she left, Tan stared at the leather saddle for a long while. She thought he could be a powerful shaper, but why did he have the sense that he wasn't doing any shaping at all? The shapings he made were different than what Cianna created, regardless of how they looked.

What if he wasn't shaping anything? What if what he did came from the elementals rather than himself? And if that was the case, how would he ever learn enough to help Lacertin stop Incendin?

CHAPTER 7

A Rescue

THE SMOKE HANGING OVER ETHEA left pockets of clear air. Tan made his way through the streets, not really certain where to go for the night. The master shapers all had a place at the university. Roine likely would stay at the palace with the king. Through his connection with Amia, he sensed she still shaped, though it was a soft and gentle sort of shaping, nothing with much strength. Hopefully she could free the king from his shaping.

And then what? Was he ready to leave Ethea and follow Lacertin into Incendin?

Tan sighed. What he needed now was rest. The room he had stayed in when last in Ethea was gone, destroyed by fires, but there was a place he knew he might be able to sleep, a place Elle had shown him before they left Ethea.

Moving through the city proved difficult. Crews of men wearing the king's colors worked diligently to clear the mess of debris and burned buildings, blocking the street in many places. None bothered to more than glance at him. In other places, the streets were impassable, rubble forcing him to climb over or work his way around, always aware of how shaped fire simmered beneath him.

Few other people were out on the street. There were those dressed in rough clothing, some singed and torn, likely without much of a place to go now that parts of the city had been destroyed. Then there were others, still dressed fairly well, hurrying through the streets. They all wore brightly colored scarves around their faces to protect them from the smoke.

Tan shook his head when he saw the scarves. He didn't remember seeing anything like that the last time he had been in Ethea. It seemed an entire fashion had sprung up since the attack, but only for those able to afford it.

He wondered how he appeared to everyone else. Still wearing his heavy cloak and stained from travels, he looked more like the now homeless.

Tan weaved through the streets, troubled by what he'd learned of shaping from Cianna. He should be happy—he'd finally found someone willing to work with him to understand shaping—but instead, he felt uncertain. The way he shaped was different than what Cianna did, and different enough that he wasn't sure he would be able to learn anything more from her.

Orange light flickered from around a corner. Sounds of shouting and a few screams rang out. Tan hurried toward it.

Flames crept up the wall of a nearby building, slowly consuming it. A woman stood in the street, bent over with her hands on her thighs, head tilted as she stared at the fire. Dark soot smudged along her cheek. One side of her face was reddened.

A man crawled from the building, flames engulfing him. The stink of burning flesh gagged Tan. He needed to stop the flames.

He tried pulling heat from the flames around him, but the fire didn't answer as he called. There was the seductive pull of it begging him to release it. Tan resisted, ignoring it.

Fire would be no help.

Could he use wind?

He called to the wind, quickly asking it to press down around the man. Nothing happened.

The woman looked over at him. Tears streamed down her face, creating patches in the soot on her cheeks. "Help him!" she cried.

Tan rolled the man, trying to smother the flames, hoping his ability to shape would protect his hands from injury. The man screamed as he rolled him.

"What happened?" Tan asked.

No one else came into the street. Either they were gone or no one was willing to help.

The woman shook her head. "I don't know. No fires had come through here before. Our home was safe!" She finished in hysterics, crying loudly. "Jayna is still inside!"

Rolling him had slowed the flames, but the fire had been shaped and would not be easily put out. Without being able to reliably shape, there was nothing more he could do.

"I'm sorry."

"My daughter," the woman said. "He was trying to reach her—"

Tan looked over at the fires. Heat radiated outward, pressing painfully against him. Even when he'd ridden on Asboel, he hadn't been aware of the heat. What did it mean for him to be aware of it now?

He wouldn't be able to get inside the building, not without ending up like this man.

Whatever shaping still held in the city had flared. If this was draasin fire, there was little Tan would be able to do.

A scream, high-pitched and panicked, came from inside the building.

Tan turned quickly. The girl, Jayna.

He started forward without thinking. As he did, he drew in on a wind shaping, praying ara would answer. *Protect me*, he demanded of the shaping, not certain whether he shaped or whether the elementals helped. Pressure built as he surged through the first line of flames.

Heat pressed on him, almost knocking the wind out of him. He held his breath and pushed forward. Bright orange and yellow flames snaked across a wooden floor, working up stone walls. Cracks formed in the walls and the stone crumbled slowly, giving an ominous groaning sound. Much longer and the building would collapse.

He focused on the stone and tried to push out with an earth shaping to hold it intact. He felt the pressure of a shaping but couldn't be certain it worked.

"Jayna!" He said the name and let it out on a shaping of wind.

Thankfully, the shaping worked. Jayna cried nearby.

Tan turned, stepping through another line of fire. The wind shaping dragged the flames away from him, keeping him from being burned. Smoke still clogged his throat, searing his lungs with each breath. Strange the shaping didn't protect him from that.

He found her lying crumpled on the ground in the next room. A table rippled with fire and the remains of chairs had collapsed near her. Blisters formed on her cheeks and much of her hair was charred, leaving her with a jagged appearance that reminded him of Elle.

Flames pulled on him, begging for him to feed them more energy. Tan pushed away the urge. He scooped her off the ground. She moaned with the movement but didn't move otherwise.

He pressed out with the wind shaping, wrapping her inside it like a blanket of air. It smothered the smoldering flames along her clothes and skin. She cried out again, but softer this time as she tried to take a breath but coughed.

Tan ran through the fire to the front of the building. The groan coming from the stone sounded louder and then the wall started to collapse.

Hold! Tan rumbled the demand.

He had a moment where he knew the command would take.

Each command—each shaping—drained him. After working with fire throughout the afternoon, he had little strength remaining.

Tan shouldered through the door and stumbled into the street.

Another woman stood consoling the woman now. A man crouched next to the burned man but not closely, as if afraid he would get burned.

The first woman saw him emerge and ran over to him. She reached for the girl but the shaping kept her back. Another flash of panic crossed her eyes. Tan released the wind and handed the girl to her mother.

"She will need healing. Possibly shaping," he said.

"Shaping?"

"Water shaping could heal her."

The woman laughed in a high-pitched sort of way. "Where I am to find a shaper? If I go to the palace and demand it from the king, you think he'd send a shaper out to me?"

Weakness left him irritable. "Yes. Tell them Tan sent you. Ask for Roine."

She looked at him as if he was mad. Possibly he was. Why should one of the Athan help this woman?

Another woman ran forward to help lift Jayna. Tan shook her away. "Go! Run to the palace."

The other woman looked from Tan to the burned girl before nodding and darting off.

Tan took another step and stumbled again. Someone lifted him under his arms and pulled him to the other side of the street. He heard a snapping sound, like that of thousands of branches breaking, as the building collapsed in a blast of stone and smoke. Debris scattered all around.

Without thinking, he pushed out with the wind shaping, sweeping forward.

The debris bounced off his shaping, held back by the protection he—or ara—had created.

Heat pressed on him and flames surged. Without thinking, Tan drew the flames through him, pushing it through his connection to the draasin, letting the elemental absorb the fire.

The effort of the shaping was more than he could tolerate. Tan leaned forward and drifted to sleep.

CHAPTER 8

Seeing Zephra

HE AWOKE TO SOMEONE SHAKING his shoulder.

Tan looked blurrily around. Flames still flickered on the other side of the street, but they were lessened, now simply smoldering rather than burning brightly. Heavy smoke drifted over the street. The stink of burning flesh still lingered.

He turned to see Roine leaning toward him and felt the shaping he worked, but didn't have the energy to sense what he shaped. Tan wasn't certain he would even be able to sense it with Roine.

"What happened?" Roine asked.

"Did you help her?"

Roine glanced behind him before looking back at Tan. "I did."

Tan took a deep breath and let it out slowly. "I wasn't sure you would come."

Roine stood and laughed. Relief flashed across his face. "A woman said a shaper named Tan demanded Roine's presence. What choice did I have?"

He shifted. "I never told her I was a shaper."

"You run into a burning building and come out without any sign of injury. What else would they think you were?"

Tan grunted, and it turned into a fit of coughing. When it subsided, he looked to Roine. "How is she?"

"She should be fine. Her burns were easy enough to heal, but she breathed in too much smoke. There's only so much I can do for it."

"And the man? What of him?"

Roine reached toward him. "I'm sorry, Tan."

He took a deep breath and looked away. He hadn't been able to help, not when it mattered. Before, he had relied on Asboel to help, or for Roine and then Lacertin. Even Amia helped more than him. But when he *needed* to shape, he hadn't been able to control it.

Would he ever learn how?

"What is it like when you shape?" he asked.

Roine pulled his attention back from the street. With a soft shaping of wind, the smoke lifted. The woman crouched near the dead man, cradling Jayna in her arms as she sobbed. One hand smoothed down her daughter's damaged hair. The other hand gripped the fallen man.

"The same as you, I imagine," Roine answered. He turned back to Tan. "Why do you ask?"

"Where does the shaping come from?"

Roine reached out a hand and helped Tan to stand, smiling as he did. "You a scholar now, too?"

Tan struggled to stand, wiping his hands on his pants. His head throbbed again and fatigue tried to draw him back to the ground, where he could close his eyes, but he forced himself to stay on his feet. "Not smart enough to be a scholar," he said. "But Cianna was trying to teach me fire shaping. As she did, I began to wonder where the shaping comes from. Is it the same shaping each of the elements?"

Roine nodded toward the end of the street. They started walking, passing the woman and Jayna. Neither looked up at them, staring instead at the fallen man and his burned and blackened flesh.

"Cianna tried to teach?" Roine asked as they neared the end of the street.

The smoke lessened here, a faint breeze blowing through, drawing it away. Tan couldn't tell if it was shaped or not.

He debated telling Roine they had gone to the archives before deciding against it. "She wants to know about the draasin."

"Fire shapers have always been fascinated by the draasin. They are so different than other elementals in many ways."

"How?"

"Anyone can see them, for one."

"You saw the nymid. I suspect you could see udilm, too."

Roine smiled. "But golud? And ara? I can't say I've ever seen those elementals other than at the cavern."

"That was a unique place, Roine."

Roine regarded him with a strange expression. "In many ways," he agreed and led them around a corner. The road opened up. Evidence of damaged buildings lined both sides of the street, but the damage had been cleared, leaving the street clean and passable. Some construction had begun, and the scent of sawn wood mixed with the thick tar used to seal slats between boards. It was a welcome change from the stink of smoke everywhere else.

"Do you draw your shapings from within yourself?"

Roine turned and met his eyes. "Why do you ask? What does it feel like when you shape?"

"It doesn't feel like anything. Some of the time, the shapings work as intended. Most of the time, they don't."

"When they do. What do you sense?" Roine asked.

Tan wasn't certain how to answer. Did he explain that the only time shapings seemed to work for him were when he treated them as if speaking to the elementals? Most other shapers couldn't speak to the elementals, so it seemed unlikely that he shaped the same way.

"I don't really sense anything."

Roine sniffed and nodded. "Perhaps you are still too early in your education. I should have taken the time to work with you—you deserved that much—but with everything that happened since our return, I never had the time."

They continued down the street. Tan didn't recognize this part of the city. No lanterns were lit, leaving moonlight as the only light by which to see. More people were out on the streets. Most were dressed with clean clothes and a colorful scarf swooped around their neck. They seemed to move away from the palace, but also away from the university.

"I teased you about being a scholar because scholars have wondered about the source of shapings for a long time. Most agree the shaping comes from within, the ability to tap the power of the elements something shapers are born with."

"Is that what you think? Do you pull your shapings from within you?" Tan asked.

Roine frowned. "In a way. I'm not certain I'm even aware of where my shapings come from."

Tan stopped along the street and turned to Roine. The walk had refreshed him. He still felt weakened, but nothing like before. The pain in his head had subsided. More than anything, the conversation left him more alert than before.

"Try a shaping," he told Roine.

"Tan—you're not going to solve the philosophical debate of shaping in the middle of the street."

"Humor me, Roine. Perform a shaping, but slowly."

Roine snorted and shrugged. "What would you like to see?"

"Anything but fire."

Roine nodded solemnly, eyes flicking to the buildings behind them.

Tan didn't want the buildings to ignite, but that wasn't the reason he didn't want to see fire. He had already seen how Cianna pulled fire from within her. What he wanted was to see how another shaper drew their shaping.

Pressure built as the shaping started.

The ground shook softly beneath his feet.

Tan focused on sensing the ground. As he did, he felt the shaping and how it rippled the deep layers of earth far beneath his feet. Nothing strong enough to damage anything, but enough for Tan to feel. He followed the shaping, tracing it back to Roine. Like with Cianna, it originated deep within him, only this time pressing out through him and into the ground.

"Satisfied?" Roine asked.

Tan nodded. "For now. Thanks."

Roine laughed. "It's not often any longer I'm asked to show off my shaping skills."

He started forward again and Tan followed. Where did Roine lead him?

"Amia is still with the king?"

Roine shot him a look. He lowered his voice. "As I feared, Althem was shaped. And from what she tells me, the shaping is complex. She needs more time."

"How much more time?"

"The Great Mother only knows. I pray she will be strong enough."

They continued down the street, working their way through darker and darker streets. Tan did not recognize where they were, and his earth sensing didn't give him answers, either. "Why earth?" he asked, breaking the silence.

Roine looked over and smiled. "You were an earth senser first. I thought that fitting."

First. And now he could sense the other elements; he could speak to the elementals. What did that make him?

"Where are we going?" Tan asked.

"It was good you had me summoned," Roine answered. "I needed to find you tonight anyway."

"Why?"

Roine kept walking without answering.

"Roine?" Tan said. When he still didn't answer, he asked, "Theondar?"

The old warrior turned and met his eyes. "There's someone you need to see."

"Who?"

"Your mother."

Tan's heart fluttered as he hurried after Roine. "She's here?"

Buildings on either side of the street seemed to press in on him and a dizzying sensation raced through his head. Lanterns shining through windows seemed to blur around him as they passed.

Roine nodded.

"How do you know?"

Roine turned. "Either she's here or a dead man left this marker in my quarters." He held out a small circle of stone. Engraved on it was a single mark, a rune like on Roine's sword. And like on the door in the archives.

"What is it?"

"Something from a long time ago."

They hurried through the streets, turning onto smaller and smaller roads. Fewer and fewer people were out as they made their way through. Buildings pressed closer together, but the damage from the fires wasn't nearly as bad as in other parts of the city. Most had nothing more than soot smeared across them. A few had broken windows that had been boarded over.

Roine stayed silent. Every so often, he paused and closed his eyes before snapping them open and changing direction. Tan chose not to bother him. Since learning from Lacertin that his mother still lived, he had wondered what he would say if he saw her again. Would he be angry that she hadn't come for him when they ran from the lisincend? Or would he only feel relief that she still lived?

Finally, Roine stopped in front of a tall building.

"Is this it?" Tan asked.

Roine nodded. "This is where the connection ends."

Tan frowned at him. "What sort of connection?"

Roine showed him the stone circle again. The rune on it had started to fade, but as it did, it glowed softly. "This is like the key for the artifact." He lowered his voice as he spoke, pitching it so that his words didn't carry down the street. "A shaping connects this to another. A shaper who knows the right shaping can use it to find the other."

Tan eyed the stone. "How did you know she would be in the city? What if it had led you to Galen or someplace farther?"

"The mark tells the place," he said and craned his neck up at the building. A stair led to a door built halfway up the building, as if the street had sunk over time.

Tan hesitated as Roine approached the door.

"Aren't you coming?"

Tan swallowed. He wanted to see his mother, but after everything that had happened, was he ready to see her? What would she say about the things he'd seen in the time he thought her dead? What had *she* been doing in that time?

And part of him wanted Amia with him, more than simply for support. She had been with him for most of what had happened over the last few months. He may once have wanted—and needed—his mother, but now Amia was the person he shared his life with.

How would his mother react to the person he had become?

Finally, he started up the stairs after Roine. At the top, he examined the door. Made of a dense and heavily lacquered wood, it felt out of place with the rest of the street. Roine touched the door but drew back his hand as if burned.

The door shimmered and changed, fading into a dark iron.

"Still hasn't lost her skill," Roine muttered to himself.

He glanced at Tan before raising his hand. Using a shaping that Tan could sense, he knocked on the door.

It opened barely a moment later, as if the person inside had been waiting.

Tan gasped. The person on the other side wasn't his mother. "Sarah?"

He hadn't seen her since she helped guide Tan and Elle toward healing. Had she known his mother? If she had, why hadn't she said anything to him?

She fixed him with furrowed brow and touched the corner of her eyes. Her auburn hair hung over her shoulders. Light from the street reflected off her pale skin. She wore a long, navy dress that hung to her feet.

"What is this?" Roine frowned, looking from Tan to Sarah. "You know her?"

Tan swallowed his surprise before speaking. "She's the shaper who helped Elle and I. She's the reason I ended up reaching the draasin."

Sarah snorted. "You would have reached Amia sooner had you held nymid in mind more firmly."

Tan blinked. "Amia? How did you know about her?"

Sarah smiled. A shaping built quickly, pushing out from deep within her. It swept over her, and as it did, she changed. Her hair darkened. Pale skin took on color. Piercing eyes stared at him.

Tan gasped again. "Mother?"

CHAPTER 9

Reunion

WITHOUT SAYING ANOTHER WORD, his mother led them into the house, pulling the door closed behind them on a shaping of wind before sealing it closed. They made their way down a long hall with slatted walls. She did not look at them as she hurried through the hall. The soft staccato of her feet over the wood felt strangely familiar.

A single tapestry hung on one of the walls, faded beyond any recognition. Tan could see no other decorations. She turned through a doorway, disappearing from view.

Worry creased Roine's brow as he regarded Tan. "Tan?"

Tan shook his head, making a point of not looking over at the warrior. "I'm fine."

Roine started to say something more but cut it off. He followed Tan's mother into the room.

Tan took a deep breath. How could Sarah have been his mother? If she were alive, why had she not revealed herself, especially as she had been in Ethea? Why had she not helped him more?

Answers would come. He would demand them.

His mother led them to a room where a single lantern glowed atop a well-worn table with four chairs circling it. Roine sat at one end of the table. His mother stood behind another. Curtains were drawn closed over a window on the far wall. Books stacked atop a narrow shelf across from the table.

"Sit, Tannen," she said.

Tan flattened his mouth, the corners pressing down mercilessly. His hands clenched into fists. "I'll stand."

Her mouth tightened and she shifted her hands where they gripped the top of the chair. "You're angry."

"That's the first thing you say to me?" he yelled. "You were *dead*!"

"It will take more than the lisincend to kill me," she said, quickly dismissing the idea of her death. "Though I admit I had not expected them to come so quickly. Had you not warned of the hounds, I may not have known."

"You knew they were coming?"

"Not at first. I had been… disconnected… from the wind for many years. When I sent you with Theondar, I knew it was time to reconnect."

"You could have saved them."

She frowned. "Who?"

He closed his eyes, remembering the crater where the town had been. Everyone gone. Everything he knew, gone. Only Cobin and Bal remained, and he had not seen them since leaving Velminth. And Lins, except Tan wouldn't mind if Incendin took Lins Alles. "Everyone."

"Tannen—"

"Don't," he snapped, opening his eyes. "If you wouldn't save them, why else had you been in Galen? Why would the king have sent you there?"

"I told you why I was in Galen. Before you left."

"No. You told me you fought in the Incendin war and that your reward was coming to Nor. You said nothing about Father. Nothing about what *you* were doing in Nor."

His mother cocked her head in Roine's direction. "You didn't tell him?"

"That wasn't my place, Zephra."

"Tell me what?"

His mother sighed. "Your father was sent to Galen. He chose to settle in Nor."

She met his eyes, and the warmth he remembered from his childhood was there, but also the strength he remembered from watching her serve Lord Alles.

"Nor is close to the border, close enough for what the king needed."

"And what did the king need? For him to fortify the barrier?" Tan asked.

She glanced at Roine.

Tan snorted. "I know. Roine told me."

"So you know your father was a powerful earth shaper?"

Tan nodded. Talking about it brought back the hurt he felt at never having the opportunity to know his father as a shaper, to learn from him. "I know that he kept his ability from me."

"Did he?" she asked. "How many times did you go out with your father? How much did he teach you about earth sensing?" She shook her head. "Your father taught you as much as he could. Until you showed signs of shaping, there wasn't anything more he *could* teach you."

"That's why you pushed me to come to Ethea after he died?"

She closed her eyes and nodded. "You needed to be around others like you."

"There are no others like me," Tan said. He hated how he sounded, the sullenness he knew that had crept into his voice. Seeing his mother made him feel like a child again, searching for her approval.

But he didn't need her approval. Not anymore.

"Tannen—"

"Why did you go to Lacertin?" he asked.

"You asked why I didn't save them. You deserve that answer first." She pulled a chair out and sat. "The attack came suddenly. I had barely touched the wind. Wind shaping is delicate. Difficult at times. Part of me wasn't certain it would respond as it once had. But it all came back quickly. As soon as I shaped the wind, I sensed something off." Her eyes were reddened; tears welled in them. "I tried, Tannen. I did what I could, but I was not strong enough."

A hollowness settled through him. Of course his mother would have tried. Nor was her home as much as it was his. "How did you…" He swallowed, needing to get the question out. "How did you get out?"

"A wind shaping. I took to the sky to search for the lisincend. I warned you about them."

"You didn't tell me what they were," Tan said.

"Would you have believed?"

Tan didn't know. Short of seeing the lisincend, he had no way of really understanding how terrible they were. Only after seeing what they did to the Aeta had he really understood. "You saw it, didn't you?"

He took a step toward his mother. Roine moved over by the window to give Tan a measure of privacy with his mother.

She nodded, her eyes going distant. "I saw the attack. An explosion of fire unlike anything I had ever seen. There was no reason for the lisincend to risk crossing the barrier. No reason to attack with such brutality."

"Why didn't you come find me?"

She glanced at Roine and nodded. "You were as safe as you could be with Theondar. And you were needed."

Had she come for him, he might not have attempted to free Amia. He might not have encountered the nymid. They might not have freed the draasin. Tan had learned he could speak to the elementals *because* she never found him.

He closed his eyes, eager to share this experience with Amia through their shaped connection. *I found my mother.*

Sending the message to her took less energy than it did with the draasin. He didn't expect a response from her. If she remained with the king, she might still be occupied.

"And Lacertin?" he asked softly.

His mother swallowed. She glanced over at Roine. "They were close once. Did you know that?"

Tan nodded. Roine admitted that much to him.

"Back when I first came to Ethea. They were powerful shapers, both of them. When Lacertin left, it... changed something with Theondar. More than Ilianna's death would explain."

"Mother?"

"I never believed the rumors about Lacertin. He had always served Ilton loyally. For him to violate the death chamber, there had to be a reason. Lacertin had been away from the palace for months before the king fell ill, gone on an errand of the king." She smiled but didn't turn away from Roine. "Lacertin always had been his favored warrior. Much like Theondar is to Althem. For Ilton to send him from Ethea for so long must have been important. It has troubled me, all these years. I never learned the answer."

"You knew where to find him?"

She finally turned back to him and snorted. "Lacertin has never really hidden himself, not to those willing to listen. I suspect if you ask, Theondar knew where he was. Maybe he was unwilling to admit it."

"You knew he was in Incendin?"

"I knew he went to Incendin. Lacertin was a fire shaper first. It made the most sense."

Tan's eyes widened. "You went after him?"

She nodded once. "When the lisincend attacked in a way that made no sense, I needed to know. I sought out Lacertin. I learned the lisincend discovered what Theondar sought. And I asked that he intervene."

"Intervene? Lacertin attacked Roine! The lisincend nearly killed Amia and I!"

She nodded. "And he recognized his mistake. He thought Theondar had the artifact and sought to claim it." She turned to Roine. "Lacertin still did not trust him. Or Althem. And it seems for good reason."

Roine looked back at her. "It was not my fault the artifact was stolen."

"No. It's only your fault Incendin found the artifact."

Roine turned to face her. "Is this why you summoned me here, Zephra? To admonish me? Maybe I should leave so you and Tan have time to reconnect."

She stood and faced Roine. "I summoned you here to discuss the king. You brought Tannen into this."

Roine glanced at Tan, an amused smile parting his lips. "I think Tan brought himself into this. You haven't asked what happened since you last saw him."

"I have no need. I know he speaks to the elementals. The last time I saw him, he was to have healed Elle Vaywand."

"You're the reason he left Ethea?" Roine asked.

"Not the reason. That would be the archivists. I am the *way* he left Ethea." She looked over at Tan. "Elle needed the help of water elementals, and he knew the nymid. I thought he could help her and Amia at the same time."

"I didn't reach the nymid at first."

"What happened with Elle?"

"She…" He trailed off and frowned. "Wait. How did you know her?"

"I knew her grandfather. We were friends a long time ago. He motivated me to come to the university to learn." Her voice caught. "You didn't reach healing in time, did you?"

Tan took a deep breath. "Your shaping took me to Incendin," he began. He should have questioned how Sarah would have been able to shape him so that they could reach the place of convergence. A shaping like that would have been more than Roine could do. But his mother was Zephra, the most powerful wind shaper seen in generations.

"Then you lost focus."

"I was drawn there," Tan said.

Her eyes widened slightly. "The draasin you freed. You have bonded it."

Bonded. How would she have known? "How did you know of the draasin?" Had he spoken of the draasin with Elle? "And how did you perform that shaping?"

She ignored the question. "What of Elle? You left her in Incendin?"

"No. A—" He caught himself before revealing Asboel's name. "The draasin drew me to them. He brought Elle to where she could be healed."

"Where?" his mother asked.

"Doma, I think. Or beyond Doma. I'm not certain."

"How can you not be certain? Where did you leave her?" she

demanded.

"Why do you care so much about her? You didn't seem to care that I was under attack from the lisincend, that I nearly died fighting with Incendin. Why Elle?"

She tossed her head and let out a soft sigh. "She is family."

"Family?"

"Our fathers. They were brothers." She took a deep breath. "So, Tannen, what happened to my cousin?"

Cousin. Elle was family. After losing his father—and then thinking he'd lost his mother—he thought he had no family left. Now, his mother still lived. And Elle was a cousin.

"With the udilm. They healed her before I left. She remained with them."

His mother let out a shaky breath. "She speaks to udilm?"

"She does."

His mother did something then that surprised him. She smiled. "All these years Doma has sought to find another able to speak to udilm. All these years fearing Incendin and it is Elle who manages to do it."

"Why was Elle so important?"

His mother paced across the room, her feet drumming on the wooden floor. Tan remembered how she would pace when discussing things with his father, or, after he was gone, how she paced when working through problems for Lord Alles.

"One area your father and I failed you was in geography. Sarah and Elle told you how Incendin attacked Doma, taking shapers from them and leaving them unprotected."

He nodded. He suspected Doma shapers were the reason Incendin had weakened the barrier.

"It is more than that. Only a small swath of Doma borders Incendin. Not like the kingdoms, where Galen and Nara run along its border. But

Doma has never had the same protections as the kingdoms. Those who can shape had always come to the university to learn. Enough would return to keep Doma safe. Such a small border didn't require much shaping. But that wasn't the only reason Doma survived as long as it had against the constant pressure from Incendin."

"Udilm," Tan said.

His mother nodded. "Most of Doma juts out into the sea. Waves crash along almost all her borders. Udilm had always been a friend to Doma."

"Had been?" he asked.

"There has been little contact with Doma and udilm over the last hundred years. At first, the continued threat of udilm kept Incendin back, but over time, that failed. And when the number of shapers dwindled, Incendin no longer feared invading. Those with any shaping potential were taken, torn from families and dragged into Incendin."

"I don't understand what Elle has to do with any of that."

"Elle Vaywand is the granddaughter of the last great water shaper from Doma. And he was the son of the last person with the ability to speak to udilm. Elle came to learn water shaping, but she came for another reason, one she wouldn't have completed if not for you."

Tan thought of what it felt like when swimming with udilm. He had the sense of massive power, the depth of the elemental, but also a sort of indifference. Not like the nymid. "I'm not sure udilm will help."

"You spoke with them too." She nodded to herself. "Of course, you have Thea's blood in you as well." She looked over at Roine. "But why would this suddenly manifest again? Why after all this time would the ability to speak to the elementals reappear?"

Roine shook his head. "I don't know, Zephra. I am no scholar. I am only a simple Athan."

She shot Roine a look. "Only an Athan? You spent years studying in the archives. You're the closest the kingdoms has to a scholar anymore."

"That was a long time ago."

She frowned. "That's right. You're Roine now, not Theondar. So I suppose Roine managed to find the lost artifact after all the years he spent searching when few believed it existed?"

"Lacertin believed."

"Only because he found the key."

Roine glanced over at Tan and shook his head slightly.

Tan's mother followed the direction of Roine's gaze. "He doesn't know?"

Roine turned back to the curtain. "I never told him."

His mother faced Roine. "Theondar, he deserves to know. You involved him in all of this."

Pain pulled at the corner of Roine's eyes. "I didn't mean to pull him into this. That was never my intent."

His mother snorted. "Never? You came into Galen searching for the artifact. I would say that was exactly your intent."

"Not your son, Zephra."

She smiled, her eyes settling on Tan. "When you came to Nor, I knew what you sought, just as I knew what the hounds likely meant. Why else do you think I suggested Tan go with you? He would have been your best option for getting through the upper passes, but I also wanted him to be safe."

Roine grunted. "By sending him into the middle of everything?"

"I didn't expect you to let the lisincend get so close. I thought you better than that, Theondar."

Roine tipped his head toward Tan. "Not my choice to get so close to the lisincend. Tan wouldn't help otherwise. He was the reason we went after the Aeta."

"And if we hadn't, you never would have found the artifact," Tan interrupted. He began to get a sense of how others viewed Theondar: there was a certain antagonism to him. He fixed Roine with his eyes. "What did she mean about the key?"

Roine inhaled deeply, staring at the curtains as if they could provide an answer. He answered slowly. "The key we used to find the artifact."

"The one damaged as we ran from the lisincend?"

"I told you how I have been looking for the artifact for many years. There is more to it than that. I wasn't the first to search for it."

Tan frowned. "Lacertin?"

Roine closed his eyes and nodded. "The scholars convinced King Ilton the artifact must be found. He trusted no one other than Lacertin to go and find it. It is what he brought back when he returned to Ethea before Ilton's death."

"You took it from him, didn't you?"

Roine shifted his attention from Tan to Zephra, eyes narrowing and his mouth tight. "After he violated Ilton's death chamber, Althem requested I learn where Lacertin had gone. You think Lacertin and I don't get along? Well, it was worse between Althem and Lacertin. They entered the university at the same time, only Lacertin quickly demonstrated his ability."

"You said Althem didn't care about shaping." Tan wasn't sure that was quite right but couldn't remember everything Roine had told him about the king's view on shaping.

"Althem doesn't choose to reveal if he can shape. There is a difference."

"Can he shape?"

"Only Althem can answer that."

He hid something more, but Tan couldn't tell what it might be.

Roine breathed. "Tell me, Zephra. Why did you summon me here? If not for Tan, then why?"

"I summoned you to understand why you returned."

Roine snorted. "Why? The archivists have shaped the king. If you knew what happened, then you understand the significance of his shaping."

"You don't know he's been shaped."

Roine tipped his head. "No? I have an Aeta shaper that says differently."

"And you trust her?"

"*I* trust her," Tan said.

His mother didn't look over at him. "Theondar. Do you trust her?"

Roine's eyes narrowed. "She helped recover the artifact. Had she not revealed her shaping, we would never have found it in time."

"Had she never revealed herself, the lisincend would never have found it, either," his mother said.

"What are you suggesting, Zephra?"

"Only that there is much we don't know about the Aeta."

Tan turned on her. "You traveled with them. You're the one who chastised Lord Alles for not treating them well!"

"You think the Aeta a threat?" Roine asked.

"I think there is more to the Aeta than we know." She finally acknowledged Tan's involvement. "And you know it, too. It is one thing to treat them well. It is quite another to entrust the safety of the kingdoms to them."

The Aeta were responsible for the archivists. They were the reason the shapers attempted to attack the draasin. They were the reason the king might have been shaped.

But Tan trusted Amia. The bond between them revealed far more than his mother could ever understand. "Amia is no threat," he insisted.

"Perhaps not, but we don't know about the rest of the Aeta. Especially after what happened with the archivists."

A mixture of emotions surged through the shaped bond between him and Amia. She was close. He turned and saw her standing in the doorway, eyes hiding the hurt she felt.

CHAPTER 10

Failure and Options

IT TOOK A FEW MOMENTS for the others to realize Amia had come.

Tan hurried over to her and took her hand. "You heard," he whispered.

She fixed his mother with tired eyes and nodded.

His mother stared at Amia as she entered, touching her head as a shaping built. Tan realized that she performed a shaping to protect her mind. Could wind alone shield her from a spirit shaping?

"Amia," she began. "I was sorry to hear about your loss."

"Zephra. The Great Mother truly blesses us that you survived," she spoke stiffly.

"You left Althem?" Roine asked.

His mother's eyes narrowed into a tight line.

Amia sighed. "There is little more I can do. The shaping was wrapped tightly around his mind and burrowed deep. I unraveled what I could, but there is much damage. I came to tell you I did all I could."

Roine crossed his arms over his chest and tapped his hand anxiously. "How much damage?"

"I cannot say. More than I can safely remove."

"So that's it? Althem cannot be saved?" Roine asked.

She looked over at Tan's mother. "I'm no longer sure you will believe me."

"Ignore Zephra," Roine said, making his way toward her.

"Are you certain?" she asked.

"Do you need me to prove it?"

Amia shook her head. "I didn't think I did."

Roine laughed softly, standing now next to her. He lowered his arms and his hands were outstretched along his sides. "Go ahead."

She tilted her head, watching him. "You aren't shielded."

"As I said, I trust you." A quick shaping built, surging out from her and washing over Roine. As it did, he sucked in a sharp breath. "Satisfied?" Roine asked.

"For now," Amia said, eyeing Zephra.

"Good. Now tell me about Althem."

"I've told you what I can. There is a shaping, but it's complex. Nothing like I've ever seen before. What they did to you and the other shapers was simple. Like giving directions, leaving you primed for further instructions. With the king, the shaping is different. It influences him in ways I can't predict. I unraveled parts of it, but there is much of it that remains. If I tried to remove more than what I did, it's likely I'll damage him. I assume you don't want him damaged?"

"I already answered that."

"You should know the shaping I can trace is old. Some of it goes back many years, impacting all of his memories."

"Since I learned of the archivists, since learning they shaped me, I have wondered how long Althem might have been influenced," Roine began. "More than that, I started thinking back to the past, beyond Althem."

His mother frowned. "Ilton?"

Roine nodded slowly. "I'm hesitant to say because I don't know with any certainty, but you know the circumstances under which he died."

A troubled expression crossed his mother's face. Tan had seen it often growing up. When his father injured his leg falling while working along the upper ridges. Or when Tan fell sick. The worst had been when his father left with his summons. The expression had stuck to her face for weeks, finally returning when the message of his death reached them.

"I remember. The king hadn't been sick before Lacertin left. The illness came on suddenly, one the healers couldn't shape," Zephra said.

Roine nodded. "And the scholars had no answers."

"Scholars? The archivists were with Ilton then?"

"Even then. They stayed with him constantly at first. When his health began to truly fail, they left him to water shapers, though by that time, most of our skilled shapers were deployed to support the creation of the barrier."

"Grethan and I were there."

"As was I, though I returned regularly then."

"There was no suspicion around his death," his mother said. "Only around..." She trailed off, brow furrowing as it did when she focused on something. "Did Lacertin know?"

"I don't know," Roine said. "If he did, why wouldn't he have said anything? Why run from Ethea if he knew the archivists had killed his king?"

"I don't think he knew anything about the archivists," Tan said. "Not at first. The Lacertin I met wouldn't have abandoned the kingdoms. I don't think he ever abandoned the kingdoms."

Roine met Tan's eyes. "I know you want to believe him. I know you think that because he seemed to help, he is trustworthy, but this is Lacertin. I have known him for nearly as long as I've been alive."

"And you haven't changed in that time?" Tan's mother asked. "You're still the same person you were when Lacertin left Ethea?"

"You know I'm not, Zephra."

A satisfied look crossed her face. "Likely you refuse even speaking to Lacertin." She raised a hand as Roine started to interrupt. "Don't deny it. I've known you a long time as well, Theondar. Your pride gets in the way. You refuse to accept others might have another way of reaching the same goal. That has always been your problem."

Roine laughed bitterly. "In that, we are much the same."

She cocked her head as she thought about what he said. "Perhaps. But I have spoken to Lacertin. When I sought him out to understand why the lisincend crossed the barrier."

"And what did he tell you?" Roine asked.

"Not everything. I don't think he trusted me fully. Lacertin has never trusted anyone other than Ilton fully. But enough for me to understand the danger of what Incendin planned. That if they acquired the artifact, more than simply the kingdoms were in danger."

"You can't believe what he says about the elementals," Roine said.

She shrugged. "I don't know what I can believe. We have not known a great elemental of fire since the draasin disappeared. I cannot begin to understand how the elemental power works. Perhaps holding them in ice preserved their influence, preventing the others from making a claim. Or perhaps the lesser elementals were never strong enough to make a claim of becoming the greater. Either way, *if* Lacertin is right, then much of the world is in danger."

"They have the artifact," Tan said. "The shaper who transformed into one of the lisincend, she took the artifact."

"There is more to the creation of the lisincend than simply the artifact," Zephra said. "Long ago, before I ever learned to catch the wind, I witnessed a transformation. It was a terrifying experience, one that drove much of my work when I still served the university."

Tan noted how she said she served the *university*, not the king.

Roine looked at Amia. "Whatever threat Incendin poses pales in comparison to what might happen with Althem compromised."

"There is nothing more I can do," Amia said.

His mother regarded her. "Perhaps not you," she agreed.

Amia frowned at her. "I thought you do not trust the Aeta."

"I don't know who I should trust. If Theondar and my son trust you, then I must, too."

Amia studied Zephra. A sense of uncertainty flickered through the shaped connection.

"There is another," his mother said. "And if I remember what I learned traveling with the Aeta, now would be the time."

Nervousness surged through Amia. "I can't…"

"No? And if you don't, what will happen?"

Tan turned to Amia and took her hands. "What is she talking about?"

She let out a slow breath and met his eyes. "I told you there was another blessed by the Great Mother? The one who taught me?"

Tan nodded.

"She wants me to ask her to heal the king."

"Can she?"

Amia sighed. "I don't know. If there is any who would be able to unravel the shaping, it would be her."

"Where is she?"

"A place sacred to the Aeta. A place no outsider has ever gone." Amia said. "And she wants me to bring him there."

CHAPTER 11

Leavetakings

THEY STOOD IN THE BROKEN REMAINS of the university, which had been ravaged by the fires that had worked through the city. Tan wondered if the university had been the ultimate target. Much of the walls crumbled, layering what had once been a grassy area with dust and broken debris. Little of the university remained, only the barest outline of its form. Unnatural smoke shimmered in the air. What few shapers remained in the city didn't have time to work on rebuilding the university. Most were deployed to defend the barrier.

The sun broke through the clouds but still didn't warm them. The hazy smoke lingering in the city drifted along the streets, almost as if it were alive. Everything stunk of ash and decay. Crews of men worked diligently, attempting to clear the streets before rebuilding could take place, but there was only so much they could do.

Tan grasped Amia's hand, holding onto her tightly.

His mother stood across from him, watching him with a hint of amusement in her eyes. For reasons Tan didn't understand, she hadn't fully warmed to Amia. "He does not need to go with you."

Tan frowned. "I'm not letting Amia leave without me."

Zephra looked over at him. "You will not be welcome. Not at the Gathering."

"Perhaps not at first, but there is another reason for Tan to go."

"You think he can shape spirit," Zephra said.

"I know he can shape spirit. And the Gathering is the best place for him to learn to control his shaping."

"And you're certain he doesn't simply pull through you?" his mother asked.

"What you suggest isn't possible."

Zephra smiled. "There are many who think the ability to speak to all the great elementals is not possible, but Tan claims to do so."

Roine, wearing a heavy cloak, made his way toward them. Cianna trailed after him. Her bright red hair hung loose, flowing over her shoulders. She radiated a shimmering heat through her tight orange shirt and leather pants. She glanced at Tan and smiled.

With the smile, he remembered the heat of her body pressing near his as she tried teaching him to shape. A flush worked through him. Amia's sharp look told him their shared connection was betraying his feelings.

"She taught me fire," he said.

"Hmm. I'm sure she did," Amia said.

"What is this?" Tan asked when Roine and Cianna arrived.

Roine looked at Tan's mother. "Zephra is right. I need to stop living in the past. If Lacertin is right, then I can't stand by and wait for an attack. If Althem won't order the remaining shapers to move, then I will."

"You think that wise, to leave the kingdoms unguarded?" Amia asked.

"They are not unguarded. Some remain, especially along the barrier, enough to hold back an attack and send warning." He pulled several small circular stones from his pocket and held one up. A single rune was carved into the surface. "Any can send warning. Each of us will carry one. If you receive the warning, you will return to help Ethea."

"I don't think Ethea is what Incendin is after," Zephra said.

"Perhaps not." Roine attention fell on Cianna. "Their end game may be to claim Nara, as it always has been. Either way, we will be prepared."

"That's not all Incendin is after," Tan said. He thought about Doma, about the information Elle and Sarah—his mother—had shared with him. "Why else would they take shapers from Doma?"

Roine holds his hands up to stop him. "One thing at a time."

"You think to simply go into Incendin and attack?" Tan asked. "All these years we've avoided Incendin, and now you think to shape your way in and attack?"

"I think to reclaim the artifact. If it is the key to what Incendin plans, then I will do what is needed to protect us."

"You can't do that alone, Roine. The only thing that could come of that would be for you to die."

"I won't be alone." He looked at Cianna. "My weakest element is fire. Cianna will help."

"And I'm going too, Tannen," Zephra said. "I know how to find Lacertin."

"Four of you?" he asked. "Against all of Incendin? Why now? What changed for you?"

His mother held out her hand. A small, smooth stone with a tiny rune glowed on one surface. "It's Lacertin. He would only call if he needed help."

Lacertin needed help. That meant something had gone wrong. Lacertin had asked him to come but he had refused. What had he risked by ignoring Lacertin's request? "Let me summon the draasin, let us have an elemental on our side—"

"This is not your battle with Incendin this time. You have something else you must do. You must learn to control your shapings. If you can't, there is little you can do while in Incendin." He smiled, but it appeared forced. "Besides, it is more than four of us. I've convinced a few others to come as well."

He tipped his head and Tan noticed Ferran, Nels, Alan, and Seanan—all shapers twisted by the archivists—standing to the side. Even they would not be enough, not against Incendin and not if they had Doma shapers working with them.

"If I bring the draasin—" Tan started.

"Don't be stupid, Tan," Cianna snorted. "You're smarter than that. As much as I would like to fight alongside the draasin, if you bring them into Incendin, you risk the lisincend getting the one thing they want. Right now, the draasin are safe. Do as Theondar says. Learn your shaping. Learn control. Then you can help."

Tan turned to Roine. "It won't be as simple as what you think, Roine. You saw her…"

"She is a creature of fire, the same as the lisincend. I have fought the lisincend more times than you, Tannen. Do not think me incapable." He touched a hand to his sword.

Tan thought of the runes in the lower level of the archives and sighed. Nothing he would say would sway Roine. Besides, what he and Amia needed to do was equally important. He didn't know exactly where they were going, but if there was anything they could do to help save the king, they needed to do it, and before whatever shaping the archivists had placed damaged him further. Maybe then they could summon the other shapers to help.

"You will bring us to the Aeta?" Tan asked Roine.

"I'll have help," he answered, nodding toward Zephra.

They stood in the midst of the damaged shaper's circle, the stones now uneven. Roine stood on one side of Tan and Amia while Zephra stood on the other.

"Be safe, Tannen," his mother said. She gave him a quick hug and stepped away, eyes flickering to Amia. "Keep him safe."

Then the shaping engulfed them, lifting them into the air on a blur of wind.

Wind whistled around them, cold and biting. Even with the cloak he had brought, Tan hadn't prepared for the weather. While riding with Asboel, it hadn't mattered. The heat from the draasin had kept him warm. Now, walking alongside Amia, he felt every gust as it blew through the trees.

"How much farther?" he asked.

Amia pulled her cloak tight around her. "I can't say with certainty. Finding this place was something Mother never taught me, though even those not blessed are able to do it. I am trying to sense my way to them."

They had been walking the better part of two days, winding their way through the mountains. Roine and his mother had shaped them part of the way, carrying them on a gust of wind mixed with fire—the lancing lightning he had always seen when Lacertin arrived.

Tan worried about Amia. She had been through so much that he wasn't sure she should take him to this gathering of Aeta, especially after what happened to her the last time she traveled with them. At least this time she went with eyes open. And after she left him with the

Aeta, what would she encounter as she returned with help to Ethea to save the king?

"Are you certain about your plan?" he asked.

"You don't need to save me, Tan." She touched his face softly. "Maybe this will be good. You can see I am capable."

"I've seen what you can do, how you shaped the draasin. Without you, none of this would have been possible."

A shadow of troubled thought crossed her face. "I've been thinking about the draasin," she started. "I think Roine is right. I should not have been able to shape one of the elementals."

"You did it in a place of power where the Great Mother brings all the elements together. I don't think it's surprising at all that you shaped the draasin in that place."

"They are creatures of power. The more I think of what I did, the less comfortable with it I am."

Tan considered of what he knew of the draasin from his connection to Asboel. The shaping placed upon them by Amia was restrictive, but not so much so that they were unable to hunt. She had simply limited *what* they could hunt.

And would the shaping hold once the eggs he saw clutched in Asboel's talons the last time he'd seen him eventually hatched? Would the hatchlings have the same restrictions as the draasin they freed from the ice?

"Will she teach me?" he asked.

Amia focused straight ahead. "I don't know. I hope so."

"And if they don't?"

"Then I will teach you as we planned."

Tan nodded. "How long do you think it will take?"

Amia shook her head again. "It's different with each person, I think. When I came, I was very young. When the Gathering took place,

Mother knew it would take longer than previous years. At that time, there were two others able to shape spirit, both older than me. One was quite a bit older, a Mother during her time, who now served all the people. The Gathering is the only time we are a People. Otherwise, we travel as families."

"How long did it take?"

"I learned the basics. Enough to control the shaping and keep from damaging others. Spirit shaping is riskier than others in that way. You often can't see the effect of your shaping. If a shaping is made accidentally, there can be… unplanned consequences." She glanced over at him, wearing a guilty expression.

"I don't blame you for what happened that night," Tan said. "I just wish I could have done more."

Amia looked away. A mixture of emotions came through the shaped connection. "You did more than you needed, Tan. Had you not arrived, I would have suffered the same fate as the Mother. I am only sorry we brought the lisincend to your village."

Once, he had wanted nothing more than a quiet life in Nor, a life spent climbing the mountains of Galen. The arrival of the Aeta had changed that. Now he had no idea what he wanted for himself, only that he wanted Amia to be a part of it.

She smiled at him. "I want that, too."

Tan laughed softly. She shouldn't have known what he was thinking, but the connection between them seemed deeper since he had carried her into the pool of spirit. And had he not, the archivists twisting her shaping would have poisoned her mind enough that she might not have survived. Or worse, Amia might have been used to create the new lisincend.

They walked a while longer in silence. Darkness began to set; the sun faded behind the trees, leaving a heavy gloaming that sent shadows skittering across the forest floor. Tan felt no fear moving through the darkness of unfamiliar woods. Years spent learning earth sensing from his father gave him a certain confidence. All around, he sensed life. That by itself was reassuring. But something felt wrong.

"Do you sense anything?" he asked.

Amia cocked her head as she listened, then frowned. "Do you?"

He couldn't tell what triggered the sense. Other than the familiar awareness of forest, that of trees and the animals living here, he sensed nothing out of the ordinary. Certainly nothing that made him think the Aeta might be near.

"What if we don't find them?" How many nights would they wander before giving up on finding the Aeta? And if they didn't find them, what then? The king remained trapped by the archivist's shaping. What would happen if he couldn't be freed?

"That's my fear as well," she said, again knowing his thoughts. "If we can't find them, I'll do what I can to help the king, but I think Roine will have to recognize he might be forever lost—"

The soft tinkle of bells drifted through the forest, interrupting her. Tan frowned. It didn't come on the wind. Had it been shaped?

Amia's face twisted and Tan paused, struck by her fear instead of comfort she was finding her people. How would she react when they reached the place of the Gathering?

After another dozen steps, flickering lights emerged from the growing darkness: lanterns hanging from wagons arranged in a familiar wide circle. Dozens of colorful wagons, painted no differently than any other Aeta caravan he had ever seen circled in the midst of the trees. Tan would almost have thought the wagons were simply parked for the night, left idle while the Aeta rested before moving onto their next destination, but none of the wagons had any wheels.

He squeezed Amia's hand. They had reached the Gathering, but how?

Chapter 12

The Gathering

AMIA LED THEM THROUGH a gap in the wagons, moving with a determined step. The muscles in her hand were tense as she gripped Tan's, squeezing harder than necessary. Soft music drifted through the trees and disappeared into the night. There was a mournful quality to it, so different than the usual happy and festive sounds he associated with the Aeta.

A large fire crackled in the center of a clearing. The wagons weaved around trees, but near the center, the trees had long ago been felled, leaving a wide expanse of open ground. A ring of rocks piled in a circle created the open pit. A dozen spits rotated over the fire, making it seem like a massive celebration. People dressed in bright clothes and cuts of many different styles stood, sat, or danced around the fire.

But as Tan and Amia stepped into the clearing, unease settled over everything; the Aeta had sensed their arrival.

"If this doesn't work, we may need to leave quickly."

He frowned. "Why do you say that?"

She lowered her voice. "We have protected our secret for hundreds of years. No outsider has ever been allowed into the Gathering. Doing so is forbidden. And now I've brought you here."

"Not even my mother?"

Amia's eyes widened slightly. "Especially not your mother."

A tall man stepped away from the fire and made his way toward them. He had closely shorn hair that set off his large silver hoop earrings. A long, hooked nose pointed toward them as he studied Amia first, then Tan. He tipped his head slightly. "Daughter," he said in a whisper.

Amia took a deep breath and straightened her back. "Once I would have claimed that title."

The man tilted his head. He smoothed one hand down the front of his maroon jacket and kept his eyes fixed on Amia. "You no longer serve as Daughter?"

She gathered herself up and thrust her chin forward. "I no longer have a family to serve."

His eyes widened. "No family?"

Amia didn't move.

The man tipped his head. Tan felt a shaping build. Did Amia perform the shaping… or did the man? After learning that some of the spirit shaping archivists were once Aeta, he no longer felt certain.

He considered readying a shaping, but earth did not respond well to him and air was fickle. He had little control of water—he'd not really tried much water shaping—which left only fire. With the blazing flames dancing nearby, he *could* try a fire shaping—especially since he seemed attuned to fire through his connection to the draasin—but fire was destructive and dangerous. The Aeta had already seen too much destruction from fire.

Tan forced himself to relax.

"You are welcomed here, of course, Daughter. May the fire grant the warmth of the Great Mother. But you should not have—" he looked over at Tan "—brought another to the Gathering. Such a thing is forbidden. You should already have learned that custom."

Amia took a deep breath and nodded. "I know the rules, Brother, but he is *my* family."

The man's eyes narrowed slightly as he considered Tan. "It is unusual for a Daughter to choose from outside the People."

"It is."

"Did you have approval?"

Amia glanced at Tan. A warning of silence flowed through their bond. "The Mother consented."

The man studied Tan for another moment and then nodded, a smile splitting his face. "Then come and find peace and warmth by the fire. Others have already arrived, and more should come shortly. The Gathering will commence soon."

He led them to the fire and motioned to an open bench made of two sawn logs with a thick, rough-hewn board thrown over top. Amia took a seat and waited for Tan to follow. He hesitated. A few Aeta watched him, and he felt self-conscious. A wide man with a tattooed neck worked at the nearby spit. The roasting meat made Tan's mouth water. A woman stood next to him fanning a long-handled blade overtop a metal grate. A nearby scent of bread mixed with a sweet smell.

As he sat, Tan leaned in to Amia. "This is it?"

"This is the Gathering."

"Is it always so serious?"

"No, but the People are sensitive. Our ability with spirit grants us a different connection. I suspect word of the lisincend attack has reached all the families."

"And the attack near the place of convergence? Would they have learned of that?"

Amia's brow furrowed as she considered. "It is possible."

The man who had greeted them made his way around the fire. He paused to speak to various people as he walked, leaning toward them as he did. Each time, Tan felt the soft pressure of a shaping.

A shaper. He was certain of it.

At times, the man glanced over. When he caught Tan watching, he smiled. It did not reach his eyes.

"What did he mean when he said you chose someone?" Tan asked.

She sat stiffly on the bench. A sense of anxiety washed through their shaped connection, but then she sighed and took his hand. "It's a shame you know so little of the Aeta. I should have explained my people to you before now. Certainly before coming to the Gathering." She nodded at the man, who had reached the far side of the fire circle. The flames had begun concealing him. "Mothers lead each family. It has been that way since the beginning of the People. And Daughters must be chosen to follow, though we are not always daughter to the Mother. By now, I should have returned to the People, but I didn't—I couldn't—because of you."

Tan pulled her close, not caring about the looks they got from others around them. Amia didn't need him to share how he felt about her. The connection they shared was deeper than words could convey. "I choose you, too," he said softly. Amia smiled. "What would happen when the Mother could no longer serve?"

"She could have remained with the family. It happens sometimes. A Mother will become frail and unable to lead. The others will see to her comfort, a way of thanking her for years of serving the family."

Tan felt as if there was something she held back from him. "But that's not all."

When she met his eyes, her deep blues reflected the firelight. "There are other ways for a Mother to step down. One is here, at the Gathering. A transition will take place, observed by all the People."

Tan thought of the other Aeta caravan, the one Amia had left with to find healing. She must have known about the Gathering then. "Is that where they were bringing you?"

"It is where the caravan *should* have been coming. I do not know if the Mother feared the fact that I am blessed or if it was simply that the archivist was *her* family."

"What happened was no fault of yours," Tan reminded her.

"But it might have been partly my fault. Had I not shared how I was blessed, perhaps the Mother would not have feared I would replace her."

Tan squeezed Amia's hand. She trembled, a different shaking than when the sickness afflicting her mind had threatened to overwhelm her. "She committed to her path when she chose her brother over her people."

Amia nodded. "And do I do something so different by choosing you over my people?"

"That's what he meant by you choosing me?"

"Custom demands that I find another family. It was why the Mother of the other caravan was willing to take me on, even though a Daughter served."

"What was she like? The Daughter."

"Are you asking if she was angry I was allowed to join the family?" Amia asked. "That is not the way of the People. Choosing oneself over the family does not happen."

"But it did."

Amia took a soft breath and let it out slowly. "It did."

They sat in silence for a moment, nothing but the snapping of the flames and the soft music behind them as distraction. The man working the spit smiled at Amia and nodded toward the meat. She tipped her head in assent and he tore off a hunk of meat and brought it to her.

"We welcome you to the fire, Daughter."

Amia smiled and took the meat. The woman handed her a hunk of crusty bread and a metal cup of water. They turned back to their stations, neither offering anything to Tan.

"Not very friendly, are they?" he whispered.

Amia tore off a piece of meat and handed it to him. "They are scared and frustrated," she said. "You must be able to sense that."

"What is it that frightens them, do you think?" Tan asked. "It can't only be the attacks."

"I… I don't know."

"Maybe the Brother shaped them."

Amia shot him a look. "The Brother is a senser, as are most of the Aeta," she said.

Tan peered through the fire, looking for any sign of him. The fire seemed to part, as if knowing what he wanted, splitting to give him a brief glimpse of the silver hoops in the Brother's ears. The man caught Tan's eyes from across the fire and his face clouded briefly.

"He shapes as he makes his way around the fire. I thought it was you at first, but it isn't."

Amia twisted, trying to see him but failing. "Maybe there is another. There would be at least one more blessed by the Great Mother among the People."

"It was him." Tan looked away from the fire and turned to Amia. "You already know the archivists were once Aeta, at least those who could shape. Why shouldn't there be another?"

"We would know. *She* would know."

"Who?" Tan asked.

Amia nodded toward an older lady with dark silver hair tied behind her head. Her skin was a deep bronze and heavily wrinkled, but the brightness in her eyes spoke of a vibrancy.

"Her. The First Mother. The Eldest."

Tan watched the woman as she made her way around the fire. She moved with a sure step, greeting everyone with a quick smile. It took a moment for him to realize that she shaped everyone as she made her way through the throng of people. Her touch was subtle, even gentler than the archivist had managed when he shaped Tan.

Thinking of the archivist, he quickly focused on a shaping, wrapping his mind in air and water to protect himself from the Eldest's shaping.

As he did, she straightened and watched him across the distance between them, lips pursed into a straight line. She *knew* what he had done.

She continued working through the people. Tan realized Amia still spoke. He turned back to her.

"She taught me the first lessons. I was barely five when I was saddled with the responsibility of my blessing, for it *is* responsibility. Told I would lead someday, perhaps that I could replace her in time." Amia shook her head. "It was a heavy burden to place on a child, but she knew I could handle it. Or maybe she shaped me to ensure that I could." A smile crossed Amia's face. "She has such control. I have never managed to work with the same level of control as she manages."

"She knows I'm here," Tan said.

Amia nodded. "Of course she does. Likely she knew the moment we landed days ago. For us to find this place, she had to lead us."

Tan watched the woman, not taking his eyes off her. She continued to move through the Aeta, touching some on the shoulder but merely whispering words to others. With each one, she released a soft shaping. Had he not been attuned to shaping from his time in Ethea and working around Roine, he might not have recognized what she did.

"She's doing the same thing the Brother did," he noted.

"The Brother serves under her. That is his role here. He coordinates the gathering."

"And he shapes as she does." Tan insisted quietly.

"He should not," Amia said and frowned.

"Do you feel it?" Tan asked.

"I've never felt shaping the way you do. But I trust you."

He turned back to the First Mother and watched her again. Even as she weaved through the people, she continued to watch him. Her expression hadn't changed, continuing to make her appear warm and motherly, but every so often, the mask slipped and a hard edge shone through. Tan couldn't help but think it was intentional.

The Brother finished his loop around the fire. He nodded at Tan and made his way over to the First Mother, pausing to lean toward her. A soft shaping built and, as far as Tan could tell, neither spoke.

"They're speaking to each other," he realized.

Amia twisted to see the First Mother. "She's speaking to everyone. That's how she welcomes people to the Gathering. It is done individually and then to the group as a whole."

Speaking like this.

Tan had to lower the shaping protecting his mind as he pushed the thought toward Amia. He focused the thought, making a point of sending it as no more than a pinprick, his connection to her making communicating wordlessly easier. Speaking to her this way was different than speaking to the nymid or the draasin. Even speaking to Elle was different.

The First Mother turned sharply, as if startled.

She had heard.

The People do not speak like this, Amia said.

Tan touched her arm and nodded toward the First Mother.

She came directly toward them, no longer pausing to speak to others as she worked her way around the fire. The light of the flames flickered off her eyes, making them dance. The Brother followed her, keeping a step behind.

When she approached, a wide smile crossed her face. She lowered her head and leaned toward Amia, touching fingers to Amia's forehead. "Daughter," she said aloud.

A shaping built as she spoke. Tan rewrapped his mind in his shaping of wind and water, aware now how he had to draw focus from the elementals. Holding it in place got easier the longer he held it. He didn't want to risk a shaping coming over his mind without knowing what she might do.

Without asking, Tan extended the shaping through the connection with Amia to protect her as well. She could not shape air or water, leaving her vulnerable. As a spirit shaper, she should have some protection by virtue of her ability, but that hadn't kept the archivist from attacking her.

"Eldest," Amia said. She made no sign that she recognized what Tan had done.

The First Mother's smile faded slightly. Her shaping built again before releasing in a soft wave that flooded over Amia. Tan held the barrier in place, protecting her.

They should be safe among the Aeta, but he couldn't help but wonder if the First Mother would attack them in some way. Would the Brother? Tan wasn't confident enough in his shaping to be able to get them to safety. The connection to Asboel was there, but distant, telling him the draasin was far away. He might answer if Tan called, but it would take him time to reach them.

As much as he hated the idea, he *could* reach toward fire. The massive flames reaching high into the night wouldn't take much for him to shape, barely more than a flick...

Tan frowned. For some reason, he felt a desire to reach toward the fire, but it had never been like that for him before. The rare time he had shaped fire, it had required focus, as if he attempted to speak to the draasin. This felt as if he were drawn to use fire, almost as if he were compelled.

Tan narrowed his eyes as he studied the First Mother and then the Brother. The pressure of a shaping remained, though it was almost too soft for him to recognize. Had they shaped him, compelling him to use fire, without knowing? But how had it slipped beneath the protections he placed around his mind... unless they had shaped him before he placed them.

If there was a shaping upon him, was there anything he could do about it now?

Tan shifted, standing and putting himself in front of Amia. Through their connection, he recognized the concern she felt over his actions. He tried pushing reassurance, but to send more than that required lowering the mental barrier he held in place. Without knowing what the First Mother—or the Brother—intended, he was unwilling to do so.

Tan stared at the First Mother before making a point of doing the same to the Brother. He couldn't tell which of them shaped, but *someone* held it. "Release the shaping," he said.

The First Mother blinked slowly. She attempted to see around Tan. When he wouldn't move, she seemed to try to see *through* him. "The Daughter should not have brought you here." She spoke softly but her words carried nonetheless, as if shaped.

The urge to shape fire intensified, pressing on him. The flames dancing behind him created a sense of warmth, almost welcoming in a way. All he needed to do was reach for it, shape it toward him, and fire could wrap around him.

Tan clenched his jaw, pushing away the strange desire.

He held onto the shaping of wind and water, wishing he knew how to heal himself. Roine must know; he'd seen him heal injuries when returning to Ethea in the past. Could he push the water shaping more strongly upon himself?

Doing so risked injury. Instead, Tan made certain to hold onto the shaping, careful not to release it.

Through the shaping came the strange compelling drive to shape fire. He could call to the draasin, use the great elemental to fuel his shaping…

Tan squeezed the thought away.

"I know what you're doing. It will not work."

The First Mother pursed her lips in annoyance. "I do nothing, son of Zephra."

He tensed. She knew who he was. He nodded toward the Brother. "Then he does. Either way it needs to *stop*."

Pressure built again as he spoke, releasing with a pop.

The First Mother tilted her head. She had sharp green eyes that stared intently at him. Her mouth pursed in a tight line. "The Daughter has shared what she should not have shared."

Amia started to stand. The other Aeta nearby, those working the spit near the fire and a few the First Mother had passed on her way toward Tan, turned to watch. They stood silently, eyes fixed on him, as if waiting for something to happen, almost as if they *knew* he was being compelled.

Had he been wrong? Had it *not* been the First Mother or the

Brother shaping him?

Could there be others of the Aeta, those he thought were simply members of the family, able to shape spirit? If so, had Amia known?

"She shared what needed to be shared," Tan said. He spoke with more force than needed, but he grew irritated. After everything Amia had been through—losing her mother, her people and then being *used* by another family—for her to suffer through the same again bothered him with a raging intensity. And if the First Mother refused to help the king, what then?

He knew what he would do then. Tan would leave, reach for the draasin, and travel to Incendin as Lacertin had suggested. The other shapers would need his help.

The First Mother frowned. "Needed to share? Are you so certain, son of Zephra? She shared to prevent Incendin from acquiring a dangerous artifact, but did she stop anything? Did her sharing do anything but delay them?"

In spite of everything, Incendin now possessed the artifact. Whatever they would use it for—however the new winged lisincend would use it—Incendin now possessed the very thing they had tried to prevent.

But not everything had been a failure. Hadn't Tan learned he could speak to the elementals? Hadn't Amia shaped the draasin to prevent them from attacking people?

"And now she brings you to our place of gathering." The First Mother shifted to stare at him. "A dangerous decision, especially bringing one such as him to this place."

"What do you mean 'one such as him?'" he asked.

The First Mother fixed her gaze on Amia. "You would see him trained. That is why you brought him here?"

Amia took Tan's hand and studied the First Mother. Her face

flashed with a hint of defiance. "There is another reason."

The First Mother shook her head. "You think I should interfere in the politics of the kingdoms?"

Amia took a sharp breath. "You will not help, even when our people were involved?"

The First Mother glanced at Tan, her eyes narrowing. "You brought the son of Zephra to the Gathering. Of all the outsiders you could have brought..."

"Zephra traveled with the People for nearly a year. She learned many secrets, yet never shared them."

The First Mother's eyes narrowed. "You claim the Mother shared what she should not have shared with Zephra?"

Amia shrugged. "I don't know. Only that the Mother spoke highly of Zephra, even years after she was gone. Zephra was a trusted shaper, one who protected the interests of the People. And Tan has done the same."

The Brother stepped closer to the First Mother, standing nearly alongside her. "It is too dangerous, Eldest."

Tan frowned, suddenly remembering where he had heard the term used before. It was the term used by the udilm for Asboel, a term the draasin had not fully embraced. Was that significant somehow?

"As dangerous as Aeta serving as archivists in the kingdoms? As dangerous as them shaping the king and the kingdom's shapers as they worked with Incendin?" Tan asked.

This time, he fixed the Brother with a hard glare. The shaping emanated from him; he grew increasingly certain of that.

The First Mother shook her head. "You are mistaken."

Tan nodded to Amia. "Am I? See for yourself what was done to her, how Incendin treated one of your people. Come to the kingdoms and see what happened to the king."

In that moment, he released the shaping held on Amia, leaving her exposed.

The First Mother studied him a moment, the frown on her face deepening, and then a soft but powerful shaping built. It washed over Amia, layering atop her.

Tan could almost make out what the First Mother did, but the complexity to it astounded him. Roine spoke of the shapings Zephra made as something of immense skill. From what he'd seen—the way she used air to mask her appearance and how she could travel on a gust of wind—she had every bit of ability Roine remembered. This seemed similar to what he imagined his mother was capable of creating, only with spirit.

When it ended, Tan could only stare. There might not be anything he could do against a shaping like that.

And it made clear the other shaping he'd been feeling was not the First Mother.

Tan looked past the First Mother, holding the Brother with his gaze. "How is it Amia didn't know? How is it you've kept him a secret?"

The Brother frowned. His body stiffened slightly.

The First Mother watched him, waiting.

Tan sniffed. "How many here shape spirit? How many are blessed by the Great Mother?"

Amia's eyes widened slightly.

Now that he felt the First Mother's shaping, it was clear there was a difference between the various shapers. He could identify at least two distinct shapings right now, probably another. All were of spirit.

Which meant spirit shapers within the Aeta were not as rare as Amia had led him to believe.

CHAPTER 13

Serving the People

THE FIRST MOTHER SAT IN FRONT of a faded wagon on a narrow chair made of brightly colored slats. Paint peeled off the wagon and where wheels had once been, there was nothing more than broken spokes. A thick log was placed underneath the wagon, as if to keep it from rolling away, but there seemed no way for it to go anywhere. As much as the Aeta could settle, this was a place of permanence.

Amia sat next to Tan, arm folded under his. The Brother had left them alone to talk and had returned to make his way around the fire. As he did, the soft presence of his shaping built. Now that Tan knew what to focus on, he sensed it easily. Others mixed with it, few with much strength, but enough that he recognized how many shapings occurred here.

The First Mother studied Tan. One hand ran alongside a long

piece of dark stone. Runes were worked into it, reminding him of the obsidian bowl used by the Incendin shapers.

"Sensing another's shaping is a difficult skill," she said.

"I have sensed shapings long before I ever managed a shaping of my own."

The First Mother frowned. She sat silently, tapping the long stone with one hand. Behind her, the Aeta music had returned. There was merriment to it, but mixed in was a hint of sorrow. Voices murmured underneath the music as the Aeta spoke.

The flames no longer called to him. Whatever shaping had been placed on him had either been removed or did not act with as much urgency.

Tan reached out with earth sensing; a large caravan made its way toward the Gathering. There would be others after it. Had Amia's people not been killed by the lisincend, she would have come here. Tan found it sad that she came under these circumstances, without a caravan of her own and everyone she cared about gone.

"You have strength but there is no control," the First Mother said. "The Daughter brought you here thinking you could learn control."

"He is blessed by the Great Mother," Amia said. "But that is not why we came."

"What you ask cannot happen. It risks too much for the People if I were to leave here."

"Even if the People were responsible?" Tan asked.

The First Mother's eyes hardened as she fixed Tan with a firm gaze. "The People are not responsible. Once, your people would have called you a warrior. Those who claim that title now are nothing like those who preceded them. They use wind and water and air and earth but cannot hear the Great Mother and cannot speak to the elementals. Most don't bother to try."

Tan wondered how much to tell the First Mother. He wanted her teaching—after seeing the control she exerted over spirit, he knew she had much to teach—but did he trust her enough to do so? Did he dare not trust her?

"I have spoken to the elementals."

"As I said, complicated," the First Mother said.

"You know?"

She laughed softly. Light danced off her green eyes. "There is little I don't know, son of Zephra."

Tan shifted in his seat. "When did you learn?"

The First Mother leaned forward. "When you awoke the draasin."

Tan swallowed, thinking of everything that had happened to him since they freed the draasin, everything that had happened to Amia. All this time, the First Mother had known about the elementals, how could she *not* have known about the archivists? How much could she have stopped? "But you didn't know of the archivists?"

She turned away. "The Great Mother has gifted me with insight, son of Zephra, but there are limits to even my abilities."

"Why would they have gone to Ethea?"

Silence built between them before she answered. "Because I sent them."

If that were true, then the First Mother was responsible for everything the archivists did… and she seemed to have no remorse. "Did you know what they would do?"

"Some of this you would not learn until you were raised to Mother," she said to Amia. "I chastised you for sharing secrets of the People, and now here I am, about to do the same." She closed her eyes. Fingers drummed on the long stone, running over a few of the runes. "Our people are blessed by the Great Mother. Some have a greater blessing than others, but all have some element of the gift."

Tan nodded. "Spirit sensing."

The First Mother tipped her head. "A crude term for something so precious, but yes. We are blessed with the ability to sense what you call spirit. Some can touch it and shape it. Those who can are rarer, and those with any real ability with it rarer still." She smiled at Amia. "You would have served your people well, Daughter."

Amia didn't say anything. She didn't need to. Tan felt the sense of loss through their connection.

"I thought only the women of your people are shapers," Tan said.

The First Mother sniffed. "Are only the women of your people able to shape? Women lead the People. It is how it has always been. The men serve in other ways. Those with ability are tested at the Gathering. If they have aptitude for shaping, they remain, protected, here."

"If they remained at the Gathering, how did some end up as archivists?" he asked.

"Those with particular strength are sent to the university to learn. The First Mother has taught for as long as the People have wandered. But there are limits. Many have gone to learn, study in a place where it is welcomed." She glanced toward the fire, where the Brother continued to walk among the Aeta. "In time, and when I have found a suitable replacement, the Brother would be among them. Like the others, he will go and learn from those who've gone before them, serving both the People and your kingdoms in a way, maintaining our connection to the ancient stores of knowledge we were once responsible for."

There was so much about what she said that he wanted to question. "Did you know about the artifact?"

The First Mother hesitated before nodding. "We have known since the beginning."

Amia gasped.

If the First Mother knew, how much could have been avoided?

How many of the Aeta could have been saved? Could Nor have been saved?

"You have held it, have you not?"

Amia nodded.

"Which means you were the one to wade through the pool."

"I have seen the pool," Amia said carefully. "We both have seen it."

The First Mother shifted her attention from Tan to Amia. "You understand what it is?"

"It is the Great Mother," Amia answered quickly.

As far as Tan could tell, it might have been more than that. When he had been in the pool of liquid silver, he had experienced an understanding of the world that had lasted only as long as he had been there. He had undone the twisted shaping on the draasin Enya and freed Amia's mind from the torments she experienced. Had he more time, he might have managed to stop all of Incendin, but he had the sense that wasn't what the liquid pool of spirit was meant for.

"It is power," the First Mother breathed. "And the device was created from that, made solid by an infusion of elemental power. It was Aeta scholars who first suggested its creation. Without the Aeta, there would have been no artifact." There seemed a measure of pride in her comment.

"Do you know what it does?" Tan asked.

"None but those scholars knew with certainty."

"But you suspect."

He needed to know. If the Aeta were responsible for the artifact, the First Mother must know what it did. Could it control the elementals, as Roine suspected, or was there another purpose for it, something greater than they yet knew?

The First Mother let out a shivering breath. "I don't know."

Tan grunted. "Theondar suspects it is meant to control the

elementals."

She blinked at the mention of Roine's real name. "Elemental power infuses the device. It is possible that by lending strength to it, the ancient elementals sacrificed something."

"But why?"

The First Mother leaned back. "To ask why is to seek and understand the world of that time. None of us today truly understand what it would have been like in a time when draasin flew freely across the sky, or when udilm crashed against the shores, or when eyris and tolmud still served as the great elementals."

The last two names struck a memory with Tan, a sense of recognition he suspected he had gained when Amia had shaped understanding of the ancient language into him.

"Ara and golud were not the great elementals of the time?"

"They were by then, but that had not always been the case. Elemental power flows through time, some increasing through generations while others lessen. The lesser can become the greater. And vice versa."

Tan nodded. "That's what Incendin hopes."

The First Mother tapped her pursed lips. "Why do you say that?"

"The lisincend. They are Incendin's first attempt to create the power of an elemental, shaping a closeness to fire they could not possess simply as shapers."

Her eyes closed. A powerful shaping built. When it released, it radiated past the Aeta, as if not intended for them.

The First Mother opened her eyes. "You said 'first' attempt."

"There is another, created at the place of convergence using the artifact."

"You saw the transformation?"

Tan nodded.

"What did it involve?"

Tan held her gaze. "She sliced the archivist's wrist and his blood pooled into an obsidian bowl with runes like the one on your stone. She performed a shaping, drawing through the bowl. As she did, she turned into—"

"One of the lisincend," the First Mother interrupted.

"Not the lisincend. At least, not as we know them. Whatever she became was different. She had much the same leathery skin and control of fire, but she had wings."

The First Mother stared thoughtfully past them. "We have often wondered what the lisincend intended. They are powerful, but not so powerful that the risk of the shaping made sense. So many are lost as they attempt to transform. If they think to gain the power of an elemental..."

"There are some who fear it will work," he said.

The First Mother took a deep breath. "There are other elementals of fire. Saldam, inferin, saa. Each with their own strengths."

"But fire is different," Tan said. It was what the draasin had told him. The elementals of fire did not do things the same way as other elementals. There was no guarantee that saa or inferin would ascend if the draasin disappeared.

"Fire is different," the First Mother agreed. "Where are the draasin now?"

Tan hesitated. He knew generally where the draasin had gone, but he couldn't pinpoint them with any accuracy. "Safe, I think."

An amused smile turned her mouth. "Strange to think we refer to the draasin as safe."

"Were they really so terrible?"

"Who is to know? It was a different time. The elementals spoke to man freely then. Not as it is today." She looked at Tan. "Where is the artifact now?"

"Incendin has it. The new lisincend took it with her."

The First Mother avoided the accusation in his gaze. "I don't think she will succeed in using it. Doing so should require shapings of each element."

"But others could use it to transform?" Amia asked.

"It… it is possible."

But there might be another reason Incendin wanted the artifact, Tan thought. If they could make it work, they could use its power for whatever purpose they planned. And Roine—his mother—would be unprepared.

"Would it work if it's shaped by several at the same time?" he wondered.

The First Mother frowned. "I don't even know what it will do when shaped. To answer what might happen when many shape it…"

"I understand, but do you think it requires a warrior shaper?"

"Since Incendin possesses the device, it matters little. Only fire shapers emerge in those lands."

"There might be another way Incendin could use the device, another way they might succeed in using it. They have other shapers. Stolen shapers," he said. "Men and women taken from Doma and brought to Incendin."

The First Mother shifted in her chair.

"You know about them," Tan said.

Amia looked from Tan to the First Mother.

"There is nothing that can be done for them. They must trust their people will protect them," the First Mother said.

"What people? Shapers taken by the lisincend, depriving them of anyone who might be able to help?"

The First Mother raised her head proudly. "There is nothing that can be done." She hesitated, and then addressed Amia. "I cannot do what you need. If Incendin has the device, I need to protect the People."

"But—" Amia began.

The First Mother crossed her arms. "You know I cannot." To Tan, she said, "And you will learn nothing here, son of Zephra. You are not of the People and will never understand the reasons for what must be done."

Tan inhaled slowly and stood. "This was a mistake, Amia. We should go and return to Roine. We can reach the kingdoms and then decide what needs to be done. Maybe with enough time, you can help the king."

Amia hesitated. "First Mother?"

There was hurt in her words, but it also came through the shaped connection. Amia didn't want to believe the Aeta could be responsible for the archivists—that the First Mother had known what they were doing and still did nothing—but as much as she might claim Tan wouldn't understand, he thought he did. She protected her people.

The First Mother turned. The hard edge had returned to her eyes. "You are one of the People, Daughter. And blessed by the Great Mother. You should stay with your people. Retake your place. Establish your family."

"I have stood by while my family was destroyed by the lisincend. I watched my family—my *Mother*—burn in front of me. And then, when I returned to the People, I was treated—" she choked back a sob "—treated as if I was no better than a dog, chained into the Mother's wagon while those who should have protected me used the gifts of the Great Mother to torment me, twisting my mind. And then, when I thought everything lost, it was Tan who came and rescued me." She stood with hands on her hips, golden hair slipping down and around her shoulder. She touched the back of her neck and there came a soft *snick*. The wide band of silver fell apart. Amia tossed it at the First

Mother. "You claim he is not of the People and that I should establish my family. Well, I *have* established my family."

She took Tan's hand and pulled him with her, storming away from the First Mother.

CHAPTER 14

Attacking Spirit

AMIA DIDN'T STOP UNTIL THE LIGHT from the fire was a distant glow. The night had grown cool and a chill wind gusted around them. The air smelled crisp, the earthy scent of fallen leaves clinging to it. But other than the wind, nothing else moved, as if the forest itself held its breath as they passed.

Soft bells tinkled. At first, Tan thought they came from the wagons at the Gathering, but then he realized they came from deeper in the trees and were moving closer, coming toward them. Another caravan coming for the Gathering.

Tan stretched out with his sensing. The caravan was not large—not compared to the Aeta family that had tortured Amia—and barely only a dozen wagons. There was something odd about the caravan, though it could simply be Tan's irritation with what had just happened tainting his sensing.

"Do you need to rest?" he asked.

Amia clutched his hand tightly. Tears stained her cheeks and she wiped them away with her sleeve. Her neck appeared bare without the silver necklace. For as long as he'd known her, it was her marker of the Aeta. Now, without it, what would she be?

"We should reach Roine," she answered. "He still needs me in Ethea. Now that you're not staying here…"

"They will need me in Incendin."

"You still need training."

He pulled her into his arms and kissed her on the brow. "Then it will have to be you. I know you worry you can't teach me, but what choice do we have?"

"I'm not sure…"

"Can you shape me again?" he asked, thinking of how she had gifted him knowledge of the ancient language.

She frowned for a moment, biting her lip, and then pulled away from him slightly. "It is different. I don't think I can share this knowledge the same way I did the knowledge of *Ishthin*. With *Ishthin*, I simply modified a shaping, one I had seen before. I can show you what I know of shaping spirit, but there is something the First Mother does, a way of opening understanding, that I can't replicate."

Tan wondered if it were anything like when he'd been in the pool of spirit. Standing there, he had seemed to know anything he wanted. All the knowledge of the world existed for him to reach, if only he asked.

Could he have learned how to spirit shape while there?

Perhaps, had he considered the question, but now he would need to summon each of the elementals to call spirit back to the cavern. Even if the others answered, he wasn't certain the draasin would. Wherever Asboel had gone, he deserved time alone, time with his family, especially if the vision he'd granted Tan with two eggs clutched in his talons was accurate.

He stopped and turned when he felt a shaping build distantly.

Roine?

It didn't feel the same, not like the spirit shapers he had felt at the Gathering. This was different.

Tan concentrated. Rather than from the south, the direction he and Amia had come after leaving Roine, this came from the northwest.

"What is it?" Amia asked.

Tan let his concentration return to Amia. "There's a shaping coming from the Gathering. Powerful, but I don't know what it is."

"Probably just from the First Mother. She is the most powerful shaper I've ever met."

Tan looked at her with surprise. With her travels among the Aeta, Amia likely had met many shapers, now including at least two of the last warriors.

"It's not the First Mother," Tan said.

"How can you be certain?"

Tan examined the shaping again. "Since helping you, I can tell the difference between shapings."

Amia frowned. "Different than before?"

"I've been able to sense shapings longer than I've been able to consciously attempt them. But it's changed since we were in the cavern. Now there's something like a signature to each shaping."

Amia pushed her hair back behind her ear, twirling it around one finger as she did. Her other hand trailed to her neck, rubbing where the silver necklace once had been. "If it's not the First Mother, who is it?"

Tan waited as the shaping continued to build. As it did, he recognized another part to it, as if another shaper added their touch.

But it was more than that.

The shaping was not spirit. Somehow, he knew that with certainty.

What, then?

It continued, becoming a painful pressure that built and built until he couldn't tolerate it. He grabbed his head, trying to hold back the pain as it threatened to split him open.

And then it released.

The shaping occurred as a flash of light and a gust of wind.

As it did, Tan recognized a part of it. He had felt it before. Incendin.

Fire and light filled the night, burning brightly behind Tan and Amia.

She gasped softly. Fear came through their shaped connection. She clung to his hand.

Gusts of wind drew the shaping forward, as if they drove the fire, feeding it as it blew through the trees.

Could Incendin really attack the Aeta a third time? Could their people truly be so unlucky as to have Incendin come after them again?

"The Gathering," Tan whispered.

Amia stared at the blooming flames. A shaping built from her but she winced, jerking back from whatever she sensed through her shaping.

"Stay here," Tan suggested. "I will go."

Amia put her palm flat on his chest. "You can't go alone. If this is Incendin, we barely survived last time, and that was with the draasin helping."

"I have to try," Tan said. "I can't stand here and watch as Incendin destroys more of your people."

Amia bowed her head. "They are no longer my people."

Tan took both of her hands and squeezed. "They will always be your people."

The tears that had dried in her eyes welled up again and she wiped them away. "Can you reach him?"

She didn't need to specify who she referred to.

"I can try, but I don't think he will come." Even if the draasin did answer a summons, he wouldn't be able to reach them in time to stop the flames.

But others of the great elementals might answer.

"What if she's there?" Amia asked.

If the fire shaper twisted into the winged creature was among the Incendin shapers, Tan didn't think he would have much of a chance of stopping them. If only Asboel *would* answer, but calling him might be more than dangerous. It might be exactly what Incendin wanted.

"I'm coming with you. If one of the…"

She trailed off, but Tan knew what she had started to say. If Incendin had an archivist with them—and how could they not, if they found the Gathering?—then she might be needed.

He took a deep breath and they started forward, running through the trees.

The forest blurred past. Tan held onto his sense around him, stretching out as his father had long ago taught him to do, listening to the sounds and sensing everything.

He pushed harder, a shaping building as he ran.

Golud.

He spoke the name in a rolling rumble, using the cadence the elemental could understand. Tan couldn't be certain golud would be found here—the elementals were not found everywhere—but if they were, he could use the earth to quench the flames.

No answer came.

Tan ran harder. Amia kept pace.

Wind whistled around them, a wind shaper working upon it, driving the fire and feeding the flames. Tan considered attempting a shaping to tamp down the wind but decided against it. Any shaping risked the attackers knowing he was here.

They came up a small rise. The soil was rockier and the trees thinner, giving a better vantage for seeing the fire as it stretched forward. Fire pressed in a ring around the wagons, as if attempting to swallow the Gathering.

"Great Mother!" Amia swore softly.

Through the crackling of the flames, he heard someone scream. The wind swallowed the sound.

Golud!

Tan sent this as a demand, rumbling through earth. This time, he felt the ground shake in reply.

The fire. Please.

Speaking to golud was difficult, different than the other elementals. He wasn't certain golud would even understand what he tried to say.

The ground rumbled again. Agreement.

Flames died down, tampered by the presence of the great earth elemental.

Incendin shapers pressed harder, a powerful shaping building again. Golud resisted, pulling much of the energy out of the flames. Golud would not be able to stop the fire shaping entirely, but it could resist Incendin enough for Tan to help.

Now Incendin shapers would know something was different.

"Please," he began. "Wait here. I can't stomach the thought of something happening to you again."

"I will go with you. We will help them together," Amia said.

Tan inhaled deeply and ran toward the flames.

As he ran, he formed a wind shaping and worked against the Incendin shaping, forcing the wind against the fires. Did he reach for ara with the shaping? He didn't really know—he had no idea what he did when he shaped, but he must if the wind shaping were to work.

Please help the son of Zephra.

This came out differently than trying to reach golud. Speaking to ara required a light touch, almost delicate. A translucent flicker came to the wind, enough to make him think ara might answer, but then it disappeared.

Wind pressed against him. The shapers knew where he and Amia were.

The wind whipped around him in a spiraling torrent, threatening to lift him into the air. Tan focused on forging a connection to ara and begged for the wind to die down.

The wind started to falter, calming enough for him to regain his footing. He grabbed Amia's hand and kept her close to him. "They know we're here!"

She nodded.

"I can't stop the shaping."

She nodded toward the fires. The Incendin fire shaper pushed against golud. With enough time, even the elemental would be overwhelmed, driven back by the force of the shaping. Tan might manage to slow it, but not enough to save the Aeta, especially not as the wind continued to wail around him.

Tan tried pushing through the trees. The wind fought them as they went, trying to stand them up, holding them back from the Aeta wagons.

The sounds of screaming worked through the howling of the wind around them.

Tan pressed harder, wishing he had spent more time in Ethea trying to understand his shaping, learning to master even one of the elementals, but his connection to each was different. He could sense earth easily, but shaping it continued to challenge him. Wind answered at times, but not always. Water only seemed to respond when he neared the elementals. Only fire had been easy for him.

Ever since connecting to the draasin, he had felt an affinity for fire. He could reach for the draasin more easily than the other elementals, but it was more than that. Like when he had been at the Gathering, with the flames dancing around him. It might have been partly the Brother's shaped influence, but Tan would have little difficulty shaping the fire, twisting it. He might not have the experience of the Incendin fire shapers, but he felt the same draw, and had even used that to defeat one of their fire shapers.

Could he do the same again?

What had he done when trying to rescue Amia? He'd pulled fire *through* him, feeding it into the draasin. Draasin were creatures of fire, born of elemental power. Fire would not harm it.

He hesitated, focusing on the flames. Doing this would be difficult, but if it worked, he might be able to quench the fire enough to reach the Aeta. At least he could slow the attack, give some of the Aeta a chance to escape.

"Tan?" Amia said, pulling on his arm.

He let go of her hand and focused on his connection to the draasin. For this to work, he would need to connect with Asboel. At least to warn him.

Prepare.

He sent it with as much strength as he could. Connecting to Asboel across the distance taxed him, leaching strength quickly. Using limited conversation might preserve his strength.

Maelen.

It came like a whisper at the back of his mind.

Tan nodded, pushing through an image of the fire. He felt the flames where he stood. They beat on him, not hot enough to burn.

Energy hummed within the fire, something he could almost touch. Within it was the shaping made by the Incendin shaper.

Tan focused on this.

And then, with a shaping, he summoned the energy of the fire and pulled it into himself.

It tore through him, searing and hot. Had it not been for his connection to Asboel, the fire might have consumed him. As it was, it threatened to twist him, writhing toward his mind, so different than the last time he had done this.

Tan pushed it back, forcing the fire through his connection and into Asboel. He had seen the draasin absorb a fire shaping from the lisincend. Absorbing this fire should not be too difficult. The difference was the distance and how Tan acted as an intermediary.

Dangerous.

The warning came from Asboel. With it, he asserted himself on Tan's mind, drawing through him, connecting to the shaping and pulling upon it.

And then the fire was gone.

So, too, was the hot pain in his mind.

Thank you.

You seek to become Twisted Fire?

I seek to stop them.

Dangerous, Asboel repeated.

He withdrew from Tan's mind without saying anything more. Tan let him go.

The wind died suddenly. Tan stumbled, catching himself on the narrow trunk of an ash tree. His head throbbed, as if his mind itself was raw. His throat was dry and he coughed.

Amia grabbed him, holding him up. "What did you do?"

He shifted and turned away. "What I could."

She touched his face, running her fingers along it. "Your face…"

Tan brought his hand up and touched the skin on his cheeks. They felt as raw as his mind felt, as if the fire had burned him. What had he risked by pulling the fire into himself?

"I used Asboel," he told her. His voice sounded ragged to his ears, rough in a way it hadn't before. "He absorbed the fire."

"That shouldn't be possible."

Tan took her hand and hurried forward. They needed to reach the Gathering. If anyone survived, the shapers might strike them again. This time, he might not be strong enough to stop them.

"It wasn't the first time I did it. When you were chained in the wagons, the fire shaper attacked me. I pulled fire through me and sent it into the draasin."

"That was different. You said you had nymid armor. They assisted."

Tan hadn't considered that, but Amia was right.

"When we get through this, I will have to see what you did," Amia said.

Tan nodded, suddenly worried. If Asboel, with all his experience, considered it dangerous, then it really was.

They reached the edge of the fire. A soft glow remained, little more than smoldering embers, but enough to see what had happened. The fire had worked in a circle through the forest, burning through trees and leaving them as nothing more than charred remains.

Amia approached slowly, covering her mouth as she did. Her skin was reddened.

Tan stepped across the ground. "I thought it would be hotter than this." He felt none of the heat that had come when he pulled on the shaping.

Amia looked at him. "It is."

Tan frowned, but continued forward, making his way through the circle of ash. He thought they might find nothing more than char, but as they went further, the trees began to have less and less damage until it stopped altogether. The ground was once again green, as if nothing had happened past a certain point. It took Tan a moment to understand why.

The ground rippled, pulled apart as if blasted by fire. Golud. The earth elementals had stood their ground, pushing back against the flames.

Thanks, he sent as a low rumble.

The ground rumbled in reply.

They moved past the border and into still-green trees and undergrowth, stepping past the rippled ground golud had influenced.

"Do you think they might have survived?" Amia asked.

"I don't know. We haven't seen any of the shapers. They might still be here."

Amia closed her eyes. Her shaping built slowly and washed out and around her. When she opened her eyes again, the surge of fear through their shaped connection matched her words. "They are gone."

"What is it?"

They reached the edge of the wagons. Soot covered them, as if flames had tried and failed to lick their way along them. Splashes of color still showed through, but it seemed muted, as if smoke layered overtop and obscured the normal Aeta painting.

Tan thought everyone had gone, that the shapers had killed all the Aeta, but then he heard voices. Soft whimpers and hushed conversation carried to them. Coughs and sobbing mixed in as well.

"The shapers are gone," Amia said.

Tan pushed out with an earth sensing but after speaking to the draasin and pulling their shaping into himself, something had changed and he couldn't sense well enough to know much more than that people stood nearby.

Amia led him through the wagons, pausing to look around.

The massive fire pit no longer raged. Spits with roasting meat were unattended. Bread that had been savory was now burned and acrid. A few wagons on the far side of the wide circle had been tipped over. One had knocked a tree down, tilting it so it leaned over the rest of the clearing, leaving people to duck under the bare branches.

Few people bothered to look back at them. Those who did had faces covered in thick soot. Many had tears staining their faces, reminding Tan of how Amia had looked as they'd left the Aeta only a short while ago.

Shapings came regularly. Tan recognized the signature of the shaping as the First Mother. He didn't sense anything from the Brother. Had he been hurt in the attack?

"Where is she?" he asked aloud.

People stared at him blankly. One woman, a wide woman with what had once been a bright orange dress, blinked slowly and pointed toward the far side of what had been the fire pit.

Tan and Amia made their way around it. The First Mother worked through the Aeta, shaping them. He recognized the shaping.

When she saw them, she froze. "You returned."

Tan let Amia answer. He felt the anger that still worked in her.

"Tan refused to let Incendin attack you without doing anything."

The First Mother frowned. "This… this was you?"

"Not the attack," Tan said.

"I'm not such a fool as to believe you capable of attacking like this. I sensed the Incendin shapers when they came."

Tan sighed. "I'm sorry I couldn't do more."

"More?" the First Mother asked. "You stopped the attack. That was enough to give the People a chance."

Had he been prepared, had he known how to craft shapings effectively instead of relying on his connection to the elementals, he might have been able to do something to help the Aeta. Instead, he had felt nearly helpless. And worse, from what he'd learned from Asboel, what he'd done was dangerous.

"Where are the others?" he asked. "Where did the shapers go?"

The First Mother met his eyes. "They are gone."

"Who?"

"All of them."

Chapter 15

The Effect of a Shaping

TAN SAT ON THE COOLED ROCKS that had once formed the ring of the fire pit, chewing on a piece of still-warm hare he'd pulled from the nearby spit. After shaping and speaking to the draasin, he felt not only exhausted but famished as well. Amia stood across from him. Every so often, she would glance at him with worried eyes and then look away. She couldn't hide the concern that flowed through their shaped connection; Tan felt that acutely.

The First Mother looked around at the rest of the Aeta. Her eyes had a weariness to them that hadn't been there before. Like so many of the others, soot and ash stained her clothes. Somewhere during the attack, she'd struck her head. Dried blood crusted on her forehead and she winced occasionally as if experiencing the pain anew.

All around him, the Aeta seemed in a daze, but something felt strange. Tan scanned the Gathering, looking for what bothered him until he realized what it was. It looked as if the wagons were readied to move, but that meant uprooting the Gathering. How long had it been since the Aeta had moved from this place?

"Where are the others?" Tan asked the First Mother. "What happened to the Brother?"

There were other spirit shapers when they had been here last. Now, Tan didn't sense anything from them. Perhaps they were as exhausted as he felt, drained after the battle with Incendin.

"They are gone."

A pained expression worked across Amia's face. "I'm sorry we couldn't be faster."

The First Mother coughed and touched her head. She blinked slowly, swallowing. A soft pressure built as she made a shaping, then she released it slowly, sweeping it out and across the rest of the Aeta. "They are not dead. Not yet."

"If they're not dead, then where…" Tan sucked in a breath. "The Incendin shapers took them?"

The First Mother nodded. "Five fire shapers came. Five of the People were taken."

Could they be after spirit shapers again? Was that why Amia was abducted from Ethea?

"Were they all shapers?" he asked.

The First Mother hesitated, as if uncertain whether she should answer. "All. They had differing strengths, though none were as gifted as the Brother."

Tan's heart sunk. Incendin would try to create more of the twisted lisincend using them. One was frightening enough, what would it be like with more? "We need to save them," Tan said.

The First Mother stared toward the trees. "They are gone. There is nothing you could do."

Tan considered the wreckage of the Aeta Gathering. "I could have done more. Had I been stronger… better prepared…"

"You did more than you should have been able to do," the First Mother said. She considered Tan for a moment. "How *did* you contain them? The fire shapings. What did you do?"

As she watched him, intensity returned to her eyes. Tan had the distinct sensation that he needed to be careful with what he told her. The problem was, with as tired as he was, he no longer cared about caution with the First Mother.

"I pulled their shaping through me and into the draasin," he answered. He took a bite off the meat he held and chewed it deliberately.

Her eyes widened slightly. "You *absorbed* the shaping of five fire shapers into yourself?"

"I did what I needed," he answered. "I could think of no other way."

The First Mother shifted her attention to Amia. "Did you know he did this?" Accusation hung in the question.

Irritation flared within him. Tan stood and faced the First Mother. "Rather than thanking, you still berate Amia? It wasn't her fault Incendin found your Gathering. It wasn't her fault this place nearly burned. She deserves more kindness than what you're showing her!"

An angry shaping built quicker than Tan could process. It burst from the First Mother, rolling over him. He made a quick attempt at water and air shapings to protect his mind, but failed.

"You're a fool, son of Zephra. You who have faced the lisincend more times than most men claim—even when your kingdoms warred with Incendin—you still don't understand the gravity of your actions."

He couldn't tell the intent of her shaping, but the irritation that had been building seemed to ease. Perhaps she simply sought to calm him. "I don't understand."

The First Mother grunted. "That much is clear. You didn't tell him, did you?" she asked Amia. "He must know. What if he does it again?"

"It wasn't the first time," Amia said.

The First Mother's eyes widened again. "He's done it before? Perhaps *you* are the fool, especially as you know what could happen."

"What could happen?" Tan asked. He tried to keep the frustration he felt from his voice, but it spilled over anyway.

The First Mother fixed him with her gaze. The hard edge to her eyes passed, softening into a look of warmth. "Drawing a shaping into yourself is dangerous enough when you control the shaping. Have you ever seen one of the kingdom's shapers pull a shaping into themselves?"

Tan hadn't spent enough time with kingdom shapers to know. "I don't know. Probably not."

"Have you ever seen *anyone* pull a shaping into themselves?"

As she asked, Tan realized that he hadn't seen it, but he'd heard of it being done. And suddenly, he understood her fear. "But I didn't draw fire into me to serve it. I didn't try shaping myself into the lisincend."

"This may be why you survived. Even were that not the issue, you pulled fire from five fire shapers that I saw. Perhaps there were more. That is more than you would be able to handle alone. Had it not been for the draasin accepting the shaping, I suspect you would have been destroyed."

The First Mother touched his arm, running her fingers across his skin. It felt deadened where she touched, the sense muted. "Even with your bond pair helping, you still suffered. I don't know how much can be healed."

Tan looked at his arms, almost as if seeing them for the first time. The skin was rougher, thickened, and almost leathery. He had seen skin like it before on the lisincend, though it was much tighter and almost scaly.

"Could a water shaper heal this?" he asked.

The roughness to his voice made more sense now as well. What had he done?

"Water can heal, but I don't know if any shaper can help." She left unsaid that an elemental might be able to. "It's possible you will heal on your own. The damage is not too far gone, at least what I can see." The First Mother shook her head. "Perhaps *I* was the fool, refusing to teach, leaving him untrained. Not only a danger to others, but to himself." She spoke almost to herself. "But without him, we would all have perished. Perhaps the Great Mother knew what was needed." Her hand squeezed over her mouth as she lifted her face toward the sky. Her eyes closed and Tan felt a shaping build with the force of her contemplation. When she opened her eyes, she brought her chin back down in one strong motion. "I will offer what help I can to you, son of Zephra."

With that, she lifted herself off the stone she had been sitting on. As she walked away, her gait was unsteady and she wove through the remaining Aeta, who absently reached out a hand to steady her. Not that they appeared very steady themselves. Their eyes had a haunted look, as though they were devastated by the attack.

"If Incendin has Aeta shapers, we don't have much time," Tan said. "We need to get the First Mother to King Althem to release the spirit shaping. I need to help Roine and the others." Anger boiled within him at the thought of his friends facing more of the twisted lisincend without him.

"The king can wait. I will go and do what I can. You need her to teach you. You need to have mastery in part of your shaping. Look at what it almost cost you."

"I thought I could use Asboel." The answer sounded weak to him.

Amia came and sat beside him. She took his hand and looked into his eyes. Worry wrinkled the corners of her eyes. "Did he help?"

Tan nodded. "He reached through me. I felt him absorb the

shaping. The First Mother is right—had he not been there, I might not have survived."

His mind still felt raw and painful from the fire shaping, but even that had begun to fade.

"I'm afraid of waiting too long," he admitted. "If we fail, the kingdoms will fall."

Amia patted his hand. "We all do only what we can."

CHAPTER 16

Learning Spirit

THEY STOOD ATOP A SMALL PEAK. A valley spilled out below, not unlike the valley at the place of convergence. Tan's head hurt from focusing on shaping, a throbbing ache that reminded him of the pain he had felt while in Ethea before bonding to Asboel.

"You let yourself grow distracted," the First Mother said from the small boulder she sat on. Wind caught her silver hair and twisted it in the breeze. The thick band of silver at her neck reflected the fading light more strongly than he would have expected, making it almost seem to glow.

"I'm sorry," he started.

But he couldn't help it. As he tried to focus as she taught, he found his mind wandering, drifting back through what had happened. He had to force it away from memories of his parents and thoughts of his time in Ethea.

"Spirit is different than the other elementals," the First Mother said. "It is sensitivity and understanding. You need to know yourself before you can use it effectively. It's why the youngest learn spirit the fastest."

He pulled back in surprise. "You're saying I don't know myself?"

"I'm saying it's harder to know yourself as you age." She turned her back on him and gazed over the valley. "Some think it easier. That as we age, we get set in our ways, making our decisions clear, but isn't the choice of a child much easier to gauge than the choice of a toddler? And aren't both much easier to understand than someone your age?" She waved toward the trees. "Think of your connection to earth sensing. Without these trees, what would there be?"

He shrugged. "Dirt and rock. Maybe some birds."

The First Mother faced him, eyes flashing annoyance. "Simplistic, but not untrue. And if you were to sense this without the trees, would you find it easier or harder?"

Tan thought he understood. It was the same reason his father had taken him to abandoned iron mines when first teaching him to sense. He had to learn basics before he could add layers of complexity to his sensing.

"You want me to pretend I'm a child?"

"If only it were so simple."

With a light touch on his still-leathery forearm, she shaped him. A wave of relaxation flowed through him. Doing so only delayed his understanding, and he needed to learn as quickly as he could.

"You need to peel away layers of your experience. Only once you have mastery over your spirit will you be able to shape another's."

"Every time I try to 'peel away' my experience, you tell me I'm losing focus," Tan said.

"You haven't reached deep enough."

He looked away. "Isn't there another way to do this? The king needs your help. Your people are suffering. And Incendin could be growing stronger."

"My people are likely already dead," she said softly. "And if Incendin has reached the point where they openly attack, taking the People like that, then I fear what will happen elsewhere."

"I have friends who are in Incendin now. They can help."

"As I said, they are likely dead."

"And when they create more of those—" he paused, uncertain what to call them "—lisincend, Lacertin thinks they will attack the draasin."

The First Mother studied her hands. "If you're right and their intent is to replace the draasin, to *become* elementals, then they would be better served attacking while the draasin are weak."

What would Asboel say about anyone calling draasin weak?

A thought troubled him. "Lacertin thinks they will try to replace the draasin, but they wouldn't be able to do that unless they were elementals already, would they?"

"When you suggested the lisincend goal was to become as powerful as the draasin, to eventually replace the draasin, I knew there must be more to it."

Tan thought of how the Incendin fire shaper had pulled her shaping through the artifact, drawing the archivist's blood with it. "Is that why they need spirit shapers? Can we do anything to stop them?"

"I don't know."

The admission troubled him for some reason. "Is that why she wanted to reach the pool of spirit?"

"There are many ways to reach the Great Mother. I suspect they have learned another."

"Your shapers?"

"Each touches the Great Mother in a different way. It is possible that collecting enough shapers of spirit, they will be able to draw in enough of the Great Mother to fully create their transformation."

"You knew about this, didn't you? That's why you were moving the Gathering."

She met his eyes. "I feared it possible. If they had convinced the People serving in the archives to help, they could easily learn of the Gathering."

"But why? Why would the archivists sacrifice their own people?"

"There must have been a reason, though I cannot see one." She shifted her attention back to him. "But that is not why you are here now. Focus. Master your shaping—your spirit. Only once you learn it can you help those you wish to serve."

Tan gazed over the valley, thinking of what it had been like before there were trees and life and all the animals he easily sensed roaming through it. Could he do the same with his mind, with his experiences? Would he really be able to peel away his experiences to learn who he was?

And if he couldn't, what would happen to him?

Tan sat by the small, crackling fire. The fire pit didn't dance as before, only a few logs burning, keeping back the chill of the air. The fire called to him, differently than it had when he suspected the Brother shaped him. Tan ignored it.

He let his mind wander, trying to do as the First Mother instructed, but doing so was difficult. His head ached from wasting time trying to shape spirit throughout the day. Nothing even closely intentional had come from the time he spent. He would be better off going to Lacertin and helping him remove the Incendin threat.

Except there wasn't much he could do until he was better trained. Before he had feared he wasn't a shaper like the others; his power came from the elementals. Now he grew more certain. None could really help him, not like he needed. With Asboel gone, he had no one to guide him.

And if—*when*—he failed to help the king, what would become of his friends in Incendin?

As he struggled to shape spirit, memories of Nor kept creeping up, but not the ones he thought he should focus on. Flashes of Lins and his friends slithered through his mind and made him angry. He thought of the day the Aeta had first came to Nor, of when Lins called Amia a rat. Or earlier, when Lins beat old Hildon's dog because it stole scraps from the kitchens. Memories of Bal came to him. Annoyance at finding her hiking alone in the mountains the day he first discovered tracks from the hounds, or when she followed him throughout the village until he had to sneak away to get privacy from her. Even Cobin, first Tan's father's friend, and then his friend, too. How many times would they hunt together, getting lost through the woods, relying on Tan's ability to sense their way home?

It hurt that he wouldn't see any of that again. Nor—his home—was gone.

He needed to focus on better—happier—memories. Times when he'd followed his father into the woods, trailing after him as his father had taught, using his earth sensing to search for him. He never managed to find him until his father *wanted* to be found. Only now did he understand why. There were times in their old family home when his parents had still been together, when his father would work at his whittling while his mother cooked, happily tending to the kitchen.

And then there was the memory of the day his father received his summons. He'd held the letter for a long time, simply sitting by the fire, staring at it. Tan remembered looking over his shoulder, seeing the wax seal and not understanding. Yet his father had gone willingly. He'd hugged Tan and kissed his mother the morning he left. It was the last time he'd ever seen his father.

"What are you thinking about?"

Amia watched him. He wiped his eyes, pushing back tears threatening to well up in them. "The First Mother wanted me to peel back the layers of my experiences," he said. "She said it's harder to teach someone with many experiences."

Amia laughed softly. "Since I've met you, you certainly have managed to have many different experiences."

He reached over to her and took her hand. "Not all bad."

"Not all," she agreed. "You look troubled. What was the last thing you were thinking about?"

He took a deep breath. Likely she felt emotion through the bond the same way he did. That meant Amia would know how he felt. "My father and the day he left. He got a summons from the king. Incendin attacked to the north. And he went. At the time, I didn't know why he had to go. Nor is so far from the rest of the kingdoms that you sometimes forget you're a part of them. Other than the manor lord, there's no real influence from the throne, and even the manor lord rules as he sees fit. When my father received his summons, I think he almost didn't believe it came. He stared at it for nearly an hour, sitting by the fire. At the time, I didn't really understand it." He shrugged. "Maybe I still don't understand. At least now I know why the king summoned him, if not why he went so willingly."

Amia frowned. "Don't you? He was an earth shaper. Don't you now do the same thing he did?"

"I never answered the king's summons."

"No, because you don't need the king to tell you what you must do. You went against the worst of Incendin twice, facing the lisincend."

"For you."

She laughed again. "Was it all for me?"

The shaping might have compelled him at first, but he'd done what he needed. "I won't serve the way my parents did. I won't go blindly off to follow his command."

"Are you so certain your parents did?"

Tan hesitated. Years living with his parents hadn't told him anything about them. They had secrets he would never know, parts of their past they kept from him. Had they done it for his protection, or could there have been another reason?

Even now, after seeing his mother again, he didn't know anything about what had motivated her. She claimed to have gone to Nor because of him, because she wanted to raise him in a place where he could be safe and where his father could continue to fortify the barrier, but Tan couldn't help but think there was more to it.

"We need to convince the First Mother to go to Ethea," he said.

"She delays."

"Why?"

She shrugged. "To teach, presumably."

"And what happens if I can't master spirit shaping?" Tan asked.

"You will master it. You're too strong not to."

Tan closed his eyes. He needed to tell her what he feared about his shaping. Too much was at risk if he didn't. "There is something you should know," he started. "I learned something in Ethea when I was working with Cianna."

At the mention of the fire shaper's name, the pull of irritation worked through the bond. "I'm sure she managed to teach you something."

Tan frowned. "She wanted to help me learn to control fire. She thought since I bonded to the draasin, I had the potential to be a strong fire shaper."

"You will be a strong fire shaper. You don't need one like her to prove it to you."

"That's just it. I don't know that I shape the same way."

Amia crossed her arms over her chest. One hand went to her neck. Tan was reminded, again, of the silver Aeta band. She'd taken it off for him. "How can you tell that you shape differently than anyone else? You can't *see* someone shaping."

"But I can sense it. I've always been able to sense it, at least since meeting you. At first, I thought it had something to do with how you shaped me, but now I'm not sure. You know that anytime there's a shaping, I sense it. Sometimes it's stronger than others. For the longest time, I couldn't use it to tell *who* was shaping, only that there was a shaping. With Cianna—" Amia tensed slightly when he said her name "—I could determine the direction of the shaping. I sensed the fire as she drew it out of her. Roine said it is the same for him."

Amia nodded. "Shapings come from within. The shaper is connected to the element. That is why those who can shape spirit are considered so blessed. We are connected to the Great Mother herself."

"Or another elemental," he said softly.

"There is no elemental of spirit."

Tan wasn't as certain. What else but an elemental did they summon in the place of convergence? Unless the Great Mother *was* the spirit elemental.

"Why do you bring this up? What does it matter how a shaping is drawn from the shaper?"

"Because it's not the same for me. When I have shaped, I don't draw it from inside. When I try to do it as Cianna showed me, nothing happens, but when I try to shape as if speaking to the draasin…" He tipped his head toward the fire pit. With a thought, he instructed a small fire to ignite. "When I do it that way, I have control. The shaping works. Any other way and it doesn't."

"So you don't think you're shaping at all. That you simply *control* the elementals?"

"I don't have any other explanation. I just don't think I shape the same way. It's why I'm not certain the First Mother can teach me to control spirit. Other than when I was in the pool of spirit, I haven't ever managed to intentionally shape spirit."

"You've shaped it before. The draasin said you did."

"What if I didn't? It happened at the place of convergence, the same place you managed to shape an elemental. I think you and Roine are right—that shouldn't have been possible, but the shaping took. It held. But other shapers would have tried to control the elementals. Why would it work for you and not for others?"

"Because we were in a place close to the Great Mother, a place where her power was augmented."

"And if I can't shape without the elementals, I'm not a shaper at all, am I?" Tan looked over at Amia, knowing she had no answers but wishing that she did, that she knew how to explain to him what he was. "And if I'm not a shaper, what am I?"

CHAPTER 17

Twisted Fire

THE FLAMES CRACKLED SOFTLY in the fire pit. None of the previous intensity burned there, nothing like the fire that had danced before Incendin attacked. It didn't push back any of the cool in the air, leaving it with a bite that stung Tan's cheeks. The skin of his arms and legs felt taut and itchy. He shifted, trying to get comfortable, but since absorbing the Incendin fire shaping, he couldn't really get comfortable.

"If what you say is true, then we shouldn't stay here," Amia said. "You need healing and we need to return to Ethea. The king—"

"You said you couldn't help the king," he interrupted. He didn't want to think about the healing he needed. Other than the way his skin pulled tight on him, he didn't *feel* any different, but that didn't mean the shaping hadn't changed him.

"And I can't." Amia stared at the fire, a worried look on her face.

"The shaping that has enveloped his mind... only the First Mother could unravel it. There are layers of shaping, more than any I have ever encountered."

"That would be Jishun."

They turned. The First Mother stood to the side of the fire. There was a distant look in her eyes as she stared into the darkness. Her arms were crossed over her chest, hands stuffed into the long sleeves of the cloak she wore. Her hair hung loose around her shoulders, almost giving her an unkempt appearance.

How long had she been standing there? Had she heard Tan admit that he wasn't even a shaper?

"Jishun served as Athan," he said. "He would have been able to stay close to him, but as Athan, he spoke as the king's voice. He was the reason Amia was taken. The reason she nearly died."

"Instead, he died, did he not?" the First Mother asked.

"Taken by Incendin," Tan said.

The First Mother's face twisted in a frown. "Taken. Sacrificed. Used to transform into an abomination to the Great Mother."

Twisted Fire. The elementals all detested what the lisincend had done to themselves. Could they know what they might become? Could the elementals know the lisincend had the potential to become elementals?

Tan took Amia's hand, thinking of how she had been chained inside one of the Aeta wagons. Would she have been the sacrifice instead, or had they some other plan for her? "He earned his fate."

"You sound so certain, son of Zephra."

"I saw what he did."

"Yet you still do not know his mind. Could it be Jishun had a reason for what he did?"

The First Mother still refused to believe that one of the Aeta could have caused such devastation, but Tan had witnessed what they were capable of doing. He had seen the way they attacked Amia in the archives, how they abducted her when she went with the Aeta. Whatever happened to Jishun was deserved.

"You taught him," he said.

The First Mother took a quick breath, pulling her arms more tightly around herself. "I trained him, as I train all blessed by the Great Mother. Had he been born female, he would likely have replaced me in time." She looked at Amia. "But his was a different purpose and destiny. He was the most skilled of any I have ever taught. If there was a shaping he made, it would have been done skillfully."

"I have sensed the shaping on the king, but it is too complex for me to remove. I began unraveling it—"

The First Mother shot her a look.

"But stopped when I saw how deeply it wrapped around his mind."

"What will happen if the shaping is not lifted?" Tan asked.

The First Mother spread her hands out, palms up. "Without knowing the intent of the shaping, I cannot answer."

"Could you determine the intent?" Tan asked.

Her mouth tightened as she considered the request. "Doing so would involve me leaving my People."

"You had to leave anyway," Amia said. She swept her arms around the wagons. "I see preparations beginning. Wheels replaced. Wagons getting hitched. The People and the Gathering are moving."

"And do you know the last time the Gathering moved?"

Amia shook her head.

"Because it has not moved in your lifetime. This is as settled as the People will ever be. And now we move, uprooting ourselves again."

"That is the price we pay for the bargain."

The First Mother sniffed. "You speak as if you understand the bargain. Made in a time of fear, it might have protected our people once, but it does nothing but force us to wander. Tell me—would you have settled had you the chance?"

Amia cast her eyes over Tan. They lingered on his mouth, on his hands. At last, she gave a single nod. "I have settled."

The First Mother studied Tan. "With the son of Zephra, you have not settled."

A slight smile turned Amia's mouth.

"We need to know what Jishun planned. We need to know about the shaping he placed on the king. And if there is any way to remove it," Tan said.

"What you ask…"

"*You* trained him," Tan said. "He was of the People."

The First Mother sighed. "You speak of things you do not understand, son of Zephra. And now you ask me to bring the Gathering to Ethea?"

Tan took a step forward. "Not the Gathering. You."

She tilted her head and met Tan's eyes. "As I said, you don't know what you ask."

"You're right. I don't. But I know what one of your people did to mine. I would think you could recognize the need to make amends."

The First Mother stepped up to the fire pit and set her hands on either side of it. "You claim the king as yours?"

"I claim Amia as mine."

The First Mother studied them both. "You would formalize this?"

Amia stared at the First Mother with an unreadable expression. "I am no longer a Daughter of the People."

"Because you took off your mark?" She coughed, eyes looking weary. "You will always be a Daughter, but you will have to choose whether you wish to be Mother."

Tan didn't fully understand what they meant, but now wasn't the time to fill him in. They had a more pressing matter to attend to. "Will you help the king?"

The First Mother considered the Aeta working at the wagons or cooking or sewing. None were singing tonight. Few even bothered to speak. The pall over the Aeta was nearly the same as when they had come to Nor, chased out of Incendin by the hounds. "We are the Landless. We are Wanderers. And we have hidden ourselves for hundreds of years. We have kept ourselves away from the politics of nations. Doing so has kept the People safe." She shifted her gaze back to Tan. "I can't do what you ask. I can't leave the People."

Disappointment filled him. As it did, the pressure of a massive shaping built.

He stretched out with his sensing, straining to listen for what happened around him. It wasn't the First Mother. Her shaping had a different feel. This came from outside the reach of the firelight, and stronger than should have been possible for any one shaper.

That meant several.

"Tan?" Amia must have sensed his unease through the connection.

"Someone shapes nearby," he said.

"You have already seen that we have many shapers," the First Mother said.

He leaned forward and pinched his forehead as he considered. "This is different. Earth. Wind. Fire?"

A chill worked down his back. If they were kingdoms' shapers, he should have known. They would have announced themselves in some way and wouldn't have any reason to come upon the Aeta by surprise.

The shaping continued to build.

Now he felt it beneath his feet. The earth trembled lightly, enough for him to sense. He could tell from Amia's face that she felt nothing.

Shaped wind whipped down through the trees, sending the scant flames in the huge fire pit dancing with more intensity. And then the fire leapt toward the sky, fed by another sudden shaping.

Tan jumped to his feet. "You need to end this!"

Amia's eyes widened and she tried looking everywhere at once. "I can't tell where they are."

The First Mother took Amia's hand. "Come, Daughter, we will work this shaping together."

The shaping continued to build. If Tan did nothing, it would strike soon.

With a quick whisper to the wind, he asked it to fall silent. Ara was fickle and playful, but listened to his request. He stomped a foot onto the ground, calling golud's attention, and the elemental silenced the rumbling within the earth.

The effort of the two nearly wiped him out. After working with the First Mother throughout the day, trying to shape spirit, he was left weakened. Even simple requests of the elementals were almost too much.

The fire twisted, spiraling as it raced toward them.

He spoke to it as he spoke to the draasin.

Nothing happened.

It was then Tan realized the fire didn't come for him. It came for the First Mother.

Like a bolt of lightning, it streaked toward her.

Amia stood next to her. She would be hit by it, too.

Tan jumped.

The flame struck his chest. As it did, he had no choice but to pull the flame—the shaping feeding the flame—inside of himself.

Searing pain seared through him, nothing like he had ever experienced before.

Everything felt raw. He screamed.

The fire snaked toward his mind. Part of him recognized that if it reached its goal, what remained of him would be destroyed.

He pushed against the fire but was too weak to hold it back.

Asboel!

He cried out the draasin's name, unmindful of who among the Aeta might hear him. He felt a faint stirring and he sent the shaping through the bond, toward the draasin.

And then he collapsed.

The pain burning in him eased somewhat, barely enough for thought.

I warned you. Dangerous.

Asboel admonishing him hurt almost as much as the smoldering fire he felt within his veins, in his mind.

The Daughter…

I will come.

Not yet. Tan couldn't let Asboel see him like this. That was not how he would maintain the bond.

I care not for appearance, Maelen. You and I share—

Tan didn't get the chance to know what he would say; a shaping washed over him, a shaping he was unprepared for.

All the elements converged on him: water and wind and earth and fire. The last he felt most strongly, as if drawn to it. Without meaning to, he pulled the fire shaping into him again.

This time, he felt nothing. It was as if he was already numb, yet he sensed fire easily.

He opened his eyes, his gaze drawn to the fire pit. The flames swirled in a funnel, working their way toward the First Mother and Amia. The ground trembled, shaking beneath them. A storm raged overhead, too violent to be anything but shaped. But it was fire that called to him most strongly.

It sang to him, almost demanding he reach for it.

Rage worked through him. They had been attacked, again and again. Each time, he felt helpless.

Not this time. This time, he could use fire. He might not have the control Cianna wanted him to master, but he had the strength. He could twist the flames to his will.

He forced a shaping, turning the fire away from them, pushing it out toward the trees.

Distantly, he recognized his shaping was different than before. This time, it came from within.

Someone yelled.

The earth's rumbling ceased. The earth shaper had fallen. Tan felt no remorse. Nothing but hot and angry rage boiled within him.

Wind still threatened to steal the fire from him, trying to push it down. The wind shaping felt weak and he traced it to where he knew the shaper to be. With a force of a shaping, he sent fire at the shaper. A cry rang out and quickly fell silent.

How many shapers had come?

Tan didn't dare release the energy of the fire shaping. He couldn't if he wanted to. The flames danced around him—within him—and he pushed it out, letting the fire he felt burning inside roar away from him.

Another shaper fell and the storms silenced. The water shaper.

That left only fire.

Holding onto fire, Tan sensed the shaper, tracing along the shaping that tried to wrest control away from him. Wrapped as he was within fire, they could no more take fire from him than he could have let it go.

With another push, he sent the flames back at the fire shaper, pushing out and away in an angry torrent of flame, filling the shaper with so much fire, his opponent couldn't sustain the shaping and was consumed by it. A burst of light down the slope was his reward.

He turned, looking for another shaper. Incendin must have sent another, and now that he embraced fire, now that it consumed him, he would use everything he had against them.

But the night was silent other than the crackling of flames.

Tan considered what the fire was doing to him. Heat shimmered from skin that had turned a flaming red. His clothes had burned away, now cracked and fallen to the ground. He held out his hands. Steam rose from them.

What had he done? What had he become?

He tried releasing his connection to fire, but he couldn't. It called to him, seductive and strong—stronger than his will to resist. All he had to do was pull more fire within him, draw in the shaping, and he could serve fire more fully. The shaping was easy; he sensed what he needed to do, if only he was willing to reach…

A lancing pain shot through his mind. A shaping of spirit.

He had released his protections. Why would the First Mother attack him?

Unless she had planned this. Could all this have been her intent? She sent the Aeta to the kingdoms to become archivists. She had tried drawing Amia to the Gathering, letting Jishun and the archivists abduct her. She had drawn him to the Gathering, forcing him to pull fire into him in an attempt to save the Aeta.

All of this was her choosing, her way of removing Tan from Amia. He would not let her.

He built a shaping, readying to send it toward the First Mother. All he needed was a single burst of flame—a single shaping that he had seen before—and he could destroy her, keep her from harming him anymore.

The shaping twisted in his mind, forcing him to release fire. Only then did he realize what happened. It was Amia who shaped him.

He turned to her with anger still burning inside.

Amia's face was a mask of emotions, none of which came through the shaped bond very clearly.

Anger coursed through him. Why would she stop him as he fought back Incendin, especially now that he finally had the strength to oppose them? She had experienced the same loss at Incendin as him, losing everything—her family, her home, and her entire life taken by the lisincend. Now that he had found the strength to fight…

Stop!

She sent it as a command, shaping through him.

Fire called to him, but distantly and with less urgency than before. He didn't know if he could reach it if he tried. Worse, the sense of the draasin was a muted itch in his mind, shielded from him.

Tan turned, looking at the Aeta around him. Most hid, having run for protection when the attack began. Those who remained stared at him.

But it was the look Amia gave him that hurt the most. She watched him with an expression of sadness and pain.

Tan followed her glance over his body. His skin had changed, leaving him looking more like one of the lisincend than himself.

What had he done?

Amia hesitated and then came over to him. She hesitantly touched his arm but jerked her hand away. Tan felt nothing where she touched him.

"Tan…" The pain in her voice pierced through the remaining anger he felt.

"I only wanted to stop Incendin." His voice was rough and painful, so different than he remembered.

"You did. They won't harm us again."

He swallowed and nodded. At the back of his mind, anger tried pushing back in, almost as if it wanted to draw fire with it. "What did I do?"

The First Mother stepped over to him. Her eyes were hard. "You began a transformation."

"I didn't… I only wanted to protect Amia…"

But he knew what had happened, had felt it each time he pulled fire and the shaping within him, drawing it away from Amia. Fire burned away part of him, leaving him raw and changed, pulling him closer to fire, but destroying him at the same time.

"What have I become?"

The First Mother took a deep breath before pursing her lips into a thin line. "Nothing yet. But you have changed."

Changed. Like the lisincend. Like the Incendin fire shaper who wanted to become more like the draasin. Tan had begun a similar change. With it, he felt the draw of fire. It would be so easy to reach for it, shape it. Nothing like the difficulty he had before.

It was not the only change he felt.

No longer could he easily sense everything around him. The wind did not pull at his hair. And if he lost the sense of earth and wind, likely water had left him, too. Changing with fire had sacrificed his ability to use the other elements.

He might not have been a shaper like those of the kingdoms, but he had a connection to the elementals. Whatever he had done had damaged that connection, possibly severing it permanently. That loss hurt more than anything.

"What can I do?"

"There is no longer anything you can do, son of Zephra. You serve fire now."

"No," Amia said. "There must be something we can do, some way of saving him."

The First Mother started away. "You sacrificed yourself for the Aeta, Tan. For that, I will do what I can to help your king. But there is nothing more for you that can be done."

CHAPTER 18

The Draw of Fire

DARKNESS HAD FALLEN AROUND the forest, but Tan saw with a different light. Hints of red and oranges radiated from the trees. Birds, glowing with a soft internal light, perched on branches. A squirrel scurrying overhead leapt in a blur of red. Even his eyesight had changed.

He stood alone, uncertain what to do next. Transformed by his shaping, he was more lisincend than anything. The sense of anger burned within him, begging for release. The only way for him to release the rage was through fire.

It ate at him, seething through his skin. Heat radiated out from him, shimmering against the night, shielding him.

"You should go with her."

He faced Amia as she approached. He had sensed her coming—had somehow *smelled* the heat of her body as she approached. The bond shaped between them was still there, but twisted. Without it, he suspected the anger working through him would overwhelm him.

"You need me."

Tan grunted. "I need nothing."

"Tan—"

The transformation had damaged him, but he could not deny that it had strengthened him as well. For the first time, he felt as if a shaping would come easily. All he had to do was twist the heat he felt around him, the heat he *saw* around him, and it would respond. Why shouldn't he revel in this ability?

And powered by fire, couldn't he stop the lisincend? He could help Roine and his mother as they worked against Incendin. They might have served fire longer than Tan, but he had a connection to the draasin. That connection would make him more powerful. Probably powerful enough to stop the lisincend altogether.

"Those thoughts are not your own."

He pressed against the shaping Amia worked on him. It tingled within his mind, a constant irritant. The fire working through him wanted it gone. Or he wanted it gone. Perhaps they were the same.

"The thoughts are mine." Her body glowed with a delicious light, the heat radiating from her filling the night. He could find her with his eyes closed. "I can shape easily now. It wasn't always so simple. Now, all I have to do is reach for fire and it is there."

"But what has it done to you?"

"It was worth the price."

Amia took a step toward him "Was it?" she asked softly.

"You're alive."

"Tan—"

"Had I not stopped the shaping—had I not stopped the shapers—you and the First Mother would have been killed by them. This?" He swept his hands over himself but didn't look down. "All of this is the price I was willing to pay."

"Did you know what would happen?" she asked. "Did you know that you would become one of the lisincend?"

"I'm not like them. I won't simply kill like they did."

"Then what do you think you did to the shapers?"

Tan took a deep breath. He had done what had been needed to stop them. Had he done nothing, the shapers would have reached the remains of the Gathering. They would have attacked and killed Amia and the First Mother. Or worse: they might have abducted them as the others had been taken. And then what would happen to them?

Instead, he had been changed.

"I did what I needed. They were going to take you or kill you. I did what I needed," he repeated.

Amia took another step toward him.

Heat pulsed out through his skin, pressing against the night, fueled by the raging fury within him. This close, she would be affected by the heat, but still, she came.

"Tan." She said his name with a sharp crack of a shaping.

He didn't feel it as he once had. This was different but it still pressed on his mind, threatening him.

This time, he didn't fight the surge of flames. He let it work through his mind, burning away the shaping. "Don't," he snapped.

Amia jerked back, as if he had burned her.

More than anything, her response shook him. The fury eased somewhat, replaced by fear. "Amia?" he said. "What happened to me?"

Her reaction made him aware of the way fire influenced him, the way it pressed on his mind.

She held out a hand as if to touch him but stopped herself. Fear slid across her eyes and as it did, she tried to shield him from feeling it through their connection. He could not only feel it, he could smell it, too.

"You did what you needed. And now I will do what I need to save you, as you once did for me."

"What are you going to do?"

Pain shot across her face. Then he felt her shaping as it surrounded his mind.

The attack came suddenly. From anyone else, he would have struck out with more violence. Since it was Amia, he hesitated, but only for a moment, only long enough to register what she tried to do.

She worked to separate him from the fire.

Without thinking, he built a shaping, pushing against Amia's spirit shaping. Hers built and pain came with it, matched by the expression on her face.

Tan pushed back harder, pulling on the fire burning within him, trying to push back what she had done. The lisincend had managed to withstand her shaping. So could he.

But the lisincend had experience working with fire that Tan lacked.

Amia continued to push. Fire grew more distant.

With one more violent attempt, he thrashed against the shaping, but it was too late. Amia's shaping settled on him fully, separating him from fire.

The colors of the night faded. No longer did he see streaks of orange and red. No longer did Amia glow near him. The warmth radiating from his skin eased, leaving a biting wind that gusted through. Without fire, he felt empty.

"What did you do?" he demanded.

"What you needed. I will see you get help whether you want it or not."

"What 'help' do you think will work? The First Mother said nothing can be done. What I did changed me and instead of thanking me, you've shaped me," Tan growled.

She tried to hide the hurt on her face. "There is much that can be done for you, Tan. You can speak to the elementals. There will always be help available for you."

He closed his eyes. He could still smell Amia, the heat radiating from her. Part of him felt angry at what she had done, at the shaping that restricted him, separating him from fire. Another part wanted nothing more than to hold her, tear off her clothes, and…

He shook off both thoughts.

"I can't speak to the elementals. Not like this," he said.

"Even the draasin?"

Now that the fury raging through his mind had died, he knew he couldn't let Asboel find him like this. What would the draasin say, knowing he was twisted by fire, no different than the lisincend? What would happen to their bond?

"Not the draasin," he said.

Amia touched his hand. This time, she did not jerk back.

"There is nothing that can save me."

"You have risked yourself for others more times than I can count. You have faced impossible odds, daring to go against Incendin and the lisincend. You have convinced the First Mother to travel to Ethea and unravel the shaping working against the king. Do you really think there is nothing that can be done?"

He nodded.

"Thankfully I do not feel the same way."

Amia no longer seemed bothered by heat radiating from him. Before she shaped him, it had pressed out of his body, as if fire itself was trying to escape from within. Now, he didn't feel the same heat. Nothing other than thick and stiff skin pulling with every movement.

Amia kissed him lightly on the cheek.

Could she be right? Could she really find a way where he could be healed? And if she could, did he dare refuse?

"What do you have in mind?" he asked.

She whispered it to him. Tan prayed briefly to the Great Mother that it would work.

CHAPTER 19

Water Elementals

IT TOOK ONLY A FEW DAYS for them to make their way through the mountains and reach the high peaks overlooking the rocky shores below. For the first time, Tan realized he had been wrong in thinking they were in Galen. The shaping his mother and Roine had done on him and Amia had taken them far from the kingdoms.

"We were in Doma," he said.

"The Gathering. It is protected here," Amia said. "The families can move through easily, passing along the northern edge of the Vatten to reach Doma without needing to cross into Incendin. Others come from Chenir or even the outskirts of Incendin. But it is a place few else travel. We are protected, left alone here. Or were."

Tan took in the scene, lingering on the massive rocks below. The ocean pounded against them, crashing in massive and violent waves. He stared at the water, wondering if he could truly reach the udilm like

Amia thought or if he would simply drown. Either way, the pain of what he had done would be over soon.

His skin ached. It pulled against him, straining with each step he took. His mouth felt constantly dry and his throat felt raw.

Worse than all that was the pain in his mind, the constant reminder of Amia's shaping that separated him from fire. He could do nothing against it. After days feeling the same, he wanted nothing more than to remove the shaping, to let fire come to him again, but it could not while Amia held onto her shaping.

"I am not certain this will work."

"It worked for another," Amia said. "If we were closer to the place of convergence, I would bring you to the nymid. Instead, we must come here."

"I can't hear them anymore," he said.

"You will. We simply need to get you the help you need."

"I will die."

"Can you really live like this?" she demanded. "Can you really live fighting against the draw of fire every day, knowing that one day you will hurt someone you care about? Knowing that one day it will consume you and you will become like *them*?"

"I can…" He trailed off. He had been about to say that he could control the fire within him, but he wasn't certain that he could. Before she had wrapped him with her shaping, the fire had threatened to consume him with its fury. What would he have done then?

He let out a frustrated breath that steamed against the air.

"The kingdoms still need you, Tan. Not this creature you could become, but *you*. The man who speaks to the elementals. The man who can draw the Great Mother. You are the person the kingdoms needs."

"I'm no shaper. Before this happened, I could not shape like you or Roine or my mother. But now? Now I could reach fire more easily than any fire shaper. Cianna would be impressed with my control."

Amia gave him a brittle smile. "You have no control, not over fire. It has the control."

He shrugged. "Does it matter?"

She fixed him with a hard gaze. "Yes."

"I will die attempting this," he said again.

"Then you die trying to be the man the Great Mother intended you to be." She met his eyes. "The man your father wanted you to be. The man I want you to be."

Tan bit back the anger surging through him. "Come. Help me to the rocks. Help me swim to my death."

Everything was numb for him; he didn't care how his words hurt her.

Atop the rocks, salt spray struck him, stinging against his still-raw skin. Tan enjoyed the sensation, thankful to feel anything again. Since the transformation, he had felt little. Or maybe it had been Amia's shaping that left him feeling nothing.

He raged against it again.

She glanced over. "You are so close now. Why would you fight?"

He sighed. "I think… I think that fire would always fight."

"Fire might fight, but you can't control it. I've said it before. Without control, there is nothing keeping fire from consuming you."

"It doesn't consume the draasin."

"No. It doesn't. Yet you aren't one of the elementals."

Tan could almost imagine what it must be like for the draasin, to have the power of fire without the fear of loss of control. If he had that, he could truly stop whatever Incendin planned. There would be nothing the draasin could do to stop him.

And why should he want to seek healing? What had he done when healed that he couldn't do now? Now, he at least had control over one of the elements, control that few others could rival. With that power, he could do much good, regardless of what Amia feared.

"The shaping is failing," she said.

Tan blinked, recognizing what she meant. Fire's fury threatened to return. With each passing moment, he began to lose more and more control. Or fire regained more and more. How much longer before he could be rid of Amia's shaping altogether? How much longer before he could be free of her?

A shiver worked through him. That had been the fire, he felt certain of it.

"Amia." She met his gaze with fear in her eyes. Tears welled up. "I choose you." He jumped. It felt like an eternity passed as he fell, slicing through the air, before he plunged into the water.

Cold swirled around him. Tan felt it distantly, a part of his mind registering the change in temperature. He kicked, pushing against the water. Steam bubbled around him as water touched his fire-shaped skin. His head popped above the surface briefly and he sucked in a deep breath before another wave crashed down on him.

In that moment, he caught a glimpse of Amia. She stood atop the rocks, watching. Hope had replaced the fear.

He could almost feel.

Since the transformation, the bond between them had been damaged. He felt none of her emotions, nothing that told him how she felt. For the first time, he realized he missed it.

This had to work.

Tan plunged beneath the water, kicking his feet as he went and driving himself forward. Cold and dark water surrounded him. Shifting currents swirled around, dragging him toward shore and then back out to sea. Salt mixed in his mouth, burning his throat and eyes.

Fire surged against Amia's shaping, demanding release. Her shaping fell.

The suddenness of it was jarring. Fire surged from him, boiling the water around him.

Fury raced through him. He kicked, trying to drive to the surface. As he did, he shaped the water around him, pulling heat from the water itself and turning it to steam. There was too much, more than he had the strength for.

He screamed. Water spilled down into his lungs.

The shaping faltered, failing as water pulled him down.

Tan flailed, panic setting in. Another shaping failed, water pressing too quickly around him, quenching the flame before he had the chance to begin.

He would drown. Harsh laughter burst from him.

In that moment, a memory of Amia standing on the rocks flashed before him. The panic eased; he had chosen this.

If he could not be healed from this shaping, he would not want to continue living. Amia would not stay with him, and then what would he have? He would be emptier than he was now.

A sense of peace flowed through him, quenching the fire raging within. He closed his eyes, letting the water claim him.

Udilm.

He called out, pushing out to the water elemental.

There was silence.

Udilm! It is He Who is Tan!

Water shifted around him, swirling back and forth as it dragged him with its current.

No answer came.

Tan's chest burned, and not from a shaping. He could not breathe.

Water would not answer him. The transformation had changed

him too much, left him altered in a way he could not be saved. Maybe he didn't deserved to be saved, not like this, not twisted into a form of fire he had seen cause so much destruction. Did he really want to live like that, turned into the very thing that had caused him so much pain?

Tan sighed out the last of his breath. He did not.

Water continued to pull him down, and he did not fight it.

I'm sorry, Amia.

He pushed it out with all the energy he could summon. The sending felt difficult and different. He could not be certain she received it.

Water pulled him, and he drifted.

Spots of color swirled around him. Tan swallowed the salt water still in his mouth as he readied for death. The Great Mother would claim him, and the colors were the last visions he would have before she did.

As much as he wanted to live, as much as he wanted to go on with Amia by his side, he didn't want to do it as a lisincend.

He felt it as death came to him. And then stopped.

He Who is Tan.

The words came as a wave, soft and slow, touching his mind lightly, nothing like the udilm had the first time he reached them. This was soft and delicate and barely touching his consciousness.

I failed.

You have changed, He Who is Tan.

The sense of the udilm drifted, disappearing for a moment before returning.

Tan recognized that he drifted at the edge of death as he had when he first met the nymid. Then, they had healed him from the blast of fire thrown at him by the lisincend. Now such a blast would not harm him.

I did what was necessary.

You are nearly Twisted Fire.

Tan laughed bitterly. *It was the only way I could have saved her.*

The elemental drifted away for a moment before sliding close again, rolling in with each wave. Unlike before, he could not see anything about the elemental. Udilm had had a face of sorts when he last saw it.

Not the only way. The only way you knew.

Tan snorted again. Even dying, he was taunted. *Is there a difference?*

Much difference.

Tan closed his eyes, letting the water play around him.

Why did you come, He Who is Tan?

She thought you could heal me.

A pause. *And you did not?*

How could he answer? How could he explain that his mind felt different, changed from before, that every thought seemed tinged by the influence of fire and that he didn't even care? If it gave him the strength necessary to do what was needed—to save Amia and stop Incendin—then he welcomed the change.

You think you did not have the strength before?

I could not shape without the elementals. What strength is that?

He Who is Tan. He Who Speaks to the Elementals. There is much strength there.

The connection to the udilm sounded closer. Tan opened his eyes, looking for evidence of the elemental, but still saw nothing. Water continued to swirl around him, pulling him around, swirling him violently in the water.

What would you do if healed?

I would stop the lisincend. I would stop Incendin.

The udilm seemed to withdraw, leaving him in darkness. For long moments, he felt nothing.

Is that all you would do?

What else was there? He wanted Incendin to leave the kingdoms alone. He wanted the lisincend to pay for what they had done to his family and Amia's. And the archivists to suffer…

But those weren't all his thoughts.

He wanted time with Amia. He wanted to learn about his abilities. And though he thought about vengeance for what the lisincend had done to him, more than that, he needed to protect the draasin from Incendin. Asboel may not fear the lisincend, but Tan did. As often as Asboel had helped him, he needed Tan's help now.

A soft voice seemed to sigh.

You have bound to the Eldest.

Tan nodded. Asboel would be disappointed in what had happened to him.

Perhaps he *should* die rather than see how Asboel would react.

Time passed in silence. In that time, water swirled around him. It began to burn against his arms, as if the salt in the water threatened to peel back his skin.

Pain surged in his mouth and throat and lungs. His mind went cold. Silence and blackness surrounded him. The water elemental would not heal him.

And then he heard a voice.

You will be restored.

He opened his eyes. Green glowed around him. Not the elemental he expected.

Nymid?

He Who is Tan.

How are you here?

A face appeared out of the water, coming close to him. *You came to water. All is connected. All is restored.*

Why?

Udilm did not wish to restore He Who is Tan. Twisted by Fire. Nymid know him. The Eldest vouched for him.

Tan blinked. *The Eldest. He knows?*

He knows.

Pain tore through him.

The sensation was unlike anything he'd ever experienced. The closest comparison he had was plunging through an icy stream in the middle of winter, but even that wasn't cold enough. This was more like the frozen cold that held the draasin in the place of convergence.

He screamed but no sound came out.

His body spasmed, his back arching violently.

Everything hurt. Agony raced through his stomach. His chest tightened, squeezing as if the weight of the ocean pressed upon him. Even his eyes hurt.

Worse was the pain in his head. Wave after wave of pain raced through his mind.

The sensation was unrelenting. The only thought he could clearly come up with was that the nymid tortured him, but the thought left him. The pain pounded through him, rolling through his body over and again. Tan was aware of nothing other than pain.

And then it eased.

He opened his eyes. Light filtered through to him. He felt drained, but no longer did the rage wrack his mind. No longer did anger seethe through him, threatening to boil from his skin.

Had the nymid healed him?

Nymid?

The response came immediately, louder than it had been. *He Who is Tan.*

The voice sounded like a shout deep in his mind. He struggled to shield himself and without intending to, he wrapped a shaping of air around his mind to protect himself.

After it was done, he realized what he had done and released the shaping slowly. *You healed me.*

Swirls of green shimmered toward him. A face appeared within it, forming the features of the nymid he had seen before. *You were restored.*

He wasn't sure how to ask the question he needed to have answered. *What did I do? How can I keep it from happening again?*

None are meant to draw the power of the Mother within them.

I only tried to protect those I care for.

The Daughter. The Eldest.

Tan nodded. His head ached, but less than it had before.

He had vague memories of the anger working through him following the transformation, but he remembered what he had done, how he had simply destroyed the Incendin shapers.

We would not have restored you otherwise.

Tan swam in place, letting the water pull on him. There was a certain warmth to it that tingled across his skin. Shame worked through him at what he had done—and what he had nearly done. Could Amia ever forgive him?

What am I?

The nymid seemed amused by the question. *You are He Who is Tan.*

I am not a shaper, not like those of the kingdoms.

The nymid's face twisted. Tan couldn't tell emotion from the nymid, but there seemed a sense of confusion. *You are the one the Mother chose. And you are needed.*

It was Tan's turn to feel confused. *The Mother?*

Water pressed upon him and he slid against something soft, sticking him in place.

Sand.

Light filtered through the water. His chest started to burn, but differently and in a way he had felt before.

He sat up and pierced through the water's surface. Bright sunlight shone down on him. A slow current pushed against him, rocking him back and forth. He turned, noting a shore on either side. Whatever river he had drifted into emptied into the vast expanse of the ocean far downstream.

Tan dragged himself out of the water and sat along the nearest shore, staring at the water. He tucked his knees against his chest, letting the cool breeze dry him, pulling goose pimples out onto his skin. He shivered and smiled as he did.

He dipped one foot into the water, making a connection to it. Pale green swirled in the water, nothing like the bright concentration of nymid he'd seen while still underwater. *Thank you, nymid.*

Their response came slowly and quietly. *No thanks are needed for one who serves the Mother.*

Tan inhaled deeply. *I will serve.*

He had no idea how, but he would serve.

CHAPTER 20

Bond Pair

DAYLIGHT HAD FADED by the time Amia found him.

She touched his shoulder, waking him from a dreamless sleep. A cautious smile pulled at her mouth as she did. "Tan?"

He sat up. His body ached and he stretched, trying to pull the stiffness from his muscles. His skin still felt raw, but not like it had when he had transformed. "You found me?"

She handed him a roll of fabric. He took it and shook it open. A cloak. Not his own—that had burned when he nearly transformed—but one of the Aeta, and made of a thick green fabric. Tan pulled it around him, thankful for its warmth.

She touched his arm hesitantly at first, but then she pulled up against him and kissed him. "The udilm healed you."

"Not the udilm. The nymid." He motioned toward the river. "The udilm wouldn't restore me. I must have been carried here by the current." He took a deep breath and let it out slowly. "I'm not sure what would have happened had I not made it upstream."

Amia stared at the water for a moment. "The river runs into the sea. You shouldn't have been pushed up the river."

Tan watched it and realized she was right. "Maybe the udilm helped some."

The connection between them felt as it had before fire transformed him. Amia hesitated. "I didn't know if it would work."

"Thank you for trying."

She turned her face up so he could see that tears welled in her eyes. "You were so different. I… I didn't know if I could save you."

He pulled her against him, hugging her tightly. "But you did. Had you not believed I could be saved, fire would have…" He trailed off, uncertain how to finish. What would fire have done? It had changed him, twisting within him, but it was more than that. He had felt strength and power that he didn't feel now. Fire gave him that.

Now… now it was lost. He was nothing more than he had been before. Possibly less. Without the ability to shape easily, what was he?

Amia rested her head against his shoulder. "You are Tan. You are enough."

She had heard his thoughts.

He sighed. "What now?"

"The First Mother planned to go to Ethea. You saved her twice. For that, she agreed to help the king."

"I need to find Roine and Lacertin. They fight Incendin and—"

Amia shook her head. "Leave them to their fight. You have many skills, Tan, but you nearly lost yourself. You…" Amia stepped away from him and met his eyes. "What would you accomplish by going? What would you do the others could not?"

What would he do? He couldn't battle the lisincend, not like Roine.

Had fire still consumed him, still worked through him as it had, he might have had a chance, though the lisincend had served fire for longer than he could imagine. And after what had happened, he feared fire's pull. What would happen were he attacked by another fire shaper? Would he manage to protect those he cared about without drawing fire into himself, without twisting it like the lisincend did?

More than revenge for what the lisincend had done to him, he knew there was another task for him, one that was more important. "I need to protect the draasin."

Amia's breath caught. "How?"

"I don't—"

Soft laughter interrupted what he was about to say. He tried again, this time to rebuke Amia, but it didn't come from her. Concentrating, he realized it came from…

Asboel.

Maelen.

A warm gust of wind swirled over him. Tan looked up to see Asboel drifting to the ground on a quick flap of his wings. Golden eyes studied him and seemed to see through him.

Amia jumped back. "Did you know he was coming?"

Tan turned back to look at Asboel.

You were damaged, Asboel told him.

The nymid restored me.

Asboel snorted. Steam streamed from his nostrils. *So I have heard.*

I am sorry.

Asboel lowered his head until he met Tan's eyes. *You still have not learned what you have done, have you, Maelen?*

And what have I done?

We are bonded to each other. It happens rarely. Few bond with the pure spirits. Impure frequently bonds, though I think that has not happened for many years.

What does it mean that we're bonded?

Asboel snorted again. *Only the Mother knows. There is always some purpose. Mine is likely to protect you. Yours would be to explain what has changed in the millennia since I last hunted these lands.*

Tan didn't think that was his only purpose. The nymid had seemed interested in him protecting the draasin. *I haven't explained anything that has changed.*

Asboel tipped his head back. *You have explained Twisted Fire. That is enough for now.*

They are a danger to you. They seek to serve fire in your stead.

Fire would not allow them to serve.

Tan wasn't so certain. After feeling the effect of fire as it worked through him, fire didn't seem to care who served, so long as it was allowed to burn. The difference for the draasin was their control.

Why did you come?

You were in danger. When udilm sent word...

You came for me?

You are like the hatchlings with your questions.

A vision of the other draasin came through the connection he shared with Asboel. Through the vision, he saw the two eggs Asboel had clutched in his talons had been set onto a heated stone. The other draasin—the female, though Tan didn't know her name—perched over them. Days or weeks passed and then the eggs began to crack. Two small lizards crawled from the eggs.

Hatchlings? They are safe?

What would happen if Incendin discovered the hatchlings? Would they try to twist them and shape them into something they were not? Would they try and destroy their elemental connection?

And what did it mean for the world that the hatchlings existed?

Amia's shaping would not be in place for them and, if what he suspected about the shaping was true—that Amia had only managed to shape the draasin because they were in a place of convergence so close to the Great Mother—there would be no way to duplicate it. The draasin would be free to hunt as they pleased, guided only by Asboel.

How long before the draasin became the hunted once more?

Asboel twisted and his tail twitched. *The hatchlings are well cared for, Maelen.*

Twisted Fire—

Will not harm them.

Tan wished he could believe that to be true. *They have taken those who can shape spirit.*

This time, Tan sent an image of the Aeta, pushing to Asboel what had happened when the Aeta attacked, how they took the Brother and others of the Aeta able to shape spirit.

There is one who fears enough spirit will enable Twisted Fire to accomplish what they seek.

Asboel seemed to frown and dipped his head toward the ground. *I do not fear them. Do not fear for me.*

Tan met Asboel's eyes. In them, there was great experience and power, so much that Tan couldn't imagine the depths of what Asboel understood about the world. Yet he did not understand the lisincend—particularly the twisted lisincend, Alisz.

I cannot help but worry for your safety. That is my burden with the bond.

Asboel stared at him for long moments, his tail twitching. *Then we will hunt them together.*

There seemed a weight to the comment that Tan didn't fully understand. Perhaps it had to do with Asboel offering to hunt with him, or maybe it was the acknowledgement that he didn't fully understand the lisincend.

He turned to Amia. *The Daughter must return to Ethea.*

Amia glared at him. "No—I will go with you."

Tan frowned. "How much of that did you hear?"

She pressed her hand against his chest. "I hear you clearly. More clearly than ever before. And there is another who answers, though the voice is distant and faint. There is something else," she started, frowning at Tan. "I'm not sure how much I fully understood."

"He wishes for me to hunt the lisincend with him."

Amia's eyes widened. "You can't… you were just healed by the water elemental and now you want to run back to attack the lisincend? What happens if you draw in fire again? Will the nymid save you again?"

"They have to be protected. I can't let the lisincend attack."

Asboel lowered his head to meet his eyes. The massive spikes on his back steamed slightly in the cool air.

The Daughter speaks truly, Maelen. You are barely healed from the transformation. Twisted Fire can wait. Grow stronger. Learn. Then we can hunt.

Tan clenched his fists. *There isn't time—*

Asboel snorted. *Time? I have spent a millennia trapped beneath the ice. There is always time.*

But Twisted Fire!

Asboel looked from Tan to Amia. Ancient knowledge shone in his eyes, more wisdom than Tan would ever know. *Come, Maelen. I will return you to your home.*

Tan sat atop Asboel. Amia sat behind him, gripping his shoulder. She would not—or could not—touch the spikes on Asboel's back.

Wind whistled past him. Translucent faces of ara occasionally flashed by and Tan studied them, wondering if he would ever speak as easily to ara as he did to Asboel. Mist swirled around them as Asboel flew, practically shrouding the draasin in a fog. It reminded Tan of the smoke hanging over Ethea, the remnant of draasin fire.

Amia clutched his shoulder but said nothing. Asboel said nothing either, guiding them quickly toward Ethea.

They crossed over high, peaked mountains. Far below were thick green pine trees rolling over the mountains. It took a moment to realize they flew over Galen.

Asboel claimed he took Tan home, but Galen had been Tan's home. Ethea was no more home to him than Nor could now be. He had no real home, but at least he had Amia. And once his mother returned from Incendin, he would have a semblance of a family again, especially if he could find Elle.

Amia squeezed his shoulder and slipped an arm around his waist. "Did you feel it?"

He craned his head around to see her and frowned. "Feel what?"

She stared down toward the ground. Her brow furrowed as she studied something distantly. "As we crossed into the kingdoms. Did you feel it?"

Tan blinked, slowly understanding. "The barrier."

Amia nodded. "We should have felt it when we passed into the kingdoms. Always before, I feel it like a tingling on my skin. I didn't know if it was different when flying."

Tan thought about what he'd felt before when traveling with Asboel. When he crossed the barrier on Sarah's—his mother's really—shaping, he had felt the tingling. And then when returning to the kingdoms with Asboel, he had felt it again. This time, he felt nothing.

The barrier had fallen.

CHAPTER 21

The Last Visit

TAN HELD ONTO ONE OF ASBOEL'S spikes and leaned toward the ground. He stretched out with earth sensing, listening as his father had taught him years ago. Even then, he had felt the barrier, though he hadn't always known what it was he sensed. Over the years, its presence had been a comforting thing. When he stretched out through the forest around him, he could reach the barrier and stop, knowing nothing dangerous could reach him with it in place. Ever since the hounds had crossed over into Galen, that had changed. The barrier was still there, but the sense of safety had disappeared.

Now, even the barrier was gone. What did it mean that it fell now? Lacertin had been instrumental in creating it; did he know that it had fallen? Would he know what it meant that it was gone?

We must hurry, Asboel.

The draasin's tail twitched. *Now you wish to return home?*

Through the connection, Tan pushed through what he could sense of the barrier. Doing so was difficult. Putting words to a concept like sensing and shaping—especially of one of the elements the draasin couldn't use—felt nearly impossible. Instead, he shifted it, turning it into something the draasin could appreciate and drawing on his experience changed by fire to do so.

He sent Asboel the sense of heat glowing along the border, and then removed it, as the barrier no longer existed.

I am familiar with this creation. It does nothing to hold back the draasin.

It was not meant for the draasin. It was meant to hold back Twisted Fire and ones like it.

You fear that it is gone?

I fear why *it is gone.*

Asboel snaked his head around so one golden eye could look at Tan. When he straightened out, his wings flapped with more intensity.

They raced through the sky. The fading sun fell beyond the horizon, the sunset prolonged by their flight. Amia held tightly to him. Worry drifted through the bond between them.

"Where do you think they will go?" he asked.

"If Incendin lowered the barrier, they could choose to attack anywhere," Amia said.

"They have attacked twice in the last few months."

Amia tensed. "And both times in the same place."

"That's what I fear as well."

We need to go to the source of the Mother.

Asboel twitched. Having been frozen in the lake for a thousand years left him anxious about returning. *That is not home.*

No, but Twisted Fire will seek to return there. They have the artifact.

A spurt of flame came from Asboel's nostrils as he snorted. *They cannot reach the Mother. They cannot call the others.*

And if they could?

Asboel snorted again, this time with frustration.

We should know for sure, Tan sent.

Asboel twisted and banked, turning them away from rolling hills, veering instead back into the mountains. The air gusted against them, blowing cold and biting against Tan's cheeks as they flew faster than before.

"He fears why Incendin would go to the place of convergence?" Amia asked.

Tan nodded. "You and I know that there is something about the place that gives it power."

The lake appeared below them, a smear of glittery silver moonlight shining from below. It seemed they had only just come from this place and were now returning. And why must it be here? Why did everything happen in this place?

Asboel dove toward the lake, descending rapidly. With a tip of his wings, he turned them toward the mountain cavern, swooping past the lake and quickly into the mountain itself.

Tan shivered. Each time he came to this place, something changed for him. The last time he had been here was when the fire shaper transformed. The time before, they had rescued the artifact. What would happen this time? How much would change for him now? Could he prevent anything from changing?

Asboel landed on the hard stone with a brief flutter of wings. Nothing but darkness surrounded them.

Amia formed a shaping and faint light bloomed from hidden shapers lanterns. Dust swirled around them from Asboel's landing and the air smelled musty and bitter. The shaped trees and grasses that once filled the cavern had begun to wither. Tan wondered if the elementals had once fed the shaping. Now that they were gone—now that the elementals no longer formed the pillars creating a barrier that protected the artifact—did the shaped creation die?

Tan leapt from Asboel's back. Amia climbed carefully down. They looked around but saw no sign of the Incendin.

Tan stretched out with earth sensing. There was nothing else within the cavern. "How long ago did the barrier fall?"

"It was intact when we left. I felt it as we passed through it."

"How long has that been?"

Amia's brow furrowed as she considered. "Two weeks?"

Could it really have been only two weeks ago he had been in Ethea? What had happened to his mother and Roine in that time? Tan wished he shared a connection with them as he did with Amia. At least then he could know what happened to them, he could know if they still lived.

"Long enough," Tan said.

"For what?"

"If Incendin planned to return, they would have enough time to reach this place. Wherever they're attacking, it's not here."

"What if they haven't reached it yet?"

They couldn't stay here, not if the lisincend planned a return. The lisincend weren't here now, but that didn't mean they wouldn't come at all. Tan had every reason to believe this was where they would attack. And if that was the case, they needed to do something to stop them from being able to reach for the Mother.

His being here—*Asboel's* being here—put that at risk. If Incendin needed to draw on all the elementals to call the liquid pool of spirit, then having the draasin in this place put that at risk.

Unless they had another way. Tan had no way of knowing whether Incendin had figured out a different way to reach for that pool of spirit. If they had, he would need to block it somehow.

He would need to send the elementals away.

The small stream running through the cavern burbled. Tan touched a foot to the water. Cold water swirled through his boot. He sucked in a quick breath. *Nymid!*

He waited.

Amia watched him. "You think to call the Great Mother again?"

The temptation was there. When he had stepped in the pool of liquid spirit, he had known more about the world than he had ever imagined. He felt a part of it, connected in a special way, as if he were an integral part of that world, rather than simply someone it acted on. As if he mattered. While in that silvery liquid, he had known Amia, had shaped spirit to free her from the effect of the archivist's shaping. He would give anything to return to that sense of knowing. Perhaps then he could understand shaping, could learn what the Great Mother intended of him.

But now was not the time.

"I need to ensure she cannot return here," he said.

Asboel stayed silent. Tan didn't know if the draasin agreed with what he planned or not. He didn't doubt the great fire elemental understood what he did. If Asboel were captured—if the archivists or other spirit shapers tried to use the draasin—Tan might be forced to use his connection to the elementals and draw spirit forth once more. He couldn't take the risk, not if there was something he could do about it.

Nymid. Twisted Fire may return. This place becomes dangerous. They will seek the power of the Mother.

A flickering sensation came at the back of his mind.

The nymid answered, soft and faint. *The Mother must be protected. This place is no longer safe.*

The nymid sent a quiet assent before receding. The water running through the cavern gradually slowed before stopping altogether.

Be ready, Tan said to Asboel.

The fire elemental snorted.

With a rolling, rumbling sort of speaking, he sent word to golud. The earth elemental was hardest for him to communicate with, a fact he always found strange given that he was an earth shaper first.

This place is no longer safe. Twisted Fire comes.

At first, nothing happened.

Then the ground began slowly rumbling. Slowly, the rumbling expanded, moving from the ground to the walls. The sound was a painful, heavy thing that shook deep within his bones.

Maelen?

We should go.

You ask golud to destroy this place?

Then Twisted Fire can no longer use it, Tan said.

"You convinced the elementals to depart?" Amia asked.

Tan turned, feeling guilty about the imminent destruction. So much effort and shaping had gone into into its creation that seeing it destroyed felt wrong in some ways. Its purpose had been served. The place of convergence would be lost, but perhaps that was only right.

"The nymid left. Golud chose to destroy this place. I suspect they will depart when it falls."

Asboel lowered his head so Tan could climb atop and reach out to help Amia. Once settled, she squeezed him around the waist, again refusing to grab one of Asboel's heated spikes.

The draasin leapt skyward, toward the opening in the cavern, as the ground continued to shake. Walls of the massive cavern began crumbling, stone spilling out and around as it collapsed upon itself. They reached the open peak of the cavern as stone from this part of the mountain began falling, dropping into the space below.

Asboel pulled higher, climbing into the sky. Tan looked down to see the entire mountain collapsing inward, spilling dirt and dust from destroyed stone into the air.

He sighed. Now he would never be able to again stand in the pool of liquid spirit, never feel the connection offered her, the sense of knowing he had while there.

There are other such places, Maelen.

You know of them?

Of course.

At least he had not destroyed the only place of convergence. With Asboel's help, they could find another if needed. Hopefully, Incendin could not.

Asboel twisted, flying over Galen and toward Ethea.

Fatigue caught up to him and he drifted, resting his head upon Asboel's spikes—the heat not bothering him as it did Amia, trusting the draasin to carry them where needed. Amia held onto him and leaned into him after a while. Her body felt warm and comfortable. As strange as it seemed, sitting atop Asboel gave him a sense of home. He hadn't realized how much he'd missed that sense before now.

Maelen.

Tan shifted, blinking open his eyes. Through the darkness, he could not easily see where they were, but his earth sensing told him they neared Ethea.

You should not bring us all the way to the city.

Asboel twisted his head so that one golden eye studied him, practically glowing in the night. He blinked and then started down, bringing them toward the ground.

Amia stirred behind him and squeezed him tightly.

"Are we here?" she mumbled.

Tan took her hand. "How long will it take the First Mother to arrive?"

"From Doma? Weeks, probably."

Tan breathed out a sigh. Weeks. Too long if the king remained shaped by the archivists. Too long if his mind remained twisted toward whatever their end goal had been.

As they landed, Asboel twitched. His nostrils steamed more heavily as he tasted the air.

What is it? Tan asked.

Something is not right. I must return.

Tan used earth sensing but didn't find anything unusual. He jumped off Asboel's back and helped Amia down. Strange tension worked through the draasin.

Asboel turned to Tan, eyes glowing in the night. *You will be safe.*

It was a question as much as a statement. Tan sensed nothing unusual and nodded. *I will be safe.*

Asboel snorted again.

I may need your help again. Tan thought of the fallen barrier, not knowing what its fall meant. Depending on what he found when they reached the king, he might need to search for Roine and Lacertin to warn them about the barrier.

Then I will come. Do not make me fear for you, Maelen.

Tan smiled. Could the draasin actually *care* for him, or was it simply some effect of the bond? *I'm sorry you needed to come. I will not make the same mistake again.*

No. You will make different ones.

With that, he leapt into the air, his massive wings catching the soft breeze and lifting him high into the night sky. He disappeared behind a wispy cloud.

The connection to Asboel didn't fade. Tan held onto it, letting the sense of the elemental fill him. He might not be a shaper like his mother or father, but that didn't mean he was powerless.

He turned toward the soft glow of Ethea. Amia took his hand and a shaping built as they started walking. After a moment, she paused, head tilted slightly.

"What is it?" Tan asked.

"I… I don't know. There is something different about this place since we were last here."

He wondered if it was what Asboel noticed, but the draasin hadn't said anything more about what he sensed. Had it been worrisome, wouldn't Asboel have commented on it? Unless he hadn't known what it was he sensed.

Tan remained on edge as they walked toward the city. The soft glowing became gradually brighter the closer they came. They crested a small rise, and the city was laid out in front of them. Lanterns and small fires burned in a few windows; nothing like the massive flames that once threatened to overwhelm the city.

Tan started forward but Amia held him back. He threw a frown over his shoulder at her.

She inhaled deeply, moonlight shining off her skin, and a shaping built from her steadily, growing stronger as it grew. When it seemed it could not get any stronger, she released the shaping, sending it sweeping toward Ethea.

"What was that?" he asked.

She ignored him and tipped her head as if listening.

Moments passed. Tan thought she heard nothing. Then she gasped.

"I hadn't thought to sense for it before. I should have, but we were with Roine and then we found your mother—"

"Amia? What is it?"

She looked over, fear in her eyes. "A spirit shaper. And powerful."

CHAPTER 22

An Incendin Return

WHAT SHOULD WE DO?" Amia asked. Her hand trembled in his as they stared toward the city. From here it seemed both so close and so distant. Amia turned and met his eyes. A steely determination shone within them.

Tan had always known her to be strong. When he first met her, she had run from Incendin hounds. Even after the attack by the lisincend, Amia had remained confident. But never had he known her to tremble as she did now. Never had he known her to show her fear, even when trapped by the archivists and the Incendin fire shaper, chained to the wagon with no way to escape. Not even when he had nearly transformed into one of the lisincend.

"We have no way of removing the king's shaping without the First Mother," he said. He should have spent more time when last in the city searching for archivists. "Roine and my mother are gone. Whatever shapers remain in Ethea have likely been influenced by whatever archivist you sense." If it even was an archivist. For all he knew, it was the Brother.

He felt as if he had been kicked in the stomach. Could that be why the barrier had fallen? Had the archivists managed to effect enough of the kingdom's shapers to force the barrier to fall? What could they do against that kind of strength?

"You need to send a message to your mother," Amia said.

"I don't have a connection to her. Not like I do with you or with Asboel."

"She is your mother. There is always a connection. Besides, you managed to communicate with Elle—"

"And she has proven able to speak to the udilm."

"You really think your mother unable to speak to ara? You have seen her shapings. She managed to mask herself from you—from everyone in the city—using a shaping of wind. I cannot imagine the control required to hold a shaping like that."

"She would have said something. Once she knew I was able to speak to the elementals, she would have told me."

Only—he wasn't certain that she would. His mother had kept so much from him over the years, what would have prevented her from keeping that secret from him, too? "It's too far. If she's in Incendin, I wouldn't have the strength to reach her."

Unless she *could* speak to ara.

He furrowed his brow, thinking.

The soft breeze gusting around him, sliding over his clothes and rustling through his hair made him consider. *He* might not be able to send a message, but that didn't mean he couldn't get word to her. The only problem was that with ara, connecting was never a sure thing.

Ara.

He spoke it with the soft flicker that he'd learned the wind required, reaching toward the elemental with a light touch, barely more than a caress of sound. He didn't ask for help with shapings—that seemed to take much less of a connection, enabling him to use the power of the wind. Speaking with the elementals took more strength, more focus. Maybe that was the reason he struggled shaping with golud.

The wind blowing around him picked up strength. He called to it again. *Ara.*

A translucent face coalesced within the wind briefly before disappearing and then reappearing on the other side of him. *Son of Zephra.*

Tan smiled. Ara was playful, but also fickle. He would need to approach the elemental in just the right way to make sure it would respond.

Have you seen Zephra?

Ara seemed to smile and the face faded, quickly appearing again on his other side. *Many times, Son of Zephra.*

Can you speak to her?

Ara flickered and began to fade. Tan worried he had been too direct, forcing the conversation more than the elemental was willing. Then it reappeared, a wide smile on the strange face. In the moonlight, ara appeared silvery, lighter than the pool of spirt but similar.

Can you? ara asked.

Tan hid the relief he felt. He hadn't upset the elemental yet.

I need to send her a message. Can you do that, or is she too far?

Ara danced around him, dozens of faces flickering in and out of existence before disappearing. *Do you test us, Son of Zephra?*

Tan laughed, trying to keep from upsetting the elemental. *Not a test. I only wondered if the distance was too great.*

The faces flickered again, more quickly this time. *What is the message?*

Tan bit his lip, thinking of how to phrase it. He didn't want to make it too complex for ara to send, but he also needed to ensure the message reached her with a sense of urgency. What would get her attention?

Tell her spirit defeats the barrier.

Ara flickered a few more times playfully. *That's not much of a test.*

Can you do it?

A face appeared, closer than before. It looked something like his mother's face, and the hair hanging around it reminded him of his mother's hair. *It is already done.*

Already?

He hadn't expected ara to be able to communicate quite so quickly.

If ara were able to do it, could he have gotten word to Elle while still with the nymid? And if he could, what would he say? She was family—his mother's cousin—but she was also his friend.

Zephra wishes you to wait.

Wait? For what?

Ara flickered again before disappearing altogether. The wind died, fading into nothing.

He looked at Amia. "How much of that did you understand?"

"Only your side. I could tell there was another, but not what it said."

"We can't do this alone. I can't do this alone."

Amia touched his cheek, trailing a finger along it. "I'm glad you finally recognize that."

"If the archivists control the king…"

He didn't know how to finish. If the archivists controlled the king—and remained in the city—returning to the city was dangerous enough. But if they controlled the remaining shapers in the city as well, then returning could be deadly. How many there knew Roine was actually Theondar? How many knew about Tan and his ability to speak to the elementals?

"We can't let them succeed," he said. "I don't know what they're after, but we can't let them have it."

Another shaping built from Amia, pulling quickly and suddenly from deep within her. She released it so it washed out and away from her, sweeping toward the city. As she listened, a troubled expression returned to her face.

"What is it?"

"I'm not certain. I sensed something from the city that I shouldn't have, but it seems to be gone now. I must have been mistaken."

Tan wished she would explain what she had sensed, but a sudden gust of wind caught his attention.

A shaping formed in the wind. It was powerful… and familiar.

"Mother."

The wind settled. When it did, Zephra stepped forward. She lowered the hood on he black cloak and revealed her face. Her dark hair was pulled back severely behind her head, bound with a strip of fabric. Shadows played around the corners of her eyes.

"Tannen."

"You speak to ara," he said. He didn't bother to hide the hurt he felt.

"It was how I first learned to shape. I should have told you before, but I didn't want to confuse you as you learned of your abilities."

"Confuse me? You haven't explained anything to me. If I hadn't thought you died, I wouldn't have learned anything about Father."

Amia pressed against him. A calming shaping washed over him.

Tan inhaled slowly, letting the irritation fade. The nymid healing had repaired much of the damage done by the fire transformation, enough to keep him from snapping as he had. The frustration he now felt was normal.

"And if you hadn't gone with Theondar, you would never have

learned of your abilities. Do you really wish to go back to the way it was before you learned what you could do? Would you really return to a life where you didn't know the nymid? Didn't know the draasin?"

More than the nymid or the draasin, he didn't want to return to a time when Amia wasn't a part of his life. Still, there had been so much change, almost more than he could survive.

"No," he began. "I don't want to return to that time. I only wish I wasn't in constant danger."

She smiled and touched his face, glancing at Amia. "I wish the same. No matter what else has happened, you're still my son. I would do anything to protect you."

"There are some things you can't protect me from."

She smiled sadly. "I have learned. Ara thought you lost for a while." Wind played around the edges of her hair and she turned to him. "I see you were restored."

Tan studied her. She used the same term the nymid had used. Could his mother speak to more of the elementals than she let on? "I am fine."

She sniffed. "Fine. You have returned to Ethea, where the king remains controlled by the archivists. Yet you have not fully returned, standing outside the city as if waiting for permission to enter. For you to summon me means you learned something and you feared returning alone." She looked at Amia and tipped her head, waiting for an answer.

"The archivists. They have returned," Amia said.

"Are you certain?" his mother said.

"There is a void within the city. I have only sensed it a few times. I should have sensed for it before…"

"Yes. You should," Zephra said.

Tan shot his mother a hard glare before turning and considering the city. Could he sense the same void Amia mentioned? He focused on the lights radiating from below, stretching out with his earth sense. He noticed no void. Then he shifted, straining with wind. That worked no better.

What would happen if he mixed all the senses together? He frowned, adding wind and water, mixing earth and fire into it.

A strange sensation rippled out from him, like a shaping, but different.

It rolled toward the city and then failed, disappearing into nothing.

The void.

His mother paced back and forward across the hillside, her cloak fluttering in the breeze. She held her hands clasped in front of her, and she fidgeted with her thumbs as she had always admonished Tan not to do.

She stopped. "Lacertin and Theondar should return soon. We will wait. Better to have numbers. I can obscure us only so much."

"What happened in Incendin?" Tan asked.

His mother's face wrinkled in an annoyed expression. Tan recognized it well. "Nothing happened. We spent the last weeks combing across Incendin, searching for lisincend. We found a pack of hounds as we did."

"A pack?"

She nodded curtly. "Hounds can only do so much. And with Lacertin…"

"What about Lacertin?"

"They… respect him. Fear him, I think. He has lived in Incendin for many years. Fire has a way of changing a person." She said the last knowingly. "And the hounds recognized him. We reached the Fire Fortress but did not dare get too close. They have shapers stationed all around it."

"Fire shapers?" Tan asked. He suspected the answer.

"Not fire. No, they use their stolen shapers from Doma."

"Do you know any of them?"

She closed her eyes. "I know many of them. Some have been captive a long time. I suspect they now view Incendin as home. Others—" she shook her head "—others are relatively new. I still don't understand why they remain."

"Unless they're shaped," Tan suggested.

Wind gusted around his mother. "Incendin has no spirit shapers."

"They worked with the archivists before. What if this isn't the first time?" he asked.

"We should have heard something if archivists had been crossing the border. The barrier has been in place a long time. Our shapers *know* when someone crosses over it."

Amia stiffened.

"The barrier," Tan breathed, suddenly remembering. It was how he had convinced his mother to return. "You understood the message?"

"I understood, but don't know how it could have fallen. The barrier has stood for the last twenty years. Shapers stationed all along the border fuel the barrier. It would take an attack all along the border for it to fall."

"At least near the place of convergence, it had fallen," Tan said.

She frowned. "You think Incendin will return to that place?"

"No. Not anymore."

She tipped her head. Wind swirled around her, flicking at the ends of her hair. A shimmer of a translucent face appeared briefly near her before fading. "You destroyed it? You destroyed the only place of convergence known?"

Tan took a deep breath and nodded slowly. "I had no choice. If Incendin were to reach it again—if they brought shapers with them, someone able to speak to the elementals—could they have drawn the liquid spirit forth again?" He met his mother's eyes, holding them so that she would understand. "I have stood in the pool of spirit. I have known the power that exists in it. Incendin will not have it."

"I would not have done the same," she whispered. "But you made the choice you needed to make at the time. You are experienced enough to make that decision." She studied him. "Are you ready to return to the city when Lacertin and Theondar arrive? We will need all the shapers we have if we are attacked."

Through their shaped connection with Amia, he knew something was not right. She shook her head. *Later.*

The air crackled suddenly. Heat built around them. Tan looked up, expecting Roine or Lacertin, but heat continued to build. Not lightning, but a different shaping, and terrifyingly familiar.

The lisincend.

CHAPTER 23

Betrayal

TAN FACED HIS MOTHER, pushing Amia behind him. As he did, he tried reaching for the elementals, wishing Asboel had not left him, but nothing responded. "Lisincend! We need to—"

His mother's eyes went distant. She spoke quickly to ara, though Tan couldn't hear what she said. With a gust of wind, she took to the air.

"Tan?" Amia said.

He held onto her, stretching out with his senses as he searched for the lisincend. Dark laughter echoed around him.

Tan turned in a circle, trying to pinpoint where it came from. The sound was dark and harsh. He could practically feel the heat the flowed through it. A cold shiver worked down his back.

"You need to run. I'll stay and do what I can—" he started. But there was no place for her to go. Had Asboel remained, he might have managed to help them escape, but had Asboel remained, the lisincend would not have come.

Amia stared at him and then *over* him.

Tan spun.

There, hovering in the air on wings of fire, was the twisted lisincend. He couldn't tell if it was Alisz, the fire shaper he had watched transform using the artifact and the spirit of Jishun, or another. The twisted lisincend descended slowly. Then another landed alongside.

Incendin had used the artifact again. How many of the stolen Aeta had been sacrificed?

Both lisincend looked much the same. Fire had twisted their mouths and faces, giving their skin a leathery appearance. Their heads were smooth and leathery like the rest of them. Both were unclothed. One stood with breasts burned, leaving nothing more than thickened folds of skin. The other was more muscular and male. Wings burst from their backs and folded back around them as they settled to the ground.

The nearest laughed.

"You led us to him, Zephra. It is fortunate we managed to find this," she said, holding out a small stone with a rune on its surface.

Had Lacertin *not* summoned Roine and his mother? Had the lisincend drawn them into Incendin? But for what purpose?

A shaping burst out from the lisincend, sizzling through the air. Fire bloomed, exploding in the night. His mother screamed.

Tan *felt* as Zephra's shaping faltered. Ara flittered away, unable to sustain before the power of the lisincend fire. His mother fell from the sky, cartwheeling as she went. Shapings failed as she tried slowing herself.

Another moment and she would strike the ground.

He sent out an urgent rolling request, rumbling it toward golud.

Ground softened just as his mother landed, absorbing most of the impact. She rolled and fell still.

The lisincend's dark smile twisted her mouth.

Tan recognized Alisz. He sent a request to golud, asking that the ground open and swallow the lisincend. More than any of the elementals, earth could contain fire.

The sending slammed against something before disappearing.

Alisz laughed. "That won't help you here. None of the elementals will help you again."

Heat started building, pressing against him. Tan had felt this shaping before, recognizing it from what the lisincend had done when they destroyed Amia's Aeta family.

"You nearly joined us once," she said. "You would have been a powerful addition."

"I would never join the lisincend."

She slithered toward him. Flames licked up and around her body. The other lisincend eyed her hungrily, staring at her naked form.

Tan remembered the urgency that burned through him with fire. The mixture of rage and desire, emotions burning within him that he couldn't control. The transformation made him more sensitive to the demands of fire, stealing control from him.

"You remember how it felt." She smiled, the expression pulling on her lips in a strange way. "I did not think it would work, but *he* did. And it nearly did. Now you would take it back within you. All you have to do is accept—"

Amia built a shaping. It came on suddenly and painfully, bursting in his ears. She pressed the shaping at the lisincend.

Dark laughter echoed from Alisz. "Your weak shaping will no longer work, little Aeta. My transformation has strengthened me even more than my brothers." She sent a streamer of fire shooting from her fingers toward Amia.

Tan jumped in front of it. He closed his eyes and *pushed* against the shaping.

It deflected at the last moment. Had it not, Tan wondered if he would have absorbed it again. Would he have begun the transformation, once more turning into lisincend?

Amia felt backward.

Tan couldn't catch her in time. Her head struck the ground, bouncing slightly. She blinked at him and then her eyes fell closed.

The lisincend laughed once more. "Now it is only us. A pity they choose to suffer. It doesn't have to be that way. They can serve as the others do. And she can serve as her people have always served."

"How have her people served?"

"You think the Accords would grant the Aeta free travels throughout Incendin?" Her wings unfurled for a moment and then curled back against her. "There was a price to their safety. A price their First Mother was all too happy to pay."

Tan swallowed. "And what price was that?"

Alisz's twisted and deformed lips pulling grotesquely across her face in a lisincend smile. "They provided a service. And we allowed them to live. A fair price. At least, we *had* allowed them to live. Now that they were no longer needed, we decided to get rid of them so they didn't think to use our shapers against us."

Tan already knew what she implied. "The Aeta would not do that."

"Perhaps you should ask her."

"Ask her what?"

Alisz motioned to the male lisincend. He turned his back to Tan and unfurled his wings, revealing his back.

Tan gasped. Strapped to the other lisincend was the First Mother. She didn't move and didn't look at Tan.

“You did little but stop those who would challenge me,” Alisz said, drawing Tan’s attention away from the First Mother and back to her. “I should thank you for that.” She stepped toward him, reaching a flaming hand toward his face as if to caress him. He jerked back. “She was to have encouraged the transformation. I thought she failed, but then you only had to find the right motivation. Once you have transformed again, you will understand. And then you will serve fire. You will serve me. As the others we took served.” She laughed again, motioning to the other lisincend.

The Aeta. Tan knew how they’d been used. But that meant it wasn’t the Brother they felt in Ethea. What was it, then?

Tan didn’t notice the shaping building until it was too late.

It settled over him, washing through him.

The First Mother stared at him defiantly.

Fire wrapped around him. Tan knew better than to resist. Doing so put the others—his mother and Amia—in danger. He wouldn’t risk them, not without knowing why the lisincend kept him alive.

Alisz crouched next to him. Heat rose from her body like a shimmery veil. She pressed it toward Tan, pushing heat and flame at him.

He resisted with as much strength as he could draw.

His mind pulsed. Whatever shaping the First Mother settled on him ached. What had she done to him?

Tan strained to sense what had happened, but felt cut off from much of his sensing ability. Much like when fire had consumed him, he felt nothing. No sense of earth, no fire, no water or wind. Nothing.

Still, he recognized something had been done to him. Somehow, he still managed to push away fire.

“You cannot resist for long. When you accept fire, all of this stops.”

His head hurt hurt, pounding in a way he had only felt once before when struggling with his connection to the draasin. Would Asboel recognize that something had happened to him? Would the draasin come for him?

Alisz smiled. "You think the draasin will save you?"

He blinked. Had she recognized what he was thinking? Was *that* what the First Mother's shaping did—had it allowed his thoughts to be read by others?

Or was it something else?

When she transformed, Alisz had drawn the blood of Jishun—an archivist spirit shaper—through the artifact. Could that have changed her in other ways?

She smiled, again as if reading his thoughts.

"We thought the archivists the key to our plan," Alisz said. "Not until we reached that place of convergence did we realize how right we were. Now… now we have less need of those like her." She motioned toward the First Mother. "Especially if she's not even strong enough to force your mind. Perhaps the elementals protect you better than we realized," Alisz said, glancing at the First Mother.

The First Mother hovered over Amia and Zephra, touching their cheeks. A shaping built, but soft and subtle. Even had he the ability to do more than sense the shaping, he wouldn't have any idea what she did.

"Once she teaches me how to control this, we will have little use for her," Alisz said.

Tan watched the First Mother. "She knows."

Steam hissed from Alisz's nostrils. In that moment, she reminded him of the draasin. "She knows. But I gain skill regardless. Perhaps we will keep her around for entertainment. Or perhaps I will put her in charge of my soldiers." Alisz met Tan's eyes. "If you serve well, perhaps *you* can be placed in charge of my soldiers. Soon, all of this will belong to Incendin. Soon all will serve fire."

Tan fought against the finger of fire she sent toward him. This one nearly touched his flesh, burning through the outer layer of his cloak. How many more would he be able to push back? "You will never do more than *serve* fire."

Alisz glared at him. Another sharp finger of flames shot toward him.

He had gotten through to her. If he could get her to lose control, maybe he could somehow manage to shape again. He had to try something. "You will never be stronger than the draasin. They do not simply serve. They control fire."

"The draasin? You think I wish to be like the draasin?"

Tan pointed toward her wings and thickened skin. "What else would you be?"

She smiled. Fire skimmed across her lips, making her look fearsome. "I don't want to be like the draasin. I would be greater than them." She sent a handful of fire toward him that he barely pushed back. "And with this," she said, taking a long, slender object made of dark silver out of a hidden fold, "I will be able to."

Alisz leaned toward him. The heat coming off her was nearly unbearable, burning his throat with each breath. "Has she told you what it does?"

He couldn't take his eyes off the artifact. The last time he'd held it had been when they had returned it to Ethea. Before that, the elementals had protected it. Maybe it would have been better had they left it there. Could the lisincend really have reached it had they not freed the draasin and relaxed the barrier protecting it?

Tan finally pulled his eyes away from the artifact and turned to the First Mother. She knelt alongside Amia. For some reason, the First

Mother had slipped the silver necklace back around Amia's neck. Tan frowned, wondering why the First Mother would even bother. Now that she admitted her betrayal, what did it matter that Amia had the necklace? The Aeta the First Mother protected were not the same as the people Amia had served—her family. She would have done anything to keep them safe.

But could he really blame the First Mother for what she did? She wanted nothing more than anyone wanted—for her people to live freely and not fear they would be harmed. The price for that, though... Tan couldn't stomach the price the First Mother was willing to pay.

And now look what it had gotten her. Aeta shapers were captured and sacrificed in the creation of more twisted lisincend. The First Mother trapped, forced into a different type of service to the lisincend.

How many Doman shapers had she forced into serving Incendin? How much damage had she done to Doma as she served Incendin, trying to keep her people safe?

Tan had to say something to distract Alisz. "She doesn't know what it does."

Alisz sniffed again. Another burst of flame pressed on him, this time with more force than the others.

Tan had to focus to push it away, pulling everything he could from himself to hold the shaping away from him. Much more and he wouldn't be able to keep the fire away.

Would he be burned? Or would instinct take over as it had before, forcing him to draw in the shaping once more, even knowing what it would do to him?

"You believed her?" Alisz asked.

She crouched again in front of him, so close he could smell the stink of heat rising off her.

The First Mother looked over. "The artifact is over a thousand years old. The ancient shapers may have known what it could do, but the records from that time are incomplete, buried in a part of the archives none can reach."

Tan frowned. None could reach? He thought the lower level of the archives was accessible to the archivists, but could he have been wrong? What was hidden there?

"What indeed?" Alisz asked.

The air crackled again and she stepped away from Tan as she raised her nose to sniff the air. She motioned to the other lisincend and he nodded, taking to the sky with a quick flap of powerful wings and disappearing into the night.

Thunder rolled, loud and chaotic. The ground trembled with it.

Tan recognized this shaping.

One of the warriors returned. Possibly both.

"You think the warriors will keep you safe?"

He shot her a look. "I have learned not to underestimate Theondar. As I suspect you have learned not to underestimate Lacertin."

She stepped toward him. With a motion quicker than he could see, she struck him in the head, knocking him forward.

CHAPTER 24

The First Archive

TAN AWOKE, BODY ACHING. Darkness surrounded him. The air smelled musty and familiar.

He blinked, trying to clear his mind. The last thing he remembered was the shaping from the warriors. Lacertin or Theondar. Hopefully both. Then Alisz striking him.

But he had been on the hillside overlooking Ethea then. Where was he now?

He shifted, trying to stand, but his hands were bound in cold iron restraints. He couldn't move, no matter how hard he tried.

Tan strained against the chains to free himself. He stretched out, reaching for golud, wishing for the earth elemental to help free him, but no sense of the elementals came.

No sense of anything made it through the shaping the First Mother had placed around his mind. It separated him from the elementals, but seemed to do nothing else. He felt no urge as he had when Jishun shaped him while at the place of convergence, nothing forcing him to serve fire.

The only reason he could think was that she hadn't wanted to force him to serve fire.

Whatever she intended served the lisincend.

Tan focused on the shaping. It circled his mind, settling atop it, creating a barrier that prevented him from reaching out. Not only separating him from the elementals, but from Amia as well. It hadn't separated him from shaping, though, or he wouldn't have been able to resist Alisz's fire. But that would mean he had shaped on his own, without needing the help of the elementals.

Could he do it again?

Tan tried the shaping he used—the shaping wind and water had helped him use—to free his mind. Nothing seemed to change. The shaping the First Mother placed on him held firm.

She was stronger than Jishun—stronger than any other spirit shaper.

Maybe wind and water weren't enough to remove her shaping. Maybe he needed each of the elements as he had when he tried sensing the void over Ethea.

He inhaled deeply and focused on fire first. As much as it had nearly destroyed him, he could shape fire. He *knew* he could now that he had survived Alisz's attempt to force him into transforming again.

At first, nothing seemed to happen. Then fire built, smoldering within him. All he had to do was push it out.

Holding onto the sense of fire, he reached for earth. He was an earth senser first; he didn't need golud to help him reach earth shaping.

Nothing happened at first. He searched through his memories, thinking of the lessons his father had taught him, the way he had taught him to sense. Tan stretched through his earth sense, listening for the way it called to him. With enough focus, he could reach through his sensing. Had his father taught him more than he realized?

Shaping earth required strength. Tan drew it through him in steady rumble.

The ground trembled slightly as the shaping built within him. Tan smiled, adding the budding earth shaping to fire.

Next he focused on the musty air, working on a wind shaping, drawing it from him like a soft breath. Speaking to ara required a gentle touch. Shaping wind likely took much the same.

It came slowly, first flickering around his hair, then stirring the dust beneath him. Tan added this to his shaping.

That left water.

He had spoken to the nymid and to udilm, but he had never really tried shaping water.

Tan swallowed, thinking of moisture in his mouth, of the blood in his veins, of the humidity of the air. Shaping seemed much like speaking to the elementals. Pushing like a soft wave rolling from him, he formed a shaping and added it to the others.

The shapings mingled together, growing stronger. Tan held them for a moment, wanting to remember what it felt like to create a shaping of his own, and then pushed this against the First Mother's shaping.

Her shaping bent but held.

Tan reached out and the shapings held.

The next time, he tried pulling more of the shaping from within himself. At the same time, he stretched out, as if speaking to the elementals, calling for their assistance to aid his shaping. The First Mother's shaping bowed and flexed like something tangible. Tan strained, pushing with everything he could muster, demanding the elementals aid him.

The shaping strained and finally snapped free.

A flood of sensations came to him.

The first was the sense of Asboel demanding to connect to him. The draasin pushed against his mind with a furious urgency, digging against his mind as he tried to reach Tan. Asboel nearly overwhelmed him with the power of his sending. It was the same as the first time he had reached out to Tan, though Tan had more experience pushing him away now.

Maelen!

Tan breathed in, releasing pent-up tension that eased now that his connections were reestablished.

Draasin. Twisted Fire is here.

A snarl of rage came through. *Twisted Fire has come through here as well.*

An image of the hatchlings came to Tan. They were small and lean, tiny, thin wings lying against the ground. It took him a moment to understand what was wrong. The hatchlings didn't move.

Twisted Fire?

Asboel snarled again. *It will not go unpunished. Twisted Fire will suffer for what they did to the draasin.*

The anger from Asboel reminded Tan of how he had felt when fire consumed him. *You should not come here. You know they seek to replace you.* And if not the lisincend, then the king would still try to hunt the draasin. The shaping still held enough that he would want the draasin destroyed for the attack on Ethea.

Twisted Fire will suffer. Do not oppose me in this, Maelen.

Tan closed his eyes, inhaling slowly. He could almost feel the anger coming through the connection with the draasin. If he could, he would draw the anger away, help Asboel find the sense of calm he once had known.

But doing so was dangerous. Tan could no more draw in the anger than he could draw in fire. Either opened him to a transformation he was unwilling to endure again.

There was something he *could* do for Asboel, just as Asboel had once done for him.

I will help.

Asboel fell silent. The connection between them continued to grow stronger, as if the draasin moved toward him.

Tan jerked forward, trying to move. The chains around his wrists still held him in place, preventing him from standing.

Now that the First Mother's shaping was removed, could he shape the chains free?

He focused on the metal as he struggled to think of a way free from them. An earth shaping might release the chains from the stone, but he'd be left with them still hanging from him. That wouldn't work, especially as he would need to move quietly as he escaped.

That left a modified shaping. With a small amount of fire mixed with water, he might manage to make the metal crack, but he'd need control for that to work. Control had never really been his strong suit.

If he could shape at the same time as calling the elemental powers, he *might* be able to manage enough control to break free.

Tan focused on the metal. Drawing from within himself, he sent a shaping of fire—barely more than a trickle—into the metal. It grew warm against his skin. As it did, he shaped water, cooling the metal again.

It snapped loudly.

Tan jerked his hands back, pulling against the chains. It groaned before finally giving way and releasing him.

He sat in place, rubbing his wrists as he tried to get his bearings. The air smelled familiar. And he was in some sort of building, with dense stone all around him. Where, though?

With an earth sensing, he reached out, listening for anything that would be familiar. The sensing pressed into the stone, through it. His eyes snapped open.

He was in the archives.

Tan struggled to maintain his focus as he stood. If this *was* the archives, he was likely in some lower section—possibly even the lowest level, where he had twice failed to get through the doors. Shapers lanterns hung on the walls, and he could light them if he wanted, but he held off, afraid of drawing attention to himself. Already the First Mother likely knew he had pushed through the shaping she'd placed over him.

Listening with earth sensing, he realized there was someone else trapped here with him.

Tan frowned. Could it be Amia?

No. The connection to her was faint, faded as if she slept, but not nearby. Not Amia.

His mother?

He had to risk the shapers lantern. Using fire—shaping fire came easiest to him—he lit the nearest, sensing where it hung on the wall. Dim white light burst from it.

As it did, he recognized his surroundings. It was where he and Roine had found the dead archivist. It was also where he had failed to shape his way through the doors; he was back in that aggravating circle of doors that led to hidden secrets.

Near one end of the room, opposite the stairs, another person lay in a pool of shadows. Tan hurried over to them. The person lay face down. A hood had been pulled over their head, hiding them. Chains, like the ones that had encircled his wrists, held onto thin wrists.

Tan rolled the person over and gasped. The First Mother.

He stepped back and crouched, staring at her as he struggled to decide what to do with her. She was the reason they had been captured. She was the reason the archivists helped Incendin. And now, she lay unmoving in front of him.

Tan glanced back at the stairs. He could climb them, try to escape the archives, and leave the First Mother here. Whatever fate fell to her would be deserved.

But why would Incendin would have brought them here? What did they think to achieve in Ethea?

He searched with a mixture of earth and fire sensing, listening up the stairs into the upper levels of the archives. Above him—he couldn't quite tell where above him—he sensed the heat of lisincend. Escape up and out of the archives was not an option.

Tan turned to the First Mother and nudged her with his boot.

She moaned softly and rolled her head to the side. Her eyes blinked open. "You escape."

The lack of surprise in her voice caught him off guard.

"You knew I would?"

She struggled against her restraints before answering. "I thought it possible."

"Then why not shape me more forcibly? You could have made me do whatever they wanted." And what they wanted was for him to accept fire, to draw it inside him again. Had he done that, there wouldn't have been any way to save him.

The First Mother shifted and sat up. "You think it so easy to craft a shaping like the one you suggest?"

"I don't know how hard it would be to craft a shaping like that. You didn't teach me anything about spirit shaping."

The First Mother sneered at him. "You weren't ready."

"And now?"

"You wouldn't have escaped otherwise."

Tan thought of what she had said, how she had explained he would need to shape spirit. He would need mastery over *his* spirit. She had tried having him reach back through his memories to find the necessary understanding, but that wasn't how it was for him. Like shaping the elements, he shaped spirit differently, binding it out of the other four elements, so similar to how spirit was drawn at the place of convergence.

He glanced at the chains holding the First Mother. She would never have been able to teach him. He had needed to discover the key on his own. And he had known the secret all along but hadn't really understood.

The First Mother simply sat, watching him.

"You won't convince me this was some kind of test. That all you wanted was to see if I would be able to break through your shaping."

"I would not try. You think I should feel ashamed of what I have done?" Her eyes narrowed. "You think that keeping my people alive and safe was not worth the price?"

"You forced Doman shapers to work with Incendin. You took away their ability to fight for their people, left those of Doma unprotected. You lost the Brother and so many others because of what you have done."

"And how many more were saved? Until you have the responsibility of a people, you cannot judge, son of Zephra."

Tan stared at her. She still felt no remorse for what had happened. Nothing.

"Was your capture a part of your plan? Was letting Incendin take your shapers part of the bargain?"

Defiance blazed in her eyes. After a long moment, she bowed her head. "You know it was not."

Tan crouched in front of her. "Do you know why they are here?"

Her brow furrowed as she scanned the doors. "We are in the archives."

"We are. Have you been here? Did Jishun ever show you this place?"

"No. Coming here risked revealing the secret of the archivists."

"What's behind the doors?" When she didn't answer, Tan pressed again. "What is behind the doors?"

"The archivists were only able to open two. The others are inaccessible."

Tan studied the doors. "Which two?"

"This is not the time—"

"This *is* the time. I need to know why Incendin sent the lisincend here. And if it has to do with what's behind these doors, I will learn what your archivists hid here."

"It was not them. This level precedes the People ever coming to Ethea."

The comment gave him pause. If that were true, then maybe the archivists didn't know what hid behind all the doors. Whatever was here remained valuable to them. Valuable enough that they shaped anyone trying to get too close.

"You will open the doors," he said.

The First Mother shot him a dark look. "That won't do anything for you, son of Zephra."

A surge of anger roared through him. It came from him, not from fire. "You will call me Tan. Or Maelen."

Her eyes widened. She recognized the word.

"Now. How are the doors opened?"

The First Mother closed her eyes. A shaping built, starting slowly but building quickly.

He recognized what she did. He didn't know *how* he recognized it, only that her shaping grated against him. Tan quickly forced a shaping using the power of the elementals, of fire and wind and water and earth, toward her as he severed the shaping she worked.

Her eyes opened with a snap.

"You will not shape me again," he warned. "I feel you shaping. You know I'm not the same kind of shaper as others."

Whatever he was, he accepted that he was different. The others couldn't teach him, not as they could those who came to the university. For a long time, that had bothered him. How would he learn how to craft shapings if no shaper would—or could—teach him? But now he understood. Not completely. Perhaps he never would, but the elementals guided him. All they required was him to be open to their suggestions.

"No. You are not." She studied him, eyes darkened. "The archivists could open the doors of spirit. There are two here."

"How do I know which of them are the doors of spirit?"

She moved her hands. The chains dragged across the ground as she did. One long finger traced through the dust, creating a star with a circle around it. A rune.

Tan had seen it before.

He left her and hurried toward the doors, looking at each one. The first few had several runes worked into the surface of the wood. Did that mean they required shapings from each of the elements to open? If that were the case, Roine should have been able to open those doors. Then Tan reached the door with a single rune.

For the first time, he realized how it looked different from the other doors. The stain was different. It caught the light in such a way that Tan was left with a sensation that it flowed into the rune.

Tan touched the door. It vibrated slightly beneath his fingers.

Did he try opening it? Through his connection to her, he knew

Amia remained alive. He couldn't help her if he was recaptured. And his mother?

He whispered to ara. *Does Zephra live?*

The still air of the archives stirred slightly, barely more than a whisper of breath. He waited, listening for the wind elemental.

Son of Zephra. She lives.

Where is she?

Twisted Fire. They prevent access to Zephra.

Can you help her?

He sensed amusement.

She is Zephra.

She needs help, he sent.

Ara coalesced slightly. Enough for him to make out eyes but nothing else. *We will help.*

He looked back at the First Mother. She watched him, lips pulled into a thin line.

Tan focused on the door. Now that he knew the elementals would help his mother, he could focus on this. Spirit. Could he shape spirit well enough to activate the rune?

"What are these runes?" he asked the First Mother.

She didn't answer.

"What are these? I've seen them other places. A warrior's sword. The fire shaper's bowl." Her eyes narrowed at that. She had seen the bowl before. "You had a stone with similar runes. And now on these doors. What are they?"

At first, Tan didn't think she would answer. Then she took a deep breath. "They store power. They are marks made by the earliest scholars. None have managed to recreate them with the same power."

Tan thought of the markers his mother used as he pointed to the door with the rune for spirit on it. "That is newer than the others.

Someone managed to recreate it."

"Newer. And not the same as the others. Why do you think we have failed to open the others after hundreds of years trying?"

Hundreds of years. "What do you think hides behind them?"

"I don't know."

"That's not what I asked."

"These doors have been here longer than much of Ethea. Longer than the rest of the archives overhead. Whatever lies behind them is likely important. Works of power, possibly engraved with runes like those. Ancient texts, even older than what is stored in the upper levels of the archives. Or nothing. As I said, none have managed to open any of the doors."

Tan traced on finger over the spirit rune on the door in front of him. The marking tried to draw him toward it, as if pulling on him. As it did, Tan knew what he needed to do.

The spirit shaping came together more quickly this time.

Tan pushed it at the door, focusing it on the rune. The marking began to glow. Softly at first, but then with increasing brightness. A soft *click* echoed, and the door opened.

Tan pulled it open far enough to look inside. Barely enough light leaked in for him to see the contents. It was a small room, but rows of shelves lined each wall. Books stacked high on the shelves. A few dark sculptures mingled with the books. A thick rug spread across the stone of the floor. A few plush chairs rested against the walls.

It was nothing more than an extension of the archives, a place where they could store select texts to keep away from the upper levels of the archives.

He closed the door again, letting it seal with a soft hiss. Tan made his way around the outer edge of the lowest level of the archives, looking at the runes on each door, searching for markings that were different than the others. The First Mother watched him silently. Finally he found the other door worked with the single rune of spirit. Like the other, it appeared newer.

With the same shaping as before, he activated the rune and unlocked the door.

He pulled it open. Light barely penetrated, leaving nothing but darkness to greet him. With it came a soft breath of stale air, much like the old iron mines around Nor. Wherever this door led, it was more than a single room.

With a sudden certainty, he knew this was what the archivists protected.

CHAPTER 25

Beneath Ethea

THE FIRST MOTHER WHISPERED to him. "You can't leave me here. When they find you've escaped..."

Tan glanced back at her. The shapers lantern cast shadows over her face, making it look drawn and more wrinkled than before. Her eyes had taken on a wild expression.

"I can't help the People if I'm left here for Incendin."

Tan was unable to muster any sympathy. "You have done little that truly helped the People. You only placed them in more danger."

Grabbing the nearest shapers lantern, he paused long enough to look back at the First Mother. The stones of this place were infused with golud. With a rolling, rumbling request, he asked the earth elemental to hold the First Mother in place.

The ground rumbled softly in answer.

Tan passed through the door. The First Mother shouted after him.

"Son of Zephra! Maelen?"

Tan pulled the door closed behind him, shutting her out.

It muted her voice. Almost, he could imagine her whimpering, lying on the ground, begging for help. After what she had done, he didn't believe she deserved help.

A long hall stretched in front of him. The stone was damp and slick but otherwise solid. Golud infused the wall, but he sensed something strange and surprising. Mixed within golud were hints of nymid in the moisture along the walls. Two elementals existed here, and he'd already spoken to ara, though he began to suspect ara would be found everywhere.

Tan started down the hall, holding the lantern in front of him to guide the way. With a gentle shaping of fire, the lantern glowed with even more warmth.

The hall twisted at one end and turned sharply.

He reached out with earth sensing, listening to the stone. There was a sense of age and weight heavy in the stone. Nothing else moved but he paused every dozen steps and listened. He would not be caught by the archivists unprepared.

Nothing came.

The tunnel narrowed. Walls pressed in, as if squeezing against him. When the hall turned, Tan considered turning back, returning to the lower level of the archives and finding a way out. Doing so would require him to get past the lisincend, but could he not manage that now that he had reconnected to the elements and discovered the secret of his abilities?

Yet he needed to see where this tunnel went.

He hurried forward, pausing at times to reach out with a mixture of earth and water sensing. Each time, he encountered nothing new.

Surprisingly, the farther he went, the stronger his sense of Amia.

Along with her, his connection to Asboel crawled more prominently toward the front of his mind. The draasin made his way toward him.

Tan wanted to hurry. Whatever else, he feared the draasin reaching Ethea before he escaped from the lisincend.

As he made his way along the tunnel, he encountered a few side branches. These were even narrower than the main hall. Water dripped from the ceiling of the nearest one. A glimmer of green flowed through the droplets. He continued down the main corridor.

It seemed to go on forever.

Without the lantern, Tan wouldn't have dared come this way. Thankfully, the shapers lantern glowed with a cool light and no heat burned his hand from it. Fire shaping might have protected him regardless, but he was pleased he didn't have to risk it.

After a while, the corridor turned and split into two. Water covered the ground, obscuring one of the tunnels. He followed the other and recognized a change in the stone. It seemed newer. Still ancient, but old like the doors leading from the lowest level of the archives. Like the door he had shaped, the archivists must have made these tunnels.

Farther on, the tunnel continued. Tan stopped at a stair leading down, ending in a dark door. Another rune for spirit marked the door. With a shaping, the rune glowed like the others and opened with a soft *hiss*.

Before pushing into the room, Tan extinguished the lantern. Lighting it again would be easy enough, but he had no idea what was on the other side of this door, which swung open silently. It was heavy but offered no resistance.

A soft light glowed on the other side.

Tan crossed the threshold and closed the door, waiting for his eyes to adjust. As they did, he became aware of sounds around him. There came a steady tapping, regular and harsh. The air carried less of a musty odor. The distant light drew him forward, past a row of doors lining the hall. None were like those in the lower levels of the archives. All were old, but not nearly as old as those. Standard locks kept them closed.

The tapping came from behind one of the doors. Tan stopped in front of it and listened to the regular rhythm of the tapping.

Tan twisted the handle, but the door was locked. He focused on the lock and sent a shaping of fire into it as he pulled. Soft metal bent silently with the shaping. Behind the door was a cell.

Tan blinked. What was this place?

He held the lantern in front of him, shining it around until he saw the person tapping. He almost dropped the lantern.

"Mother?"

She watched him with a patient expression. She had been expecting him.

"Tannen."

"You knew I was coming?"

"Ara suggested it likely. I didn't see how you would escape from the First Mother, especially after the shaping they placed on you."

"I broke through it."

She smiled. "Good. Then you can free me from mine."

Tan took a step back. "I don't know how—I'm not a spirit shaper like that."

"If you managed to get past the shaping of the First Mother, you are shaper enough. Now try. Then we will need to free Theondar."

"Roine is here?"

She nodded. "When they arrived, the lisincend captured him. I thought they would kill us all, but they didn't. They separated us from our ability to shape, using only enough spirit to keep us from shaping, and then threw us in here. I do not know what they plan."

Tan frowned. Why wouldn't the lisincend do more than simply prevent his mother and Roine from shaping? It made no sense.

Could they have expected him to get free? Would they have known he could open the spirit doors and make his way here?

"Tannen?"

He shook away the thoughts. Spirit—but he needed to be able to shape spirit well enough to recognize whether his mother was freed. Unless ara could help.

He closed his eyes and focused on what he had done before. This time, as he combined the elementals and shaped spirit, he called to ara, asking for guidance from the wind elemental as he shaped his mother.

Ara guided his shaping, pulling it toward his mother.

A sudden burst of wind swirled around his mother's head, and then down, as if forcing the shaping through her. Tan tried to help, but the shaping faltered when he did, so instead he relaxed, letting ara completely guide it.

His mother gasped, sucking in a quick breath of air.

As she did, Tan suddenly feared what he had done. Had the shaping been too much? Had it damaged her? Would she end up permanently changed, as he had with fire?

Wind whistled. A shaping, and not one of his.

It came from his mother.

She stood. With another shaping, the chains around her arms cracked free, destroyed by a pinpoint of wind.

For a moment, Tan feared what might happen. Her eyes were wide and her mouth drawn. The power flowing through her was enormous, more than he could imagine drawing. Ara mixed with the shaping, swirling around Zephra. Roine had called her a powerful shaper, but Tan had never fully understood before.

Now he did.

Then her face softened, relaxing into the motherly expression he knew as a child. She pulled him into a hug, squeezing him tightly.

"You restored me."

He pushes out of her embrace. "Not me; I only created the shaping. The wind elementals used it to free you."

"Have you done that before?"

"I'm not a shaper like you. That was my problem all along, I think. I tried to learn from Roine or the other masters, but nothing they taught me ever worked. And when I went with Amia to find the First Mother, she had a different way of shaping. Nothing she tried teaching made sense, either."

"How is it you shape, then?"

He shrugged again. "I'm not sure it's all me. Maybe some are, but most of my shapings are guided by the elementals. This time, it was ara. Others, I think I've used the nymid or golud." He didn't mention the draasin. He still wasn't sure how that worked.

She started forward, moving hesitantly at first. "Has Theondar told you about the ancient scholars?"

"The warriors. They all could shape spirit, too."

She paused, grabbing his arm for support. "Not the warriors. They are more like our shapers today. The ancient scholars. They were different, even different than the archivists. We've never quite known how."

"You think they were able to speak to the elementals?"

"It would explain certain things."

"But Roine said there have been shapers able to speak to the elementals."

"Perhaps that is true, but all of them? I think the fact that you have managed to speak to all the elementals means you *are* different."

Tan breathed out. "I don't know what it means. All I know is that I need to find Amia before the lisincend harm her again." And then he had to do whatever he could to protect the draasin.

"Do you know where she is?"

"I don't even know where *I* am."

"How can you not know you're in the palace?"

"The palace?" It made sense, but how had he managed to reach the palace? A shaping worked over it, a barrier much like the one that had once run along the border of the kingdoms. Without Roine or another with a ring…

Except, he had a ring.

He touched the pocket of his cloak. When Jishun died, he had taken the ring off the archivist and slipped it into his pocket. After everything that happened, he almost forgot about it. It was there.

"They brought you to the palace?" Tan asked.

She nodded.

"And the king?"

A troubled look flashed across her eyes. "Whatever has happened has removed all traces of Althem." She met his eyes. "I knew Althem once, Tan. He was different then. Competitive. Strong. But not like this. A darkness has settled over him."

"That's the shaping. The archivists could have been shaping him for years."

"And you think removing the shaping will bring him back?"

"I don't know. Amia couldn't remove it; it was too complex for her. That was why she asked the First Mother for help. She will not help. Not if it means her People are in danger."

"The People have always been in danger. It's the reason I traveled with the Aeta in the first place. Why should they have been given free access to cross safely through Incendin? It was more than trade. That was clear to me from the start, but none have ever managed to understand *why* the Aeta were given such freedoms."

"Did you know about the bargain the First Mother made with Incendin?"

"No. But it makes sense. Why else would the Aeta be allowed to cross Incendin?"

"She controlled the Doma shapers."

Anger flashed across her eyes. "And they must be freed. Control like that is the reason the Accords were necessary. For the First Mothers to allow it to continue..." She let go of his arm, strength returning. "This is bigger than the kingdoms, Tannen. Bigger than even Incendin."

"It has always been about more than the kingdoms," he said. "Especially when the lisincend became determined to become elementals."

She took a deep breath. "What will you do?"

He paused and sensed Asboel. The fire elemental was close and getting closer. "I will stop Incendin. I will stop the lisincend. And I will help the draasin."

CHAPTER 26

Rescue

ZEPHRA, WHO WAS FAMILIAR with the route out of the palace dungeons, took the lead. The place stunk of rot and human waste. Several times, he gagged as they made their way along the rows of cells until his mother crafted a tiny shaping she fitted over his nostrils, blocking the stench but not stopping him from breathing. Again, he marveled at her control.

They paused at a wooden stair at the end of the cells. Many of the stairs were cracked. Some were missing altogether.

As his mother paused, flickers of translucent ara passed in front of her, quickly disappearing. She turned her head and waited.

"Where's Roine?" Tan asked.

"Up. You should know that Theondar was injured. He managed to protect his mind more quickly than I did. In order for the First Mother's shaping to take hold, his shaping had to be lowered." She looked over at him. "I do not know how much he'll be able to help."

"And Lacertin?"

"I did not see Lacertin."

Outside the city, when the warriors came, he felt certain it was more than simply Roine. Lacertin would have come too, but what if he hadn't? If his goal was to destroy the lisincend, would he not take the opportunity to attack them here?

"Are you finished with your shaping? Can we go?" he asked.

"You knew I shaped?"

"You spoke to ara. I don't know what you said, but..." He trailed off and shrugged.

She offered a tight smile. "It is unfortunate there are none who can train you."

"Why?"

She stroked her chin, studying him. "It's curious that we haven't seen a warrior in generations. And now there's you—not only a shaper, but one able to speak to the elementals. I wish I knew what it meant."

His mother started up the stairs without saying anything more.

Tan watched her go. Rips gouged the fabric of her heavy cloak. Wind fluttered it behind her and it trailed up the stairs, reminding him of Elle and her too-large clothes. When she nearly reached the top, he started up after her.

The steps groaned under his weight. About halfway up, the wood cracked and he buckled forward, barely catching himself in time.

A pillow of wind coalesced beneath his foot, propping him up.

Tan looked to see if his mother had shaped him but she was focused on the door rather than on him. Ara then.

Thank you.

A nearly translucent face shimmered in the wind before fading.

He hurried up the rest of the stairs, meeting his mother at the top.

She held one hand against the door. A soft shaping built from her, pressing through the door. Her breath held for a moment and then she let it out with a quiet whisper. The door opened softly, inching forward.

Tan readied a fire shaping, uncertain what they would find on the other side.

His mother also held a shaping, stepping through the door. Then she grunted, letting out her breath. Her shaping disappeared in a huff as she dropped to the ground.

The door opened the rest of the way. Tan's shaping faltered as he saw Cianna standing on the other side. Energy practically sizzled off her, mixing with the heat radiating off her body. Even her expression, her gaze fixed on him, smoked, and her hair stood on end like she was electrified.

Fire leapt from her hand, shooting toward Tan.

He inhaled quickly and pushed the flame away, using a shaping of fire and earth.

A determined expression stole across her face. "It was a mistake for you to return here."

Tan met her eyes. "Why have you done this, Cianna?" He recognized the heat coming from her: the transformation had already begun.

For a moment, a struggle worked across her face. He remembered little from his time under the influence of fire, from when he strained to find some measure of control, but he remembered the battle to hold himself together, to avoid pushing too much of himself into the fire. The same was happening with Cianna.

He tried crafting a shaping of spirit to gauge her injuries.

She attacked before he could pull it together. Fingers of flame flickered from her, too fast for him to keep up. Each nearly reached him—nearly reached his mother. Tan wrapped himself in a shaping of air, sending a request to ara for strength as he did. Between his shaping and ara's assistance, he managed to hold her fire shaping away, but it wouldn't last. Not with the strength she now commanded.

"You spoke to me of control. You need to control it or it will take over."

Her eyes cleared for a moment and her shaping faltered. "I—" she began.

Tan dared not wait. He pushed the shaping toward her, wrapping her in a funnel of wind fueled by ara and his shaping. With it, she struck the wall behind her and fell, dropping to the ground.

Fire raged in her but fell silent for the moment. Tan touched his mother's cheek, checking on her. She breathed evenly.

Tan reached Cianna. She lay splayed across the ground, her bright red hair spilled around her, almost like blood pooling. Rather than touching her, he took a deep breath and forged a shaping of all the elements, binding them together to let him reach for spirit. As he did, he pressed it toward her, listening, asking again for ara to guide his shaping. Nothing happened, not as it did with his mother.

Would fire help? Would the draasin?

The sense of Asboel came closer, itching at the front of his mind: The draasin neared Ethea. As he thought of Asboel, his sense of the fire elemental came closer. There weren't many miles left before the draasin attacked the lisincend. Tan had to move faster, to free Cianna so she could help him help Asboel.

Tan needed all the help he could find. He would need to free Cianna from the spirit shaping.

Asboel.

His call went out quietly, enough to reach through the connection he shared with the draasin, sending with it a request for help.

He held the shaping on Cianna in place. Would Asboel guide it as ara had guided him?

At first, nothing happened. The shaping remained unformed and without direction. Then, with a sense of irritation, it surged toward Cianna. The shaping raced over her, flashing through her. It was there and the next moment it had burned out, pressed against her.

Cianna's eyes fluttered open.

Tan readied another shaping, prepared to restrain the fire shaper if needed.

"Tan?" she asked. "You… you *did* something to me." For the first time since he'd met her, she sounded uncertain.

"A spirit shaping worked through you. I did what I could to free you from it. I'm not certain it worked."

She shivered and rubbed her hands over her arms. "They forced it on me."

Tan didn't need to know what she meant.

He offered his hand, intending to help her to her feet. Hesitantly, she took it. Heat flowed from her fingers but Tan could tell it wasn't the same as before. The transformation had reversed. "Can they…can they force me again?" she asked.

"I'm not sure. I don't know enough about the shaping used on you—"

"You said you freed me from it."

"And I think I did." Asboel gave him a reluctant confirmation. "But the shaping *I* used was guided by the elementals."

"The draasin? It is here?"

"No."

Relief flooded through her eyes. "It doesn't matter. You freed me."

"And I think this shaping protects you." He didn't know how it would protect her—if he had more time to ask Asboel, he would find out, but he suspected the shaping had done more than simply remove the effect of the First Mother's shaping.

Cianna must have felt better because she scanned the room. “Zephra lives!” she breathed.

“You didn’t know?”

“We were nearing the Fire Fortress. A pair of lisincend approached. Zephra attacked one, drawing him off. I had not expected her to survive.”

His mother hadn’t told him about the lisincend. “And the other?”

“Theondar and Lacertin destroyed it.”

How many lisincend remained? How many had transformed into the twisted lisincend like Alisz?

“Theondar is here?” he asked.

“I… I was to guard him, I think.” She motioned toward a nearby door.

Tan jumped toward the door, shaping it open to reveal Roine hanging from chains. His face was blistered and charred. Most of one side of his body was damaged. Burns worked across his feet, peeling much of the skin away. Rot had already started to set in. Something sharp stuck out of his back. A quick glimpse showed Tan it was Roine’s own sword.

He gagged, turning away. There was no way Roine still lived—but the chains holding him stirred. Roine’s chest rose and fell slowly.

“Roine?” Tan asked hesitantly. How could he live after what had been done to him? Why would they force him to live? What purpose did it serve?

Roine twitched but then stopped moving.

“Theondar?”

One eye wouldn’t open. The other blinked slowly, peeling back to look at Tan. He opened his mouth and croaked out a word. “No.”

Before freeing him from the chains, Tan needed to remove the sword. If he didn’t, anything else would only cause more damage.

His shapings depended on the elementals. Here, in the palace, access to the elementals was limited. Ara had followed, but likely more for his mother. He could call the draasin, but using the fire elemental for a shaping was limited. If he were right, the nymid were down below, mixed in the water around the golud-infused stone.

The shaping would have to come from him.

He hated that he would have to use fire on Roine, especially after what he'd been through, but what choice did he have?

Tan steadied his breathing and grabbed the sword. He pushed a trickle of fire shaping through it and, as gently as he could, slipped the sword out of the warrior's body. Another delicate fire shaping sealed the wound. It wasn't ideal, but it would have to do for now.

Then, with a shaping of wind following how his mother had done it, Tan broke Roine free from the chains and lowered the man slowly to the ground. He had held Roine's sword before, but never unsheathed. Surprisingly, the blade felt cool.

Roine held onto him with the single eye. "No," he said again.

"You can have your sword back when you're better." Tan swallowed, finding it hard to keep from vomiting. Roine's skin felt leathery and it cracked at Tan's touch. He needed healing, but healing of the sort that was beyond anything Tan could fathom.

The elementals, however, could heal and the nymid were down in the tunnels. He could shape water and have the nymid guide him to heal his friend.

"Cianna!" he called.

She came into the cell. Her face tightened, revealing none of the weakness Tan had felt at seeing Roine so injured. "Theondar?" She spoke softly. "Did I do this to you?"

Tan jerked around. Had Cianna tortured Roine? "You did this?"

Pain shone in her eyes. "I don't know. I remember being shown shapings I had never seen before, feeling the overwhelming urge to try them. I think there was another with me, watching. Suffering." She swallowed. "I am so sorry." Her voice came out hoarse and caught toward the end.

Theondar took a struggling breath. "No!" This time, he spoke with more force than before.

"She won't harm you, Roine. She's been freed of the shaping." He twisted and called over his shoulder. "Cianna, help me lift him. We need to carry him down the stairs."

"Down? He needs healing—"

"And he'll get it. Help me."

Cianna carefully grabbed Roine's feet and helped Tan carry the warrior. They made their way out of the cell and down the hall, pausing long enough for him to glance at his mother. Roine saw her too. A surge of violence worked through him as he tried kicking himself free. "No!" Roine finally sagged, falling into a state of unconsciousness.

Cianna held onto him as they reached the door leading down the stairs, back toward the tunnels.

Cianna pulled open the door. "These stairs haven't been used in ages. Even the lisincend weren't willing to go down them."

Tan shifted Roine so he could carry the warrior more easily. "I came up them."

"Up? How did you come from below?"

"I'll show you. But we have to hurry."

Cianna started down the stairs, moving cautiously—maybe too cautiously. At this rate, they wouldn't reach the nymid in time to help Roine.

"Cianna?"

"These won't hold us."

"They held well enough—"

But they hadn't. As he said it, one of the wooden stairs cracked, splitting with a loud explosion. Cianna fell, dropping Roine.

Tan reached for her but couldn't catch her. He adjusted his grip on Roine before the warrior could follow Cianna down, but froze. Cianna had stopped falling. She hovered in the air, held up by a wind shaping Tan hadn't made. Had he?

Cianna's chest heaved with deep, fear-laden breaths. She looked up, past Tan, and said, "Zephra?"

Zephra's small form stood in the doorway, somehow filling it. "It's Roine. He needs healing," Tan said.

Her eyes narrowed. "I'll guard you from this side. Be careful."

"I will. I need to hurry." He hesitated. "Mother—" He caught himself and swallowed. "Amia is somewhere in here. Find her for me. Make sure she's safe. If anything happens to her…"

A pained expression came to his mother's face. "I will do what I can."

It would be enough.

Cianna sucked in a quick breath. Zephra's shaping carried Tan, Cianna, and Roine to the floor below.

Far above, worry and fear wrinkled his mother's forehead, but she had a determined set to her jaw.

"Where now?" Cianna asked.

Tan pointed toward the door at the end of the hall and they hurried to it as fast as they could while still carrying the unconscious Roine.

Cianna tried the door. "This is shaped closed. Like those in the lower archives."

"I will open it."

"You?"

He focused on the shaping, mixing fire and earth and wind and water together. It became easier with each shaping. As they joined, he quested out with spirit, pressing the shaping into the rune carved into the door. It glowed softly for a moment before opening with a quiet hiss.

She eyed the stairs leading into the tunnel below. "At least these are stone."

She started down. As Tan followed, he realized Roine had stopped breathing.

His heart lurched. He shaped air, copying the shaping his mother had made, allowing him to lift Roine more easily. Taking the warrior from Cianna, he pushed past her down the stairs, running into the tunnel. Without the shapers lantern, he relied on the soft glow coming from Cianna's shaping to guide them.

How far had it been before he saw the nymid? Would they be strong enough to restore him? Would they be willing to?

The tunnel branched and he knew he was close. Cianna ran behind him, not saying anything. There was nothing she could say that would help. Not with Roine dead.

As Tan reached the green-tinted water, a massive shaping built. He hesitated, turning to see what Cianna was doing, but it wasn't her. This was different. Earth and water mixed together. A touch of wind added to it. No fire.

The shaping eased, released into the tunnel. As it did, someone stood before him.

"Lacertin?"

He glanced from Tan to Roine, his eyes wide. A deep gash marked one cheek. Part of his hair had been burned off. A fresh scar worked across an exposed arm. "Tan—whatever you're planning, you need to stop."

Tan frowned at Lacertin. "It's Roine. Theondar. He needs healing."

Lacertin narrowed his eyes as he studied the water. "You can't do that. Not here."

"If I don't, he's dead."

A water shaping washed out from Lacertin. It flowed over Roine, touching briefly on Tan. A troubled look came to Roine's eyes. "He's already dead. And if you do what you intend, the rest of us are, too."

Tan let the wind shaping ease, lowering Roine to the ground. After it did, he turned to Lacertin. "What's going on? Why don't you want me to help Roine?"

Lacertin glanced behind him down the tunnel, toward the archives and not the palace. "I don't care about Theondar. He would do the same if it were me."

Tan snorted. "I know you don't care about him. Whatever happened between the two of you is in the past. You can't hold that against him anymore."

Lacertin blinked slowly. "It has nothing to do with what happened in the past. What's happening now is what matters." He took a step toward Tan. "Haven't you noticed something about this place? You of all people should have recognized the uniqueness."

"I've noticed only that my friends were captured. My mother. Cianna. Roine. Amia. And now you want to stop me from helping him." He sent Roine into the water with a shaping of air.

Lacertin lunged for Roine but missed.

Nymid! Restore him. Help us face Twisted Fire.

Tan hoped the nymid would forgive him for demanding and not asking, but Roine didn't have time for the delicate dance of courtesy.

Lacertin started into the water and reached for Roine.

Tan pushed him back, pulling from the wind blowing through the tunnel and summoning some of the strength of ara to infuse his shaping.

Lacertin spun. "You don't know what you're doing, Tan."

"Maybe not. But I will help my friend."

Lacertin let out a harsh breath. "No. You have called on the water elemental. And now all have been summoned."

CHAPTER 27

Convergence

TAN FROWNED AT LACERTIN. "Summoned? What do you mean they have been summoned?"

But he knew. He had used earth to bind the First Mother, to hold her in place. Wind to help his mother. Fire to heal Cianna. And now water.

All the elementals were here. Just like in the place of convergence.

Fear washed over him. "What is this place, Lacertin?" he asked, suddenly uncertain. Golud infused the stone. Nymid dripped with the water. Ara flowed easily here. And then Tan, with his connection to the draasin.

If the elementals were here, he could draw spirit, the same as he had at the place of convergence. He didn't want to draw spirit, but another might. The lisincend.

"They knew? They knew about this place?"

Lacertin shook his head. "None knew. I don't even think the archivists knew."

"Then who?"

Cianna stepped forward. "What's going on here, Lacertin?"

Lacertin stared at Tan. "You know what this place is?"

"This is a place of convergence, like the one in the mountains I destroyed."

His eyes narrowed. "You destroyed a place of power? Such places can *be* destroyed?"

"I don't know if they can. I asked the nymid to depart. Golud drew the wall down, caving in the mountain. Ara has always been fickle. I don't know whether ara will stay away, but the draasin will not return there unless forced."

Lacertin paced from side to side, reminding Tan of his mother. "Can the elementals be asked to leave here?"

The size of the tunnel was much greater than the cavern. The elemental power here would be even more than in the place of convergence.

He motioned toward the walls of the tunnel. "Golud infuses all of this. All this stone. It stretches into the archives." He didn't shift his gaze from the walls as he said. "It was why the archives didn't burn when the draasin attacked."

"Golud infuses the palace and parts of the university as well."

"That's much more than at the other place of convergence. If the nymid flow through the stone elsewhere as they do here, there would be—" he tried thinking of the size. "—more than in the lake there. And ara?"

"You understand my concern."

Cianna addressed Lacertin. "What do the lisincend think to gain from this?"

Lacertin answered. "That's just it. The lisincend can gain nothing."

"Why are they here?"

A quick shaping built, sharp and powerful. Tan had never felt anything like it before.

"Because I summoned them."

Tan spun. Standing in front of him was King Althem. He was dressed in simple navy pants with a jacket hanging slightly open over his chest, revealing a silver pendant in the shape of a star with a circle around it. The rune for spirit. A rune-covered sword hung at his waist.

Lacertin stepped past Tan but did not kneel before the king. "Althem. Your father would be disappointed in what you've become."

The king snorted, sneering at Lacertin. "My father wasn't strong enough to recognize my potential."

Lacertin unsheathed his sword. The runes along the blade glowed.

"Lacertin! He's still shaped," Tan said, stepping in front of the king. If he attacked the king, there would be no way Lacertin could return to the kingdoms.

Lacertin fixed Althem with a hard expression. "He's not shaped. He's never been shaped."

"But the archivists. They're spirit shapers..." Then he trailed off, suddenly understanding what Lacertin meant.

The king had attended the university. None knew if he had any shaping ability. Tan assumed it had been because he had none. But what if there was a different answer? What if the king could shape spirit to hide his abilities?

It meant the archivists had not shaped him. It meant whatever shaping Amia had thought she found wrapped around the king's mind had been faked.

"He's a spirit shaper?" Tan whispered.

The king drew a short bladed sword from its sheath. The runes along the blade glowed just as Lacertin's did. The warrior stood frozen in place, as if unable to move.

The king had shaped him.

"Tannen Minden. The first warrior shaper in centuries." He smiled at Tan, ignoring Lacertin. "And one with a particularly useful set of skills."

Everything started coming together for him.

Could Ethea be a place of convergence? How was that possible? Such places were said to be hidden, difficult to find—except the archivists had easily found the place in the mountains. And Tan had found it several times. Could spirit be the key?

If Ethea were a place of convergence, it meant spirit could be drawn to it. Given the sheer size of the tunnels, the amount of liquid spirit that could be drawn here with the help of the elementals would be massive. Amia had once called the pool of spirit in the mountains a drop of the Great Mother. How much would collect here?

Without fire elementals, none would come.

The draasin had come before, but the kingdom shapers had chased them away. Now Asboel came again, seeking revenge on Twisted Fire.

Panic surged through him. *Asboel! Stay away!*

The sending failed. The connection was there, but he couldn't reach the draasin, not as he should be able.

He tried again. *This is a place of the Mother. It is a trap!*

Again the sending failed.

He looked at the king. A dark smile twisted his mouth.

"Had the lisincend become a fire elemental, they would have served my purpose, but they do not have the necessary power. Fire still controls them." His smile widened. "I would thank you for that piece of understanding, Tannen. I thought you might serve better than the lisincend, but, alas, that was not meant to be. But had it not been for you—for your near transformation—I'm not sure we would have understood quite how fire controls the shaper following a transformation. As much as they try, they will never be able to serve fire as elementals. But the draasin…"

Tan glanced to Lacertin. A pained look on his face told Tan how he had battled the shaping and failed.

The king continued. "The draasin have returned. I sent Theondar to find the artifact. I never expected the draasin. Finding them was quite fortuitous."

Tan realized that a shaping worked over him as the king spoke. It was subtle and snaked its way into his mind, pushing past any barrier he could form. Like the one placed on him by the First Mother, this shaping blocked him from reaching the draasin and the other elementals.

He focused on his breathing. He could get past the shaping, but he had to form his own shaping of spirit. While doing it, he needed to distract the king.

"How can you shape spirit?"

The king snorted. "So little understanding of history. Disappointing that Zephra and Grethan didn't teach you better."

Anger surged through him at the mention of his father's name. His father had died in service of this king. His mother had nearly died. And for what? He still didn't know what the king intended to do with the place of convergence. If he succeeded in calling spirit, what did he intend?

"They taught me enough."

"Apparently not. Look at you. Standing and waiting. Once the draasin arrives, the summoning will be complete. And then I will draw upon spirit in a way that hasn't been attempted in over one thousand years."

"That's all this is about? Power?"

The king snorted. "I thought you understood. Haven't you touched spirit yourself, Tannen? Would you not return to that understanding, that *control*, if you could?"

Tan remembered the pull when he'd been in the pool of liquid spirit. The sense of understanding that worked through him. In that time, he'd felt closer to Amia than ever. He had freed the youngest of the draasin, had saved Amia. With enough time, he could have done *anything*.

But such power was not meant for him. He knew that. He was no elemental, not like Asboel, yet the king thought to claim that power for himself.

"The First Mother. Who is she to you?"

"She was nothing to me. But Jishun—he was a teacher. A mentor. From what I gather, he learned much from the First Mother. When he learned about my ability with spirit, he eagerly offered to teach, except there was only so much he was willing to try. When my skills exceeded his, he thought to restrain me." The dark smile returned to his face. "Instead, it was my turn to teach the lesson."

"You sent Jishun to die?"

"I sent Jishun to *serve*."

"You knew what would happen. How the fire shaper would use him."

"Him or your Aeta. Either way, a test. Incendin has plotted for nearly a century. They have sought the elemental power of fire, never quite reaching their goal. It is what led me to wonder what might happen with an infusion of spirit? Of course, I couldn't let Incendin acquire such power—at least, not until I had a way of controlling it."

The artifact. That was why the king wanted it. And now Tan understood why the king wanted Jishun to have the artifact. He *wanted* to create the twisted lisincend.

Tan pushed with his shaping, forming it together. The king's spirit shaping was different than the First Mother's. It wrapped around his mind, trying to press into his thoughts, working to blend them together. With enough time, Tan doubted he would know which thoughts were his and which were shaped upon him.

He added an extra infusion of water shaping. Had he not been so near the nymid, he wouldn't have the strength for what he needed. But the nymid were close. All he needed was to reach them… to have the nymid add their water shaping to the shaping he created.

The king's shaping built with sharp pressure, assaulting him with its power.

Tan grabbed his head. The shaping slipped over him, pressing down into his mind. He felt it mingling with his thoughts, burning through his brain the way fire had changed him. This time, he was being changed by the king's spirit shaping.

He screamed.

The king laughed.

"You are powerful. Much longer and you might have succeeded, Tannen. I admit I was surprised you managed to escape the First Mother's shaping. When I instructed her not to shape you too profoundly, I expected I would have to coerce you more myself. Instead—" He stood defiantly. "Instead, you have done everything I needed of you anyway. Once the draasin arrive—and I am fully aware that your friend is coming—I will have all I need to draw forth spirit."

Thoughts and ideas flashed through his mind, but how many of them were his? How much of it was shaped by the king? "The draasin will not help," he said through clenched teeth.

"Are you so certain? Haven't you already drawn their fire?" The king glanced at Cianna. "You used fire in your healing. I *feel* it within her mind. Once they reach the city, I already have the anchor I need. You have done everything I need of you."

The shaping working through his mind burned. Tan gritted his teeth. "Then why keep me alive?"

"Because I can't speak to the elementals. Not yet. Once I draw upon spirit with this—" He pulled the artifact from a hidden pocket. The faint light of the tunnel caught off the silver surface, gleaming softly. "I will be able to control the elementals."

The king knew how to use the artifact. And once he did, what would happen to Tan? To the elementals?

His friends could not help. Lacertin stood motionless, like a mindless soldier waiting for instructions. Cianna crouched behind the king.

And the king watched Tan. Waiting for the shaping to take hold.

Another shaping built. This came from a different direction, not from the king himself. What shaping would the king need another to create? What purpose would he have when he was a warrior too, able to shape all the elemental powers himself?

Tan felt the shaping work over him. Hope swelled in him.

He recognized the shaping, recognized the way it felt as it worked over him, washing through his mind. Amia. She had shaped him before, had used her ability to unintentionally force him to protect her. And now she worked to protect him.

A struggle began for control of his mind.

The king paused, head swiveling as he searched for Amia.

Tan needed to distract him. Wherever she was, she needed to concentrate, to have the time needed to free his mind.

He reached for Roine's sword and pulled it from where he had it sheathed along his waist. With sword in hand, he lunged toward the king.

Lacertin twisted, catching it. He swung his sword, bringing it around in an arc toward Tan's head.

Tan ducked and brought the sword in front of him to block, pushing Lacertin back. Unlike the warrior's sword, the runes in Tan's didn't glow. "Don't do this, Lacertin. Don't let him control you!"

The king roared. "You think he can simply *choose* freedom?"

The shaping pressed deeper into Tan's mind. He screamed again, working against it.

This time, he drew from deep within him. The shaping sought to obstruct him, but Tan pushed, pulling all the elements together as he had when shaping spirit. The combination granted him a sort of strength. Tan pulled this through him, starting from deep within his chest and pushing toward his mind.

A strange thing happened: the runes began glowing on Roine's sword and the power of his shaping built, as if augmented by the weapon.

Tan drew more of the shapings through him, mingling them to create a shaping of spirit. It grew, building, pushing against whatever the king had done to him.

Amia's shaping helped, weakening the shaping enough that Tan could push against it.

For a moment, his mind freed. Then the king pushed with more strength, driving his shaping back down through Tan, but that moment had been enough.

The nymid and ara added strength to his shaping. Asboel clawed through his mind, recognizing what had happened. Golud rumbled beneath his feet. All this strength added to his shaping, combining together.

Spirit surged out of him, unguided, destroying the king's shaping.

The king stumbled.

Tan turned the spirit toward Lacertin. *Amia… help guide this.*

Through their shaped connection, he felt her reach toward him, pushing through and controlling the shaping of spirit. It worked through Lacertin, pulling from him the spirit shaping the king had placed on him. He turned to Cianna and did the same.

Both blinked slowly, as if awakening from a long slumber.

The king recovered more quickly. "Impressive. Perhaps I will need to work with more strength the next time."

His shaping built, but this time, he drew through the artifact. The runes on the surface glowed with a pale white light.

Lacertin's eyes went wide. Tan felt him shape a combination of the elements and wrap it around his mind.

"Get out of here, Tan. If you stay, he can get what he seeks. Draw away the draasin."

"You can't stop him by yourself."

Cianna stepped forward. "I'll help."

Tan took the measure of Lacertin and Cianna. They wouldn't be enough, not against a shaper of the king's power and skill. With the artifact, he might be able to draw enough spirit to overwhelm Lacertin again.

"I'm not going to leave you to him. I can help. The elementals can help."

Lacertin waved him away. "That's exactly the problem. I can't let them help. Not here. Not while he has that." He grunted, pushing a shaping against something the king did. "Have you not wondered *why* the ancient shapers took the device from here?"

Tan hesitated long enough to see Lacertin start to fall.

He tried to catch him, but didn't need to.

Roine shot from the water, shimmering with green light. The nymid had restored him. A shaping built from him, catching Lacertin.

Lacertin stared at the king.

"Finally, Theondar, you get your chance to prove your worth," Althem said.

"Roine—the king shapes spirit. He's a warrior. The archivists never influenced him." Tan's words came out in a rush because he needed to get Roine's attention before the king convinced him to attack Lacertin.

Roine hesitated, studying the king. "Is it true, Althem?"

A shaping built, quickly flowing over Roine, who blinked. "Is it?"

Another shaping, this one adding to the last.

"We have been friends for a long time, Theondar. Think of what Lacertin did to my father. What he did to my sister."

Roine paused again, this time turning to Lacertin with a silent appeal.

Fear crept through Tan. Roine hated Lacertin. Now, knowing what the king was—how he shaped spirit—Tan wondered how much of what happened back then had been shaped. How much of it was Althem's fault?

"Did you kill your sister?" Tan asked.

Roine spun until his glare hit Tan full-force.

Tan couldn't tell if the king's shaping had taken hold. Roine knew how to protect himself from spirit shapings, but so had Lacertin. Whatever they knew hadn't been enough to prevent Althem from forcing them to do what he wanted.

Tan met Roine's eyes. "You blame Lacertin for what happened with Princess Ilianna, but Lacertin would never have done anything to harm King Ilton. Think of the steps he took to understand what happened. He spent part of the last twenty years living in Incendin just trying to understand what Incendin planned. Without him, we wouldn't have stopped the lisincend attack."

Roine let out a frustrated breath. He glared at Lacertin. Heat radiated from him.

Tan feared what would happen. Would Lacertin attack him? Would Roine attack Lacertin? Either way, the king got what he wanted.

Then Roine turned to the king.

"I became Roine after what happened with Ilianna. I did *your* work, served as *your* Athan. All this time, you've hidden your agenda."

Another shaping washing over Roine.

His voice raised in anger. "It was you, wasn't it? You killed your father, not the archivists." Roine swallowed and lowered his voice to a whisper. Somehow, it sounded more dangerous. "You killed Ilianna, didn't you?"

The king blinked, and then tried another shaping.

Roine ran at him.

Lacertin ran alongside, glancing back at Tan as he did. "Run, Tan. Get away from here."

Wind whistled through the tunnel, whipping around his cloak and stinging his skin. Zephra arrived.

She attacked with Lacertin and Roine. Cianna aided, but the others outclassed her.

Tan marveled at his mother. She floated on the air. Ara aided her, guiding her shaping. Each shaping was a crack of controlled air. The king somehow blocked each one.

Tan realized that he shaped *all* the elements. A warrior shaper.

Someone tugged on his arm. Tan's delight at seeing Amia was immediately tempered by the tears in her eyes. "Come on," she said.

"Lacertin is right. We need to get out of here."

Tan watched the shapers battle for another moment. Using the artifact, the king managed to hold his own against the others, but they slowly forced him back.

Amia grabbed shoulder. Tan decided she was right and together, they fled.

CHAPTER 28

The Power of Spirit

THEY REACHED THE DOOR leading into the lower level of the archives. Thunder and cracks of lightning chased them. Swirls of wind and chunks of debris followed. Amia remained tense as they ran. Otherwise, she appeared unharmed.

At the door, Tan paused long enough to pull her against him. He still clutched Roine's sword. Would Roine need it against the king? "Did they harm you?"

She shifted her traveling cloak. Patches had burned away, but it remained mostly intact. "They thought they needed me to help control you."

"Are you shaped?"

Amia leaned toward him and kissed him lightly on the mouth. "The First Mother tried. I think I was able to block it, but I don't know."

"She's on the other side of this door."

Amia cocked her head, concentrating. "I sense her there."

"And the lisincend are there. Somewhere in the archives."

She closed her eyes. Her sensing pressed out from her, much like a shaping. "One is there. Not both."

"And Asboel is coming. The lisincend killed the hatchlings."

"I think the lisincend still have another goal. More than simply reaching this place."

Tan was glad they saw the situation the same way. "As do I."

He reached for his connection to Asboel. *You should not come. It is a trap to draw you to this place.*

He sensed the draasin nearby but didn't get an answer.

Tan focused on shaping each of the elements and then mingled them together before pushing it into the rune for spirit.

Amia watched him. "You can shape spirit now."

"Not like you. For me, it is the same as in the place of convergence. I need all the elements shaped together to be able to manage spirit."

"Different," she agreed. "But it's still spirit."

"My shaping has always been different. I'm not like other shapers." But if he were, he wouldn't have the strength needed to have freed himself from the shaping the king had tried to place on him. Without using the nymid and ara, the king would have overwhelmed him. Without Amia, the king would have shaped him.

The door opened with a soft hiss. Tan pulled it open.

The First Mother assaulted him immediately.

Instinctively, Tan pulled a shaping through him—through the sword—and pushed against her attempt at spirit shaping. It snapped back against her, destroyed by the strength lent by the sword.

She crouched, still attached by the chains near the end of the room. "Daughter."

Amia stepped past Tan. "You don't get to call me that. Regardless of this." She pulled the silver band from beneath her cloak and tossed it at the Mother. "I know why you gave it to me."

"What does it do?"

Amia stared at the First Mother with contempt. "It's a marker for the People. Leaders." Her eyes narrowed. "Shapers. It lets others know who can shape, even if weakly."

"You have it wrong, Daughter."

Amia tipped her head at the band of silver. "Maybe I do. Seeing you chained to the ground like this, I think perhaps you are where you belong." Amia nudged Tan. "We should go. She can remain here. Let her serve the People from here."

The First Mother shot Tan a pleading expression. "You would have done the same. You would have done anything to save your family."

Tan put his arm around Amia's shoulders.

Amia moved against him. "I would have done many things to save my family," he said. "Not anything."

They hurried up the stairs, but Tan paused, one hand on Amia's waist. "I'm not going up here to only stop the lisincend. I need to protect Asboel. I need to protect the draasin."

"I will help. I don't know how, but I will help," Amia said.

They reached the landing where they once had been trapped. The lisincend had been here recently. The door and walls were burned, as if flames had spread through this part of the archives. The shelves inside were destroyed. Fire had ripped through here, leaving little more than smoldering ash that once had been shelves and books. A slight haze of smoke still hung over the room.

All the knowledge stored here, lost to the lisincend.

He backed out and turned up the stairs without another word. The next level was much the same. Some evidence of the shelving that once stored the books remained, but nothing more. Tan breathed out slowly, pushing back the anger rising within him. Not only with the lisincend, but the king. Althem let this happen.

They reached the top of the stairs. What remained of the door was twisted. Heat radiated out toward him, pressing from the upper archives on a breeze.

He held a hand up in a stop gesture. Amia took a step back, indicating he could go on without her. Tan started into the archives alone.

He held Roine's sword—the warrior sword—in front of him. Runes glowed as he pulled a shaping through it, keeping it ready.

The shelves were gone. Where once had been rows and rows holding thousands of texts—many centuries old—now there was nothing more than ash. The archives had survived the attack by the draasin only to fall to the lisincend.

As Tan neared the door, heat raged toward him. He spun, sword outstretched.

One of the lisincend stood waiting. It resembled Alisz. Leathery skin covered it. "Shaper," he hissed.

Tan tipped his head. "Where is Alisz?"

The lisincend's smile widened. "You wish to see her when you have found me?"

"I wish to destroy her after I destroy you."

The lisincend laughed. "You are young to be so confident. You know fire?"

With the question, a tongue of fire stretched toward Tan. He flicked the sword, pushing out with a fire shaping while at the same time drawing from Asboel's strength. The draasin might not answer him, but that didn't mean his presence wasn't still within him.

The lisincend hesitated.

Tan pushed a shaping through the sword, mixing earth and wind.

Here, at a place of convergence where golud infused the stone itself and ara blew through the halls, the shaping carried more power.

The floor itself surged. Stone encircled the lisincend, trapping it up to the waist. Wind whistled, drawing off the lisincend's heat, leaving it weakened.

"Where is Alisz?" Tan demanded.

The lisincend did not answer.

Tan used another shaping of earth, again drawn through the sword, and the lisincend sank deeper into the stone.

Its dark eyes widened. "The palace," it hissed.

Tan would have been better off going directly to the palace rather than coming here. Coming this way slowed him, putting Asboel at greater risk.

"Amia!" He both spoke her name and sent it through their connection.

She came through the door. Tan watched her scan the damage to the archive and come to rest on the lisincend trapped in stone. "Will it hold?"

"Earth will hold fire. Especially as golud infuses this stone."

The lisincend roared and struggled.

Tan shaped a gag of wind and stuffed it into the lisincend's mouth, silencing it.

"You let it live?" Amia asked.

"For now," he answered. "I don't know if they can be saved."

"Saved?"

When fire consumed him, he had thought of nothing more than letting it burn. He had practically become one of the lisincend. Now that he understood what that was like, could he not attempt to save the shaper?

Amia turned away from the lisincend. "They went to fire willingly,

Tan."

"So did I."

"They did it to serve fire. You did it to help those you care about."

Tan considered the lisincend, now held helpless in the rock. "They wanted to help their people as well. Would you have me kill the First Mother for what she did? She did the same as the lisincend."

"I have little sympathy for whatever befalls the First Mother."

The tone of her voice saddened him. So much had changed for him since they first met, but for her as well. The lisincend had taken everything from her. And now that she knew of the First Mother, what little remained of her past was gone.

Nothing he could say would help her, so he pulled her close and kissed her again. As he did, he pushed a shaping of spirit through her, much as she had often shaped him.

She kissed him back, gently at first and then with more urgency. She sighed as the shaping washed over her.

"The palace," he said, pulling away from her.

Amia built a quick shaping and pressed it upon the lisincend. Tan recognized the shaping as similar to what the king had tried using on him.

"It might hold for a while," she said.

"You're using his shaping?"

She glanced toward the lower level of the archives. "He might be more skilled than the First Mother. I think we need to consider the possibility that he escapes the others."

"I expect that he will. I only need them to delay him."

He hurried through the rest of the archives. It looked much like the lower levels, destroyed by the lisincend fires. Centuries of work were now lost. Tan would mourn the loss later. For now, he needed to reach the palace and keep Asboel from letting fire consume him.

Tan nearly stumbled as they emerged.

All the work that had gone into restoring the city, rebuilding following the draasin attack, had been destroyed. Fires burned throughout the city. Heat simmered from lisincend stalking the streets. How many had died for whatever the king planned?

Renewed anger washed over him so he touched the cool stone of the archives. Golud infused the stone but also permeated the footings of the city itself, a city reclaimed from nymid-infused water. He sent out a rumbling request. *Quench fire.*

Nothing more than that.

The ground trembled and shook. Amia stumbled into the street. "What did you do?"

"I asked golud to help."

"Aren't you afraid of what will happen if you use the elemental power here? Isn't that what the king wants?"

"I'm more afraid of what will happen if I don't."

He continued through empty streets, working around rubble and smoldering buildings. Amia followed, keeping up as he hurried through the streets of Ethea. The palace remained in sight, rising through the ash and smoke. No one else moved in the streets.

The heat from the lisincend shaping increased as they neared. Tan wished for nymid armor for protection. This time, he would have to stop the lisincend by himself.

A dark shadow swirled overhead. He looked up to see Asboel circling.

Do not do this!

The great fire elemental had to answer this time. Tan was too close for him to ignore.

Maelen. Leave this place.

They seek to draw you here. They seek to call the Mother. They have the device.

Asboel hesitated. A moment of calm returned to his mind. *Twisted Fire must suffer.*

That is fire speaking, not the draasin.

Draasin are *fire.*

No. Draasin are more than fire.

Tan may not understand the elemental powers as well as Asboel, but he had grown to know Asboel; the bond between them created a shared understanding. Asboel was no more fire than Tan was. And if he lost himself to rage, he could lose control of fire the same as Tan.

He focused on a shaping, wrapping earth and wind and water before finally adding fire. Spirit burst from his shaping and he sent it toward Asboel, hoping to provide calm.

And realized he was too late. Another shaping wrapped around Asboel's mind.

The draasin began dropping from the sky. His wings beat weakly as he crashed.

How had he been shaped? The only way Amia had managed to shape the draasin was because it had been at the place of convergence, and then they had liquid spirit to aid her. Who could be strong enough to shape the draasin?

"Tan!"

Amia stared at the palace, where Asboel finally came to rest in the courtyard.

Earth erupted and lightning cracked overhead. A warrior. Not Lacertin or Roine. Neither could shape spirit. That meant the king had escaped.

"You should go. Leave Ethea," he warned Amia. "I will do what I can here."

"I'm not leaving you to face this alone."

"I have to be here. I have to help Asboel. You can find safety."

"None will find safety if he succeeds."

He took her hand. With a quick shaping of wind—copying what he'd seen his mother perform and augmented by ara—he lifted into the air, pulling Amia with him.

Quickly, he urged ara and they sped into the palace courtyard.

It took one glance for Tan to take in the changes. Where had once been a combination of scenes from the kingdoms—a mixture of forest and water and sand and grassland—was now laid waste by flames. A winged lisincend stood near one corner of the courtyard. Not Alisz.

Alisz prowled toward Asboel. The king stood between her and Tan, a triumphant expression on his face. The artifact glowed with soft white light, still powered by his shaping. Alisz glanced from the king to the draasin, excitement practically steaming from her.

Asboel lay crumpled on the ground, one wing bent behind him at an awkward angle. Several of the spikes on his back were damaged, broken and scattered across the ground. Blackish blood oozed from a wound where a tree had pierced him as he landed. His head moved slowly.

Alisz would kill Asboel. And then? Could she use his energy to ascend to elemental power or would she have to kill the others? Would the king allow her to kill Asboel before he used the draasin in his plan?

Tan needed to stop them both.

Asboel?

Maelen. Finish me. Do not let them use—

He didn't have the chance to finish what he was saying. The king formed another shaping, pulling it through the artifact. It built with painful pressure and slammed over Asboel. The massive draasin twitched and fell still.

He breathed, but slowly. The shaping over his mind muddled his thoughts.

The king finally noticed Tan. "You served well, Tannen. Perhaps I will allow you to continue to serve."

"You don't know what you're doing. The ancient scholars kept that device from here for a reason."

The king sneered at him and slammed a shaping toward Tan. "Because they were scared."

Tan drew power through the sword and the shaping dissipated. "They were wise. The elementals should not be controlled."

The king snarled, "Maybe I was wrong about you." He motioned toward Alisz. "Finish him."

She blinked as if debating whether to obey. Althem forced a shaping upon her and she leapt into the air. The other lisincend followed.

They dove toward him.

Tan pressed through the sword, drawing upon all of the elements at the same time he drew upon the elemental power. Already, he engaged golud. Now he called ara to buffer his shaping and mixed what he could of the nymid, though they were distant.

The lisincend hit a barrier created by his shaping and bounced off.

"You can't do this!" Tan yelled at the king.

Althem ignored him. His shaping built, pulling through the artifact. Tan recognized how the shaping pulled on the elementals, drawing from golud beneath him, ara fluttering in the wind, the nymid deep beneath their feet in the lakebed that once had existed here, and lastly pulling through Asboel. He mixed that power, drawing it through the artifact.

Tan sent a shaping at the king but it wasn't strong enough, not against the power Althem now wielded.

The ground next to him exploded.

Lacertin shot from the ground, sword glowing with runes. Roine followed. His skin shone and still carried with it a hint of green from the nymid's healing. Zephra followed on a shaping of wind infused with ara. As Tan watched, ara faltered, drawn by the king's shaping.

"We need to stop the king—" Tan started, but the lisincend attacked as he did.

Lacertin twisted, sending a shaping of fire and wind and earth toward Alisz, pulling through his sword. His mother shot toward the other lisincend, unafraid and drawing a shaping of wind as she went. Only Roine remained.

"Roine?"

He stared at the king with an unreadable expression. "This is not my friend," Roine said. "This is not Althem. He *must* have been shaped."

Amia gave him a sad expression. "Althem is the shaper. What he does has been years in the planning."

"What does he attempt?" Roine asked.

Tan nodded toward Asboel. "He draws forth a pool of spirit. With that—" he pointed to the artifact "—he can change anything."

Roine took a step back. "I can't stop him."

"Theondar can."

His eyes widened. "I *am* Theondar, Tannen. And I can't stop him." He looked at Lacertin battling the lisincend, at Zephra sending whips of wind at the other, before shifting his attention back to Tan. "You're the one who speaks to the elementals. You will have to do this. You are the only one. Go. Do what you can. I will help the others."

"Your sword," Tan said, holding it toward him.

Roine pushed it back to him. "That is a warrior's sword." Roine shifted his attention back to Alisz. His shaping built suddenly and he shot toward her, leaving Tan and Amia together.

Tan looked at Asboel. He had come to save his friend, but to do so, he needed to stop the king. "Can you do something about the shaping?" he asked Amia.

She focused on Asboel, biting her lip as she considered. "There is still my shaping holding him."

Tan closed his eyes, thinking. Amia's shaping—the warning not to hunt man—would restrict Asboel. "Remove it."

"Tan?"

"Remove it."

Amia set her jaw and started toward Asboel, working around his broken wing and sidling up to him.

Tan focused on Althem.

The shaping still built, growing more powerful with each passing moment.

If he did nothing, Althem would control enough of the elementals to draw spirit here. Tan didn't know what would happen then, but if the ancient scholars were unwilling to keep the artifact here—if they were unwilling to risk that—then he would not, either.

Althem shot him a dark look. "You can't stop this, Tannen. Perhaps in a few years, you might have learned enough, but not now. And once I learned of your ability, I wasn't willing to risk those years. It's why I convinced your friend to take you to the Gathering. I thought you could be coaxed toward fire—"

He threw a shaping toward Tan.

Tan barely reacted in time, pushing it away with a shaping drawn through the sword. He took another step.

Althem sent another shaping at him. Again, Tan barely deflected it.

Behind him, someone screamed.

Tan ignored it, focusing only on the king. Another step.

A few more and he would reach him.

Althem shifted his focus, pressing all of his shaping on Tan.

Elemental power burned through him, threatening to destroy him.

Tan recognized it. He'd felt it before. Nymid. Ara. Golud. And draasin. Althem could not speak to them, could not do more than try to control them. But they were elementals, not meant to be controlled.

The last, draasin, burned strongly. Tan pulled on it rather than pushing it away, not drawing it in as he had when he had nearly transformed into the lisincend, but instead simply diverting it from the king's intended target.

The bond with Asboel strengthened. *Maelen.*

Tan took another step forward.

The king continued to push his shaping onto Tan. Fire no longer burned in the shaping.

Tan pulled on ara. *Help the son of Zephra.*

Ara swirled and shifted. Then it mingled with fire.

Another step.

Golud pushed, rumbling beneath him. Tan sent a command to the earth elemental. *Serve the son of Grethan.*

The rumbling shifted, now moving toward the king.

That left only the nymid. They were the first elemental Tan had ever spoken to. His bond might be strongest with the draasin, but the connection to the nymid had strength as well. *Help me save the Daughter.*

Tan reached the king. Althem fought, but elemental power burned in Tan. He reached for the artifact.

And then Tan pulled a shaping through the artifact, mingling all of the elemental power.

Not to call spirit, but to *shape* spirit, twisting it as he had learned he needed in order to summon a spirit shaping.

Blinding light surged around him. Time seemed to stand still as power unlike anything he'd ever felt surged through him.

It reminded him of stepping into the pool of liquid spirit, only thousands of times stronger. Awareness of everything around him surged through him. He could control everything, shape anything, turn the world into his ideal.

This was the reason ancient scholars created the artifact. This was what they feared.

For a moment, he considered shaping his father into existence. He could recreate Nor, place his family back as it was. Help Amia find her family again, shape *her* mother back into existence. The hatchlings could be shaped back into being.

The possibilities almost overwhelmed him.

Tan recognized the draw, the fury burning through him. Had he not nearly lost himself to fire, he doubted he would understand. Control of this power was an illusion.

He released earth, letting golud sag back into the stones. Then he released ara, letting wind return.

Tan held onto the nymid for a moment. Drawing and shaping through the artifact amplified the shaping more than the sword ever did.

Heal the Eldest, he commanded.

The nymid stirred. *He Who is Tan.*

Tan felt the nymid work on Asboel, surging through him. Fire surged in Tan's mind.

He released water.

Now only fire burned within him. Asboel.

Do you wish this bond?

Maelen.

I can release the bond. Do you wish it?

The draasin snorted. *The Great Mother chose well.*

Tan chuckled and released the fire he drew through the artifact. Time seemed to lurch forward. The blinding light faded.

Althem stood next to him. Anger swallowed his face. He lunged for the artifact and missed, instead grabbing the warrior's sword. He sneered at Tan as his shaping built, sharp and powerful. Too fast for Tan to react with a shaping.

But he was not a shaper. He didn't know what he was, but he was different. More.

Asboel!

The draasin reacted even faster than the king. Freshly healed, his jaw snapped forward, catching Althem with teeth sharper than any sword. He bellowed, flames shooting into the sky, as the fire elemental swallowed the king.

Tan shook and settled to the ground, more weakened than he had ever felt in his life.

Asboel nudged him with his nose. A sense of contentment worked through the bond.

Maelen.

Epilogue

The courtyard had been destroyed.

Roine crouched over someone attempting a powerful shaping. Tan rushed over, fearing it was his mother. Instead, Lacertin lay unmoving, a gaping hole burned through his chest. Tan reached for Roine. "Nothing can save him. Nothing can restore him now."

Tears streamed down Roine's face. "I… He…"

"I know," Tan said.

The remains of Alisz were nearby, arms and legs torn off as if by some wild animal. Tan gagged and looked away. His mother knelt before the other lisincend, holding it wrapped tightly in a shaping of air. It writhed but could not escape.

He is yours, he told Asboel.

You may keep him. Their flesh is bitter anyway.

Tan laughed. After everything they had been through, it felt good to laugh.

Roine searched the courtyard. "Where is Althem?"

"He's gone."

"Gone?"

Tan studied Asboel. "Gone. He will not harm this land again."

"It will take a long time to work through everything that happened here," Roine said. "It will take a long time for the city—the kingdoms—to recover."

Tan could have fixed everything while shaping spirit through the artifact, done anything. But that power was not meant for him to wield. He still didn't understand for what purpose the artifact had been created, but he began to understand what it could do.

"They will have a warrior to guide them. They will have Theondar."

Roine studied the ground. "It should have been Lacertin. All this time, he never stopped serving his king. All this time, and I have been serving the wrong king." Roine pulled his gaze up and redness rimmed his eyes. "You have the wrong warrior. I think you can lead. After what I've seen, you have done more than any to keep the kingdoms safe."

"I—" Tan started.

Amia slipped her arm around him. "Whatever we choose, we will do it together."

He kissed her lightly on the lips. "We need to understand everything that happened here. The archivists. The First Mother. The lisincend. The king. So many answers are needed."

Tan's mother drifted toward them on a shaping of wind. "You will not have to do that alone."

Asboel snorted his agreement. The great fire elemental simply waited, golden eyes surveying the sky, as if waiting for Tan to release him.

You don't have to stay.

Asboel snorted. *I will uphold my end of the bond.*

This time, Tan snorted. *You have kept up the bond. Go. Mourn. I will join you when I am finished here.*

And then?

We are not done with Twisted Fire.

A surge of satisfaction came from Asboel. The great draasin—the Eldest of the elementals—lifted to the sky on his massive wings. He studied Tan as he took off. With a twitch of his tail, he headed south toward Nara.

Tan's heart was heavy for what Asboel had endured. But the draasin was strong. He would be fine in time. They all would.

As much as he would have liked to, he could not have shaped away that sadness.

"You held power and you turned away," Amia said. "I felt it flowing through you. For a moment, *I* was tempted."

"With that power, I could have done anything. The temptation was there..." He looked around, pushing away the haunting memory. "More than anything, I think that was the reason the ancient scholars hid the artifact away from here."

Roine focused on the artifact. "I can—"

Tan held the artifact in front of him. The runes no longer glowed, not as they had when power shaped through it, but he knew the dangerous secret to using it. "I think it best if I watch over it. Besides, I think I know a place to keep it safe."

The lower level of the archives was quiet. The only sound was Tan's pounding heart and Amia's soft breathing. He stood in front of one of the doors—one of the ancient doors that had resisted opening in spite of centuries of trying.

"Are you sure you can do this?" Amia asked.

Tan focused on the runes carved into the surface. The First Mother had to be convinced, but she had taught him as much as she knew of them. Now, Tan recognized the various symbols.

"I'm not sure," he said.

The artifact weighed heavily in his pocket. Tan looked forward to hiding it away. He hoped this worked as planned and built a shaping.

Earth and water and wind and fire, all mixing together and all strengthened by the elementals at this place of convergence.

The runes slowly started glowing.

"These doors haven't been opened in nearly a thousand years," Tan said.

"That's why I'm not sure it's wise to simply open one."

"I need to know what they knew. I need to know why they created this place. I need to know what I am."

Amia squeezed his hand.

And then the door hissed open.

DK HOLMBERG currently lives in rural Minnesota where the winter cold and the summer mosquitoes keep him inside and writing.

To see other books and read more, please go to www.dkholmberg.com

Follow me on twitter: @dkholmberg

Word-of-mouth is crucial for any author to succeed and how books are discovered. If you enjoyed the book, please consider leaving a review online at your favorite bookseller or Goodreads, even if it's only a line or two; it would make all the difference and would be very much appreciated.

A Sneak Preview:

Fortress of Fire

The Cloud Warrior Saga, Book 4

The barrier has fallen. The king is gone. Tan has secured the artifact, but now the Fortress of Fire in Incendin burns more brightly than it has in a generation.

To master his connection to the elementals, Tan needs to rediscover knowledge about the elemental power that has been lost for centuries. When the draasin bonded to him is injured, Tan must rely on everything he's learned to save him and discovers a new threat to the kingdoms more powerful than anything he's ever faced.

CHAPTER 1

The Shaping of Spirit

TANNEN MINDEN SAT WITH HIS LEGS crossed in front of him, the cold stone floor of the cell beneath him and the stink of damp air filling the air around him. The shaping he performed came more easily than it once did, though still was not as effortless as what he knew was possible. For him to do what he knew necessary, for him to understand *why* he'd been given the gifts the Great Mother had given him, he would need to master not only speaking to the elementals but also shaping.

The First Mother stared at him, exasperation plain on her face. "You lose focus so easily. If you think to save this creature, then you will need focus."

"I think my focus is fine," Tan snapped. After spending the last two hours sitting across from this woman—the one who had nearly handed the kingdoms to a man determined to simply shape it to his whims—he was tired. His mind ached from the constant repetition of binding the air, water, earth, and fire together. Worse, there was the distant amusement he felt from Asboel. The draasin thought all of this quite a game. From Amia, he sensed only annoyance.

"Fine? If you're to understand your gifts, you will need to be able to hold your focus regardless of what comes. You might never know you're being shaped otherwise. And you know how they transformed. They stole from the People. This is not some simple shaper you plan to face."

He shot her a look and then shook his head. She deserved his anger, but her punishment was severe enough as it was. No longer able to serve the Aeta, she was instead confined to this windowless room, held with chains wrapped to her ankles that kept her from going more than a dozen steps, and stuck teaching him what she knew of the ancient runes and of spirit shaping. She was one of the wandering people, now trapped for her crimes. What warmth could be found in the weak lanterns flickering in the room gave only enough light to see the bare, rock walls. Somehow, she still managed to carry herself as if she led.

Tan pulled on a shaping of fire and mixed it with elemental power. He no longer knew if it came from Asboel or one of the lesser elementals. He doubted that it mattered. Fire now came easily to him, flowing from him more freely than any of the other elements. He thought it from the fact that he'd bonded to Asboel, but he wasn't certain. A nagging part deep within him worried that there was some residual effect from the way fire changed him. The nymid had restored him, but it was possible that fire still influenced him.

"I think I will do fine if needed."

Her shaping built faster than he could react. As it did, Tan's connection to the elementals was cut from him, sliced like a knife across his mind. A panic raged through him and he wrapped each of the elements together, binding spirit, and slammed it against her shaping. Her shaping snapped away from him.

"What was that?"

She fixed him with a dark stare. Flint gray eyes met his and didn't look away, still carrying the intensity and vibrancy he'd noticed the first time he met her. Her one concession to her captivity, letting her silver hair hang loose and wild around her shoulders, magnified the effect. "You rely on the elementals when you need to learn to rely on yourself. A time may come when the elemental power is unavailable." Her eyes softened, but only a little. "You have the power within you. I sense it, as does Amia. You lean on the elementals as a crutch."

"I don't 'lean' on them. That's how my power works."

She tipped her head toward the pulsing orange fire glowing in his hand. "You think your power is confined to the elementals? You shape fire easily enough, unless there's still a part of you that's lisincend?" She cocked her head at him, waiting to see if her comment riled him up, before pulling her chains to get more comfortable. "The elementals may augment your power, but you provide the spark."

Tan sighed deeply. If that were true, that meant he didn't need to bind the elementals together to reach spirit, but he knew no other way to do it. With the elementals, he could draw on their power, use it to help his shapings. That power could be bound together, woven to form the shaping of spirit he'd used to release himself from her when he'd been trapped in the archives, but it was a form of spirit that was nothing like what she shaped. The effect was often the same, but not always. After all the practice, he suspected he wasn't meant to shape spirit in the same way.

"Your way of shaping spirit doesn't work for me."

"Because you haven't taken the time to learn. Spirit is universal. All shapers have the capacity to reach it in *some* way, however vague."

Tan stared at the fire burning in his hand. The flames danced over his skin, leaving him unharmed. There was the sense of elemental power in the flames, the weak draw of saa in even that much fire. It wasn't only Asboel guiding fire for him. Someday, he hoped to reach the other elementals as easily. "Why do you say that?"

"It's the reason for our power. We are connected to the power that drives this world in ways others are not. Spirit is the binding force for that. Those of us who shape spirit may be able to use it more directly, but all shapers can touch it." She shrugged. "Most never bother to try."

"What of the warriors who've never managed to reach spirit? Theondar can't shape spirit. Lacertin couldn't either." Unless they simply had never learned the trick of binding them together. Could it be that *all* warrior shapers could shape spirit if they understood how?

A troubled look crossed over her face and she twisted on the floor to stare at one of the walls.

"Do you know why they can't shape spirit?" Tan asked.

"Not why they can't, but it has long troubled me that shaping—that the use of the elemental power of our world—has diminished. Spirit has long been rare, but the others? When your kingdoms were no more than separate lands, shapers were plentiful. The elementals bonded willingly, teaching those shapers their power. Now? Elementals ignore us." She fixed Tan with an appraising stare. "Or they had. I am uncertain why that would change."

Tan had learned to listen when the First Mother lectured. In trying to protect her people, she might have done terrible things, but she had an archivist's knowledge. "Some think power simply fades from us. Others think the elementals have abandoned us," Tan said, repeating something Roine had once told him.

The First Mother looked down at her hands. "The elementals have not abandoned all. And this power is fundamental to our world. It would not simply fade."

"Did the archivists search for that reason?"

She pulled on her chains again, dragging them across the floor. An annoyed look briefly crossed her face before disappearing. "When they first came to Ethea, it was to learn and study. Few managed to shape spirit, even then." She met his eyes. "What you do, the way you bind the elements together, is a different form of shaping. Perhaps weaker." She shrugged. "They came to study and understand. Only later did they begin to recognize the shift."

"A shift? Even in the last generation, shapers have been more and more infrequent."

"As has the connection to the elementals. They are not as unrelated as you might think."

Tan struggled to find a more comfortable seat. "I'm not saying they aren't related. Only that I have no idea why. The draasin doesn't seem to know." And if he did, would Asboel tell Tan? The draasin had once been hunted by shapers. Why wouldn't he want to keep them from the world?

"Then you need to find the reason. This place," she motioned around her, indicating the university far above ground, "once searched for knowledge and understanding." The chains rattled as she waved her hands. "Now it's nothing more than a way to power. There is a difference."

Tan couldn't argue with that. When he first came to the university, the Master shapers were barely willing to teach. Only when Tan's connection to the elementals was known had other shapers offered to teach.

She pulled on her chains again. "Enough of this talk. You are wasting your time with me." She gave Tan a pointed look. "Don't think I don't know how Zephra will react if she knew you were down here studying with me."

"Zephra would prefer I stayed out of all harm. She still thinks me the child from Nor."

The First Mother snorted. "Even in the time I've known you, you've done a poor job of staying clear of harm. But you are capable, Tannen Minden. That is the only reason I proceed with this. Now. You should focus on spirit alone. Your shapings grow more skilled, but they remain blunt. Until you manage to reach spirit without binding the elements, the shapings will always be that way."

"Most of my shapings are blunt," he said.

"You have exquisite control of fire," the First Mother commented. "There is no reason your other shapings could not be the same."

"I speak to the draasin. Some of what I've learned possible is from what I've seen from the elemental."

"You speak to all of the elementals, Tannen. Do not exclude them simply because you've bonded to the draasin. Perhaps that is why you fail to progress with the other elements."

Tan shifted. The stone beneath him made his legs ache, especially after sitting as he was for so long. "I don't speak to the others as I do to the draasin."

He wondered if he should share so openly with the First Mother, but she had knowledge about shaping that others didn't. As much pain as she'd caused, she remained willing to teach, if only in her own way. She had no remorse for what she'd done, but Tan didn't really expect such emotion of her. Her reasons had been pretty clear: she had done everything she thought necessary to protect the Aeta, even if it meant working with Incendin.

"Only because you do not listen."

"What does that mean? I listen to the elementals. How else would I have learned to speak to them?"

She tried reaching and pushing her hair out of the way, but the chains holding her prevented her from doing it easily. Instead, she blew on the loose strands of gray hair. "You think that speaking only to the great elementals makes you powerful? It makes you *weaker* to be so reliant on them. Think of how many draasin remain in the world. And not only fire, but think of water. Will you be able to reach udilm in the middle of Ter?" She tossed her head. "What you've managed with the elementals is impressive. Now try it with the others."

"I don't know that I can speak to the lesser elementals."

She flipped her hand at him. "Why should it be any different with the others?"

Tan bit back the argument that came to mind as he thought about what she was saying. He hadn't really tried reaching for elementals other than the great elementals. Here in Ethea and in the mountains near the place of convergence, they were easy to find. That was the reason King Althem had wanted the artifact that Tan now stored in the lower archives. But would he find the elementals as easy to reach outside of those places? It had been Asboel who led him to udilm for Elle, not anything Tan had done.

Then there was the issue with the lesser elementals. With fire, he thought he drew partly on the power of saa as he shaped fire, but what if it was all from Asboel? Would he be able to use the other lesser elementals the same way?

There was so much for him still to learn and it felt like not enough time for him to understand what he needed. For the safety of the kingdoms, he needed to master this. Now that the barrier was down, Incendin could attack at any time. Alisz, the twisted lisincend, might have been destroyed, but they didn't know how many of the lisincend remained.

"I can see from your face you finally see wisdom," the First Mother said.

"There's so much to learn," Tan admitted. "And I don't know if I can do it."

She shuffled closer to him, pulling the chains taut. "You need to embrace your abilities. There will always be things you don't know. That's the nature of using the elemental power. Accept that. Recognize that *someone* will always know something you do not. Even working with an element for fifty years will not protect you from that uncertainty."

Tan found a hint of unexpected kindness in her eyes and swallowed back the lump forming in his throat. "I'm sorry for what happened."

The First Mother took a shaky breath. "Not as sorry as I am," she whispered. She ran one hand over the chains, pressing down as if trying to break the connection. "It keeps me awake, you know."

"What does?"

"Who will lead the Aeta? Who will guide them now that I am gone? Always before, we had a succession in place. The First Mother would step aside as another Mother was raised to replace her." She looked down at her hands, real uncertainty coming to her voice. "When I first met Amia, when I felt the strength she would one day possess, I thought I'd finally found that person. Now there is no one."

"The Aeta have survived for centuries," Tan said, repeating the words Amia told him when they spoke about the Aeta. If the First Mother was fishing for him to commit Amia to again serving the Aeta, she really didn't know Amia. "You might have held them together during your time leading them, but another will come forward."

"I wish I believed that."

Tan leaned back, studying the First Mother. Defiance had once come through in her tone and the strength in her back when she spoke of the Aeta, but now she looked a broken woman. Her thin body no longer seemed to have vigor and instead simply looked frail. Her gray hair had lost its luster. Even the occasional steel in her voice was more and more rare.

"What can I do?" he asked.

She looked up and shook her head. "You needn't lie to me to convince me to continue working with you. I have said that I will. It helps pass the time. But don't try giving me false hope, Tannen. That is beneath even you."

"You know how I feel about Amia. I would do anything to help her."

"She has abandoned her place with the People."

"Only because she lost faith in your leadership. She loved her family. Losing them devastated her. For her to learn that the First Mother—the person who should have been responsible for guiding the Aeta and keeping the People safe—had betrayed her family to the lisincend, well that alone would have changed her. But to learn that the archivists had been Aeta, that they had known about her and chosen to bring harm to her, that took away all that remained in her of the Aeta. She may have been one of the Wandering People, but it wasn't until they abandoned her that she became homeless." The sense of Amia surged through his connection to her, strengthened as it often was when he thought of her. "I see how it pains her when we speak of the Aeta that still wander. I see how she wishes there was something for her to do. The Aeta don't have to hide. They can come to the kingdoms and we will help them find safety."

The First Mother sniffed. "All the time you've spend with Amia and you still know so little about the People. We do not *want* to have a place where we're kept. There is freedom to the wagons, to the wandering. That is the way of the Aeta."

"Maybe you're the one who doesn't understand your people," Tan suggested, thinking of the way the Gathering had felt. There had been relief in the Aeta at having a place to be together. Amia spoke of it with a sense of joy. "Does the wandering keep the people safe? You struggled simply bringing everyone together for the Gathering. Wouldn't it have been better to have safety?"

The First Mother lowered her eyes. "*I* was to provide safety. That has always been the role of the First Mother. That was my reason behind everything I ever did."

"And now? Seeing what you've done? Do you have any regret for the choices you made?"

She didn't look up as she answered. "It's all I have left."

CHAPTER 2

A Mother's Love

TAN STOPPED NEAR THE UNIVERSITY after leaving the First Mother. What had once been impressive stone buildings had crumbled, layering the ground with little more than rubble. The air still stunk from still-raging flames. He forced himself to ignore the stink, never knowing if it was burned buildings or something worse that he smelled.

He moved carefully through the stone, wondering what it had once been like to learn and study in here. This was where his mother and father had met, two of the countless shapers who had trained here over the centuries. Many had become warriors, so it was that much harder to view the pile of rock the storied institution had become. Although the draasin had done more of the damage, some had come from when Althem had let the lisincend wander freely through the city.

A pair of shapers picked through the rock. Tan felt the pressure of their shaping and recognized that they used an earth shaping to slide rock that would otherwise have been too large and heavy to lift by hand. It was a slow and steady attempt to rebuild the university. It would take time to bring it back to what it had been, if it was even possible. So much had changed. Part of him wondered if the Masters were even the right ones to teach anymore. They focused more on where the shaper came from and the threat they might pose rather than on what the shaper might be able to learn. As the First Mother had said, they focused on gaining power rather than on gaining understanding.

Yet, as much as Tan might want to help with the cleanup, there was little he could do unless golud helped. Earth shaping remained difficult for him. He could do little things, use a weak shaping of earth to tie into what he needed for spirit, but nothing of much strength. Not enough to help rebuild the university. Once it was done, he thought he might be able to help. Golud infused the stones beneath them, working through the bones of the city. If he could coax the earth elemental to strengthen the university, maybe it would hold better if there was another attack.

And another attack was inevitable. Tan felt that with nearly as much certainty as he felt the need to learn as much as he could about the ancient scholars. They had knowledge that had been lost. What could he learn from them that had not been seen in the world for a millennia?

Would he understand what it meant to bond to one of the draasin? Asboel thought the bond was all for Tan's protection, but Tan wasn't as certain. There had to be a benefit for Asboel as well, but he hadn't discovered what that might be. From Asboel, he learned control of fire, how to make delicate and intricate shapings of fire. From Tan, what did Asboel learn? Not how the world was in the centuries since he'd been frozen beneath the lake. Tan had been shielded from the world of shapers and warriors by his parents so that he barely knew that world. What, then, was the benefit to the draasin?

"Still staring like some backwoods village boy?"

Tan turned to see Cianna watching him. Her bright orange hair spiked away from her head and she wore a shimmery shirt that nearly matched her hair. Black leather pants clung to her figure.

"I *am* a backwoods village boy. And I was lost in thought, I guess."

"Well, I'm sorry you lost your thought. You know, I never really knew you to have one." She laughed and waved to the earth shapers moving the stone. Only one of them waved back. The other looked over long enough to glare at her, as if the destruction of the university was her fault.

"I don't understand them," Tan said.

Cianna shrugged. "Them? They're just mad fire burned down the city. Some are stupid enough to blame us fire shapers, as if *we* are strong enough to make the shapings that burned though here. The Great Mother knows I once felt power like that." Cianna's eyes went distant and she shivered.

Like Tan, she had nearly been lost to fire, though in her case, the shaping had been forced upon her. Tan had welcomed it almost willingly, doing what he needed to save Amia. It had changed him, giving him power unlike anything he'd experienced. But serving fire like that had a cost. There was a loss of control when you were pulled so closely into fire, and Tan had wanted nothing more than to let fire burn. It was what the lisincend felt with their transformation. Amia had managed to save him, finding a way for water to restore him. He still wondered why the lisincend chose the transformation.

"Do you miss it?" Tan asked.

Cianna's face turned serious. "I didn't have it long enough to really miss it, but there was an ease to it. A caress of fire." She shivered again in spite of the heat radiating off her. "But there was no control. It consumed me. I can't imagine what it must be like for them." Her eyes turned toward the archives, where the lisincend captured during the attack was still held. No one had wanted to move him, and three shapers were with him at all times, though golud maintained his capture.

"They serve fire willingly," Tan said.

Cianna forced a tight smile. "*I* serve fire willingly. What they do... that is something else. They have the illusion of control."

Not for the first time, Tan wondered what it was like for the twisted lisincend. As different from lisincend like Fur as the lisincend were to fire shapers, they had used spirit in the dark shaping that had created them. Following her transformation, Alisz had kept some rudimentary ability to spirit shape. Using the First Mother to teach her had increased her skill, leaving her likely more capable than Tan was now. But like him, what she managed was blunt. It wasn't natural to her, but forced.

"We should rid ourselves of that creature," Cianna said.

Tan had something else in mind for the lisincend, and though he didn't know if it would work, it would be time to try soon. Roine wanted time to try to interrogate him, as if the lisincend would give up anything useful. Tan suspected his way had the best hope of success. "Have you tried to see him?"

She shook her head. "I can't. Not after..." She didn't finish. She didn't really need to.

He touched her arm, feeling the warmth glowing beneath her skin. She burned with it, closer to the lisincend than she let herself believe. He might burn the same way now that fire called to him.

"What was it like before?" he asked, looking around the university. "When you studied here, what was it like?" His time had been achingly brief, only long enough to learn how little he really knew. And then the attack came and he left, shaped toward Incendin to find healing for his friend Elle. Had the Great Mother kept her safe? Had she reached the udilm, and did they keep her safe?

Cianna's eyes tightened slightly. "It was a place of learning. There have always been those with much power here. And then there were those who wanted power." She shrugged. "Maybe we can do it better this time."

"Which were you?"

Her smile returned and a playful light burned in her eyes. "A bit of both?" she suggested. "Though had I wanted real power, I would have gone south to learn."

South meant Incendin.

Tan closed his eyes. The distant sense of Asboel was there, as it always was. Reaching for the draasin was easier than it once had been. He could pull through the connection with the draasin, reach for the power Asboel commanded, but more than that, he could see through Asboel's eyes. Images flickered to him as he focused, those of bleak hot lands sweeping beneath him. Fire burned somewhere to the right, an orange glow in the midst of red as Asboel searched for movement while hunting. There was a contented feeling from Asboel, but a hint of worry, too. Tan wondered about that.

"You reached for your draasin, didn't you?" Cianna asked.

"He's not mine, but yes. I reached for the connection."

She laughed. "He's as much yours as anyone's. Creatures like that don't bond, at least not that I've ever heard. It's been over a thousand years since the world has seen one and you manage to make him your pet."

"I think he'd object to being considered a pet."

"Then are you *his* pet?"

Tan laughed imagining asking Asboel the question. He knew the answer pretty quickly. "He'd tell you yes."

"You still owe me a ride," she said. She pressed closer to him, the heat from her body making his skin dry, but not in an uncomfortable way.

"Sometime," he agreed. "If he chooses not to eat you, that is."

"Thought your girl shaped him so that didn't happen? Wasn't that why Theondar let him fly freely?"

Tan glanced to the sky. He could almost imagine Asboel soaring along near the sun. "If you think Roine could stop one of the draasin from flying freely, you haven't seen the draasin in its full power."

"Only because you refuse to let him."

Tan looked at her. "You haven't been paying attention if you think I control the draasin."

The serious expression returned and she lowered her voice. "Maybe you keep that to yourself," she said, eyes flickering to the two working shapers. "If you *don't* control the draasin, there might be some frightened people if they find out."

"They're elementals—"

"But elementals we can see. The others? We know they're there. With saa, I see it only in the way the flames dance. I suspect ara brushes against my skin when it blows. Golud is there, deep beneath the earth. I can't see or feel it, but I *know*. But the draasin? They're different. They always have been." She ran her hand up his arm, more a caress than anything comforting. A gust of wind caused her to look up and nod. Tan turned to see his mother coming in on a steady shaping of wind. "I would like that ride sometime," Cianna said, then smiled broadly at him before leaving him standing alone in the remains of the university yard.

His mother landed in a swirl of dirt. She seemed to whisper something to herself as she did—likely talking to ara—before turning to face him.

Zephra wore a heavy grey cloak and a hood pulled over her head. She pushed it back, letting her dark hair fall loose around her shoulders. A familiar irritation in her eyes looked something like an admonishment. “Tannen. You should be helping with the cleanup.”

Tan glanced at the remains of the university. “I’m doing what I can to help.”

“By speaking to the prisoners?” She was small but when she pulled herself up in front of him, she seemed to tower over him as she had when he was a child. Then she’d held a spoon or sometimes a pen and had tapped it in her irritation. At least now, her hands were empty. It didn’t make her any less imposing. “I know all about the time you spend with the Aeta.”

“Amia or the First Mother?”

His mother snorted. “Both.”

“What is your issue with Amia? Had she not saved me—”

“I struggle to believe that a spirit shaper had no idea what her people were up to. Not only did you nearly die because of it, you almost became one of the lisincend.”

“And she thought enough of my abilities to see me restored.”

Zephra’s eyes narrowed. A flurry of emotions flickered across them. “Why do you continue to risk yourself with the First Mother? Hasn’t she done enough?”

“I don’t risk myself. I’m using her to learn. How else will I understand the ancient runes found in the lower archives?”

“You still haven’t managed to open the inner doors?”

Tan shook his head. He could open *some* of the doors in the lower archives, but there was one that remained locked, even with his ability to shape spirit. It remained the mystery he could not solve. The runes on that door were such that he couldn’t even get them to glow as he could the others.

"Perhaps it's best. We don't have the knowledge those ancient scholars possessed. I wonder if there are things we're not meant to know."

"Why should we fear knowledge?"

His mother turned to him. "I'm surprised you wouldn't understand."

"What does that mean?"

She turned and looked at the clouds. "It was a time of war, the kind we haven't seen in centuries. Your draasin were hunted then and the shapers had power we can't even imagine. Their scholars created the artifact. What else might they have done?" She surveyed the city, hard eyes taking in the damage as she did. "It's a wonder we survived that time."

Tan had never known his mother to be scared of anything, but the way she spoke left him thinking that she was afraid and didn't share everything she might know with him. It wouldn't be the first time she hid things from him.

"And now you seek to learn from her," she went on.

"The First Mother did what she thought necessary for her people."

"She's convinced you of that? How surprising that another spirit shaper has managed to twist you to her view."

Anger surged in him and he pressed it back. "How little you still think of me, Mother. You don't think I can protect myself from a spirit shaping? I've learned how to *shape* spirit."

She sighed and started away from the remains of the university. "Is that what it is? From what I've read, you shape something akin to spirit, but maybe not spirit itself. Either way, I think you're letting your heart lead you. It places you at risk."

"Like your didn't let your heart lead you with Father?"

"That was different."

"Was it? I'd like to know what Althem promised you that made you think Nor was the place to settle."

Tan followed her as she left the university behind. He suspected she headed for the palace, but couldn't be sure. Roine would be there. Since Althem's death, Roine had taken command of the kingdoms.

"I told you that we'd done our service to the kingdoms."

"Strange that a spirit shaper like Althem would release you like that."

She glanced over and shook her head in irritation. "We served our commitment to the throne, Tannen. Peace was our reward."

"Only Father never really had peace, did he? Why was he summoned and not you?" In the time since he'd learned of his parents' real connection to the university, they'd never had the chance to have this argument.

Zephra stopped and fixed him with a withering glare. "Tannen, careful with what you say."

"Why? You've found it awfully easy to accuse Amia of trying to drag me into some Aeta plot, never minding the fact that I *chose* to help her."

"Only after she shaped you," his mother reminded. "Isn't that what you told me?"

"Her shaping had nothing to do with why I'm still with her. I would have helped her as much as I could regardless. The shaping has done nothing more than—"

"Connect you to her." She cocked her head. "Yes, I'm aware of that as well."

A translucent face drifted quickly out of the soft breeze before fading. Tan studied ara, wondering if the wind elemental would ever respond to him the way it did for his mother. Zephra had a connection to the wind he would never really know. And he couldn't be upset by that. She was a wind shaper, after all, while Tan was... well, a wind shaper also, only without the same degree of ability with it.

Why *wouldn't* ara respond for him the same as it did for his mother?

"I believe you've been keeping secrets from me far longer than I have with you," he said. "Had Roine not shown up, would you ever have told me about your shaping? Would I have learned who my parents really were?"

She reached for him, but he pulled away. The hurt on her face nearly made him reconsider. "You've always known who your parents were, Tannen. Learning we are shapers changes nothing."

Tan sighed. "Had Roine not come to Nor, there wouldn't have been a reason for you to tell me about yourself. I would never have learned *why* Father was summoned to serve, why he needed to be the one to go. All that time, I'd wondered. I understand now. And Father will never know."

His mother closed her eyes. Wind swirled around her head, pulling on her dark hair. "You've said it yourself. Had you not gone with Roine, you would never have learned what you were capable of becoming. You have gifts the kingdoms have not seen in hundreds of years. All I want is for you to have the chance to develop them. Learn from the Masters, understand your shaping. Those are the things you should be doing, not risking yourself where others are better suited."

"I've only done what was necessary. And there might not be anyone better suited. Not after what we've been through. How many shapers have been lost? Dozens? How many of them can speak to the elementals? How many have bonded one of the draasin?" Tan caught her eyes. "The barrier is down and those who remain are stretched thin. It leaves us vulnerable."

"Which is why you need to study. You're untrained—"

"*You* could train me. Teach me what you know of wind shaping. Help me speak to ara."

She hesitated, looking back at the remains of the university, as if imagining Tan trapped within there. "I… I'm not certain that is the right answer."

"Didn't you just say I should learn to shape the wind? That I should learn to master my abilities? In that, you and the First Mother agree."

She let her breath out slowly. "If you'll commit to learning from the other Masters, not only from the First Mother, I will do what I can to teach you about the wind when able."

Tan thought that learning from his mother might actually be good for them. After all the deceit between them, getting to know her—*really* getting to know her as Zephra—was needed. And she needed to know him, to understand who he was becoming. So much had changed between them since they had last spent any meaningful time together.

And he never had a chance to study with her, not as he did with his father. His father had taught him everything he knew about earth sensing. Tan suspected that was why he had such strength and control with earth sensing, though he only wished he'd managed to learn how to shape with the same degree of skill. As it was, shaping earth remained a challenge for him. Golud helped, but would the great elemental help when he was outside a place of convergence?

"Fine. Ferran has also offered to teach. I will go to him for additional instruction. Cianna will help with fire." Amia might not like it, but Cianna was a Master fire shaper. "And I'm sure I can find someone to teach me water shaping."

His mother nodded. "It's settled then. Now, Tannen, Theondar is expecting me before you attempt this."

The sudden change in topic made him pause. "If the others haven't changed my mind, neither will you."

"It will fail, but I will let you learn that lesson on your own," she answered. Then she patted him on the arm like she had when he was a child and started away, hurrying up the street. Tan stared after her, wondering if anything had really changed.

CHAPTER 3

An Attempted Healing

THE SHADOWS IN THE LOWER LEVEL of the archives surrounded Tan. The air held the musty odor of ancient books and even more ancient artifacts. A thick, plush rug woven in reds and blues stretched out on the floor in front of him. A simple wooden chair was angled across from him. The chair he sat on was made of stout oak and nothing like the other one. Tan had carried it down from the upper levels of the archives, unwilling to risk damaging anything on this level.

Pale white light glowed from shapers lanterns inset on the walls around him, giving enough for him to see. Runes glowed softly on the door he left propped open, just enough for him to leverage his fingers to pull all the way open if needed, but he didn't really have the need, not with golud worked into the walls and ara blowing through the archives. There was another door beyond that one, and he left it closed for privacy. This level of the archives was only for shapers like him, though there was still the one door he couldn't reach. Maybe he never would.

He couldn't admit it to his mother, but Tan still wasn't entirely certain *what* he was. He could shape like Theondar, the only other living warrior in the kingdoms now that Lacertin was dead, but he could also speak to the elementals and use that connection to weave each of the basic elements together, fusing them to reach for spirit. With the connection to spirit, he had managed to open the door to this level of the archives.

As far as Tan knew, none like him had been here for hundreds of years. The layer of dust hanging on everything attested to that. The heavy, musty odor in the air told the same. He hadn't known what to expect in this level of the archives and should not have been surprised with what he'd discovered: row upon row of books.

Part of him had hoped to find other items like the artifact, and if he could ever open the remaining door, it was still possible that there would be things like that. The archives were much more extensive here than he'd expected. So far, the books had kept him busy.

Tan turned back to the book resting open in his lap. He scanned the page, the *Ishthin* the ancient scholars had used difficult to translate, even with the gift of understanding Amia had given him before he'd nearly lost her to the archivists. This had been the only book on the shelf where he'd found it. That made him wonder how important the book had been to those scholars.

The first two pages consisted of a large map. The kingdoms were marked in the center, small labels marking the ancient nations of Galen, Ter, and Vatten, before they were bound together under a single throne. Nara looked as if it were still part of Rens when this map had been made. Now Rens had been divided, leaving part of it within the kingdoms and the rest annexed by Incendin. Beyond Incendin lay Doma, the thin stretch of land jutting off into the sea. A series of islands was drawn on the edge of the map, each island larger than the next.

Tan had seen Doma once, though he hadn't known it was Doma at the time. And what memories he had of the rest of Doma were faded, twisted by his time changed by fire.

The door pushed open and Tan looked up. Amia entered the room. Her golden hair was pinned up behind her ears and she wore a simple gold band around her neck, a replacement for the silver band that she'd once worn as a mark of her people. Roine had given it to her as a gift, a way of thanking her for service to the kingdoms. There was a certain defiance to the pride with which she wore it.

"You've been here a long time," she commented. She held a rune made by Tan, one of the first he'd attempted after learning of their potential from the First Mother. With the rune stamped into what had once been a coin bearing the face of the king, she could access this room. He'd managed to link the coin to the door, a shaping the First Mother had taught him. Amia had the only such coin.

"I'm sorry. I…"

How to explain to her the compulsion to understand what he was that kept him away from her for hours at a time? It was the reason he spent so much time with the First Mother, the same reason he would go with his mother, or Ferran were he to teach. Few shapers knew what it felt like to speak to the elementals, and none of them knew what it was like to stare at the udilm or feel the rumbling of golud in your bones. None had ever imagined riding one of the draasin. Tan had done all of those things.

But then he didn't have to explain any of that to Amia. With the shaped connection between them, she *felt* it, as surely as he felt the affection she had for him. She leaned over him, eyes taking in the map, and pointed to the page. “That’s not quite right,” she said, motioning toward the edge of the map.

“Why?” He knew little of geography outside of the kingdoms, a failing his mother had admitted to facilitating, but what he did know of Doma was that it jutted off from Incendin as depicted in the map.

“Doma isn’t as large as what you see here. And these islands,” she said, pointing along the edge, “are smaller. Par might be larger, but I’m not sure.”

Tan shifted her finger over to point at the kingdoms. “And the kingdoms were different. Ethea had to be claimed from the sea. That’s why the nymid infuse the rocks nearly as much as golud.” That was part of the mystery he hoped to better understand by searching through these forgotten texts. “The book on the draasin mentioned it. I think it was better known then. But this,” Tan said, pointing to the map. “I don’t think this is a map of the kingdoms as we know it. I think it maps it as those scholars planned it.”

Amia bit her lip as she studied the page. A strand of hair slipped free and Tan reached up to push it back and away from her face, brushing her cheek as he did. She pressed against him and sighed. “What do you hope to find?”

“I don’t know. Explanations. Maybe answers. Why did the ancient scholars even make the artifact?” It was the question that troubled him the most. There seemed no reason for that much power to be used by one person. “That much power is not meant for anyone, not even the elementals. Holding that power, I could have done anything, shaped the world anyway I chose.” He shivered. “I felt as if I could have returned my father. Your family. Everything.” He hadn’t admitted that to Amia before. Admitting that he’d considered and then rejected that much power made him worry how she’d react. He suspected she would have agreed with him, but what if she didn't? What if Amia would have wanted him to change things?

"What would have happened if you had?"

Tan thought about what could have been. Flashes of it, little more than hints of memories, remained. Nothing he could act on, just enough to make him aware of what he missed. "You would be Daughter, I suppose. In time, you would become Mother. And then, with enough experience, you would become First Mother."

"And you?"

That had been the hardest, and the first question he'd thought to ask. What would have happened to him?

When he'd stepped into the pool of liquid spirit, he'd known answers to anything. But he'd also held power unlike any that he had ever imagined. With it, he'd saved Amia and the youngest of the draasin, Enya. Tan recognized the power was not for him, just as the power of the artifact was not for him. That didn't mean it didn't make him wonder.

And while holding the artifact, he had *known* what would be if only a few things were changed. Were his father not to have died, would he have been driven to face Incendin? Had Amia not lost her family, would she have gone with Tan and rescued the draasin? Had Tan not wanted to save Elle, would he ever had secured the bond with Asboel?

Only the Great Mother knew for certain. And in that moment, Tan had held a piece of her power. No man was meant to experience that much power. Why, then, had the ancient scholars created the artifact?

There must be an answer here. Everything in his being told him there was. Those ancient scholars commanded so much more strength and skill and knowledge that it seemed impossible to him that they had no reason other than a search for power. Even the First Mother thought they sought understanding, not only power.

Tan closed the book. Answers would come in time, but not today.

He looked over to Amia, not certain whether he was prepared for what was next. "Is he ready?"

Amia squeezed his shoulder and stepped away. "Are you certain you should do this? Roine thinks it should be destroyed."

Tan shook his head. "What would have happened had you destroyed me when I'd changed?"

"That's not the same."

"Isn't it? I did what I thought necessary to save you. To protect you. Can't the same be said for him?"

Amia gripped the gold band at her neck and stared at him. "You don't know what it has done."

"He," Tan corrected. He stood and replaced the book back on the shelf where it had sat alone. This area of the archives had managed to protect the book against the dampness that threatened to stretch in. Likely some shaping, though Tan couldn't detect it. "And you're wrong. He's done no worse than I did. And perhaps there's a reason he transformed."

"You..." Amia trailed off with a shake of her head. "Even when you changed, there was still a part that remained. I don't know if I could have helped you were there not. I don't know if the nymid would have helped otherwise. With the lisincend... they went to it willingly. They only wanted power while you wanted to help. That matters, I think. With them, nothing good remains of the shaper."

Tan knew what it felt like to be consumed by fire. He knew some of what the lisincend had experienced. And if there was anything he could do to help it like Amia had helped him, shouldn't he try?

A small crowd surrounded the lisincend in the broken palace courtyard. The shapers guarding him had brought him out of the archives so whatever Tan attempted could be better contained. Once, the courtyard had featured scenes from each area of the kingdoms, but since the last attack—since Althem had destroyed it—it looked little like it had. In time, they might be able to shape it back into some semblance of what it had been.

The palace itself served a different purpose, as well. Since Althem had passed without leaving an heir, there was need for leadership. All had looked to Theondar—now known as Roine, the last remaining warrior. He had moved the remains of the university into the city and agreed to serve until a replacement could be found.

That was the reason Tan thought saving the lisincend was especially important. They could use what the lisincend knew, discover some way to prevent another Incendin attack, maybe understand *why* the Incendin fire shapers risked death to become lisincend. It had to be about more than power.

But it required first saving the creature.

Chains of stone infused with golud bound the lisincend's wrists and ankles in the center of the yard, anchoring him to the ground. His massive wings were furled in and held by another loop of chain. His leathery skin radiated with a surge of heat, as if fire struggled to escape from him. Narrow eyes watched as Tan approached.

Tan remembered what that vision had been like, the way everything seemed to burn, the seductive ability to see clearly in the dark. He shook away the thought.

Amia pulled away from him as he approached the lisincend. Tan stared after her but felt her irritation through the bond. After what she'd gone through with her people, first losing her family, then abducted and tortured by the Aeta, and finally to learn how the First Mother had been complicit the entire time, Tan didn't blame her. He just hoped she could learn forgiveness.

He shifted the sword hanging from his waist, still growing accustomed to wearing it. He no longer doubted he had the right to it; he was almost as much warrior as Roine, only without the same experience. The runes worked along the edge of the sword were similar to those he'd studied in the lower level of the archive. From what the First Mother explained, with those runes, Tan could augment his shapings.

A gust of wind whipped at his hair and he turned to see his mother land next to him. The translucent face of ara worked in her shaping. Ara seemed to dart around him, tugging playfully at the heavy overcoat that had replaced his worn traveling cloak, before disappearing again.

"Mother. You don't have to be here for this."

She studied the lisincend, tightness in her eyes betraying her concern. "When we spoke earlier, I hadn't known that it was today."

"It was Roine's deadline."

She sniffed, eyeing the lisincend. "I am unconvinced this is the right thing to do. Or that you should even attempt it."

"So is Amia."

She glanced over her shoulder at Amia. "In that, at least, we agree."

"I think you agree on more than you realize."

Roine approached, dressed in more finery than Tan had ever seen the warrior wear. A sword much like the one Tan wore was strapped to his waist. "Let's get this over with, Tan. The others will hold their shapings in reserve, but if I sense danger to you—"

"All I want is the opportunity to try and save him."

"Him? You know what you're talking about, right, Tan? This is one of the creatures that attacked Amia's family. The lisincend attacked this city. They were the reason Lacertin died!"

"Should they not have the chance for redemption?"

"Redemption? These creatures have been attacking the kingdoms since before you were born. There can be no redemption."

Tan stared at the lisincend. Locked in chains as he was, he didn't move. "You would have said the same about Lacertin once."

Roine frowned and bit back a retort. The emotions conflicting on his face said enough. Without Lacertin, they would not have defeated Althem. Tan wondered what Lacertin would have said, knowing what Tan intended.

Roine's jaw clenched. "I have not objected to your attempt, Tannen, but only because after everything you've done, you deserve the benefit of the doubt. I can't say I don't think this is a folly."

"All I ask is the chance."

"And if you succeed?" he asked, staring at the lisincend. The heat that would normally roll off the creature was held in check by the kingdoms' shapers. "Will you trust that you can release him?"

"Amia released me," he reminded.

Roine sighed. "There were other reasons behind that, you know. I seem to recall you sharing the fact that a bond has formed between you. I think that bond would inform her of whether she needed to fear you."

That, and the bond between him and Asboel, but Roine knew little about that bond.

"There are ways to destroy it humanely, Tannen. You wouldn't have to even be involved."

"Humanely? You don't think they'll take a little pleasure from destroying one of the lisincend?"

Roine lowered his voice. "Didn't you?"

Instead of answering, Tan took a slow breath and patted Roine on the shoulder as he stepped past, moving to stand in front of the twisted shaper.

Shapers ringed the creature, all now more familiar to Tan than they were when he first came to Ethea. They treated him differently as well. He said little, but Ferran spoke to him as almost an equal, asking questions of golud and listening, as if what Tan said couldn't simply be found in the archives. Alan, another wind shaper, nodded to him almost respectfully. From the moment they'd met, Tan recognized the regard Alan had for Zephra. Now that she had returned, she had taken her place at the head of the wind shapers; none rivaled her in skill, and none could speak to the great wind elemental as she could. He knew the water shapers, Essa and Jons, less well, but they would be instrumental in what he intended. He remembered that he needed to ask one of them—likely Jons—whether they would be willing to work with him.

And then there was Cianna. She stared at the lisincend, standing before it with a curious expression. A shimmery copper shirt clung to her, as did the deep indigo leather pants she wore. She turned as Tan approached. "It has not spoken since we brought it out from the archives."

"I don't think he said much even while there, did he?"

Cianna shrugged. "I already told you that I refused to go. Theondar is right, you know. He should be destroyed. What you offer is more than he deserves."

What did any of them deserve anymore? Weren't they all twisted in some way? "He suffers," Tan said. The thin barrier of spirit surrounding the lisincend shielded the creature from accessing fire. That didn't take away the call, the draw of fire. Tan remembered all too well how fire seemed to demand his attention when he'd been shaped. There had been only so much he could resist.

Cianna grunted. "You think it should not suffer after what it has done?"

"I am not sure anything should suffer." He turned to the other shapers. "Are they ready?"

Cianna gave Tan a half-smile and shifted her focus to the other shapers. "They are ready."

"Theondar has given me only this one chance," Tan said. He didn't think he could ask for another opportunity. If this failed, Tan would have to trust Roine and let the lisincend be destroyed.

Cianna touched his hand. Fire streaked with an uncomfortable familiarity beneath her fingers. Annoyance surged through Amia behind him. "I don't think it will work," she said.

"If it doesn't work, then we can destroy him." Better that than releasing the lisincend to attack once more.

"You keep calling it a him."

Tan nodded tightly. "And you keep calling him an it."

He stepped away from Cianna, steeling himself for what was to come. He had learned to control his access to spirit, but that didn't mean he had the same level of skill as the First Mother, or even Amia. Tan would have to be ready for whatever it might try to do to him once the spirit barrier was lifted. Had he trusted the First Mother, she should have been the one to lead this attempt.

He faced the lisincend and stood with arms crossed over his chest. The lisincend's eyes drifted to the sword at Tan's waist. Tan shook his head. "I don't intend to harm you."

A long, thick tongue slipped out of its slit of a mouth. Scaly lids blinked. "You should finish me and be done, warrior."

"It might come to that," Tan admitted. Better to be honest than to lie about what might be to come.

"Whatever you think you will accomplish will fail. You think Alisz was the only one of power from the Sunlands?"

Tan hesitated. He'd not heard Incendin referred to that way before. "Fur is gone. I defeated him."

The lisincend laughed. "You? You think highly of yourself, little warrior."

Tan jerked back at the comment, so similar to what Asboel had once called him.

The lisincend worked its long, thick tongue over its lips again, thin eyes flicking around before stopping on Tan. "You will fail. These kingdoms will fall. Fire will burn once more, as it must."

Tan leaned toward the lisincend. "Fire tried to consume me once. *It* failed," he whispered. "And I can free you as I was freed, only I can't promise it won't hurt."

"By freeing me, you only place yourself in greater danger."

Tan twisted to see the other shapers watching him. All of them doubted he would be able to do anything, that he would even manage to save the lisincend, but how could Tan *not* try? "Freeing you puts the kingdoms in less danger."

The lisincend wheezed out a dry laugh. "You are a fool if you believe that, little warrior. When the lisincend are gone and the fires fail, you will see how little you know."

Roine watched him impatiently. Tan closed his eyes. Heat radiated off the lisincend in a way that left his skin feeling tight. Tan ignored the sensation, focusing on what he needed to do. With a whispered summons, he called nymid, golud, ara, and draasin, binding the elementals together as he had learned to do. It was possible that he shaped them without needing the elementals, though Tan no longer knew the difference. The power of spirit formed within him, different than the other elements. Taking this power, Tan shaped it atop the draasin.

Spirit held in place.

Tan reached to the nymid. *Nymid!*

The great water elemental infused the bones of Ethea, worked deep beneath the city in greater strength than Tan would have thought possible. He didn't have the same connection to the nymid as he had with Asboel, but he was better connected than with any of the other elementals. As far as Tan knew, there were individual nymid, but he didn't only speak to the same one each time, not like he did with Asboel.

He Who is Tan.

Tan let out a tense breath. Everything he intended depended on him reaching the nymid. Standing in the palace courtyard, he hadn't been certain that the nymid would respond.

He gathered his thoughts. With the nymid, it was best to be direct. *Twisted Fire. Can it be healed?*

Why would you heal Twisted Fire?

I would restore him if it's possible.

Twisted Fire consumes the shaper.

It once consumed me.

You were not so far gone that you could not still feel.

Is that the key? Tan asked.

The nymid didn't answer.

Tan took a deep breath. *Will you help?*

There was more of a sense of great thought. Then, *We can try.*

Something about what the nymid said tripped an idea for Tan. They were right: when he'd been consumed by fire, he still had felt something. The bond with Amia had been there, but weakened. She had held onto him; her affection for him had preserved him. And because of that, he had risked failing in order to return.

Pulling on the focus with spirit, Tan surged through the lisincend. There had to be something—anything—that he could reach that might allow him to save the person he had once been. Spirit was difficult for Tan. He found nothing within the lisincend other than the draw of fire and a vague sense of fear. Nothing that would allow him to reach who he had been.

Nymid?

The nymid pressed up through the ground, drawn up by Tan's command. They moved hesitantly, sliding over the lisincend. Power rushed through Tan, power to shape and control the water, power to heal.

He pushed this through the lisincend.

The creature howled. Pain surged through the spirit connection Tan now shared with him. Fire beat at the connection, straining for freedom. Tan and the nymid fought back, resisting. All he needed was an opening, something to reach through. But he found none.

Nymid pressed, sensing Tan's need. The sense of the elemental roared through him, filling him with an awareness of their power. Combined with spirit, Tan knew he could save the lisincend, that he could shape the creature back into the man he had been.

The lisincend howled again.

Stone groaned as the lisincend strained at the chains binding it. Fire consumed the lisincend, as it had once consumed Tan, coursing through the creature with an intensity he couldn't match.

The spirit barrier failed.

In a moment, the lisincend would be free to attack. Those watching might be injured, all because he had been arrogant enough to believe he could save this creature. Amia was in danger.

Fire surged, roaring from the lisincend.

Someone screamed behind him. Tan felt Amia's alarm. He would *not* risk her.

Asboel!

The sense of the draasin roared through him. Asboel was always nearby in his mind but could slither quickly to the forefront.

Twisted Fire!

You are a fool, Maelen.

As Asboel spoke, the surge of power roared through him, the great fire elemental pushing on the fire consuming the lisincend. Asboel had not the strength to draw it away, but he could augment it.

In that moment, Tan knew what he had to do.

Pulling on water and air, he created a barrier around the lisincend as flames consumed the creature. A surge of joy raced through the lisincend as fire consumed him, drawing the flames out of the barrier, pulling more fire than he would have shaped on his own. Dark laughter worked through Tan's mind from the spirit connection.

Then it immolated. Flames burned to nothing, overwhelmed by fire.

Tan stared, unable to look away until it was nothing more than ash.

Amia came from behind him and touched his arm. He shook her off as he turned away and staggered from the courtyard, ignoring the stares he knew followed him.

Made in the USA
San Bernardino, CA
12 May 2015